I0773436

PRICE TO PAY

CORINNE ARROWOOD

Price to Pay. Copyright © 2022 Corinne Arrowood All rights reserved.

Text: Copyright © 2003 by Corinne Arrowood, All rights reserved.

No part of this publication may be reproduced, stored or transmitted in any form or by any means, electronic, mechanical, photocopying, recording, scanning, or otherwise without written permission from the publisher. It is illegal to copy this book, post it to a website, or distribute it by any other means without permission.

This is a work of fiction. Names, characters, places, and incidents, either are the product of the author's imagination or are used fictitiously. Any resemblance to actual persons, living or dead, events, or locales, is entirely coincidental.

Published by Corinne Arrowood
United States of America
www.corinnearrowood.com

ISBN: 979-8-9851087-7-4 (eBook)
ISBN: 979-8-9851087-8-1 (Trade Paperback)
ISBN: 979-8-9851087-9-8 (Hardcover)

Cover and Interior Design by Cyrusfiction Productions.

TABLE OF CONTENTS

JUST A TIDBIT OF INFO

(and if you're a local, just skip this part!)

The New Orleans culture is unlike most cities in the world. Of course, each city has its own twist on life with interesting customs, nuances, and dialects that make them unique. The answers from travelers and people from other parts of the country about New Orleans tend to be a current theme—Mardi Gras and Bourbon Street. Some people talk about the food and music, and while those are integral elements of the city, it hardly defines or paints an accurate picture of the Big Easy. (which we, for the most part, don't say)

So many times, when watching a movie set in New Orleans, the actors might speak with the lovely drawl of Mississippi, Alabama, Georgia, Texas, or even north Louisiana. Still, those accents are far from the dialect of our fair city. Locals actually can hear the differences between Uptown, the Lakefront, Old Metairie, new Metairie, St. Bernard, and by all means, the transplants from bayou country. One might speculate that we, yes me, the y'ats (as in *where ya at?*) of the city sound more like we're from the Bronx but with a different edge. We speak slower, for the most part, turn "r"s into "w"s, rarely pronouncing a word ending in "er" as it is properly spoken; no, we drop it to an "a." Call it lazy, inarticulate, or ignorant; I reply, "*Whateva!*" We are, for the most part, not lazy or ignorant.

Now, as you read *Price To Pay*, pronounce the words as they are written—it is the dialect of the characters in the book. You'll come to appreciate our "Dawlin'," "wanna," and "coulda, shoulda, woulda!" The Cajun, or Coon-Ass dialect, is altogether different. To help you along, for those who don't know, sha (known to some as chere) is a term of endearment and sometimes just a word thrown in, and yes, we have a propensity to end our sentences with a preposition. If you find it offensive, one can always add "bitch" to the end of the sentence and solve the problem. My coon-ass friends rarely use a "d" if the word ends in "s." (ex. Spends converts to spen's) Just read as written. "Mais oui" is known to be used by my frien's (friends) as "of course" or "but yes."

Like everywhere, we have our good guys and bad, but our city is one of the places you can make a new best friend waiting for a bus or in line for the restroom. We love life here, and for the most part, *Laissez les bon temps rouler!*

AND SO
IT BEGAN

That was his third cigarette in fifteen minutes. Beads formed on his brow as he paced up and down the loading dock. He knew things didn't always go on schedule, but he'd reserved his dock space three months out, confirmed it the week before, re-confirmed it four days ago, and then re-re-confirmed it just the day before. He went to the house phone and dialed "0."

With the usual sickening greeting, the operator picked up.

"It's a beautiful day a—"

He interrupted, "Yeah, yeah. Hon, page Dick Dixon to the loading dock," and hung up. He walked down the loading dock, where he could see all four of his trucks waiting in line. His production lead was getting out of the first truck.

"Yeah, I know, Percy. I paged Dick. Hang tight."

"Eli, we awready an hour late an' ain't at dock yet. Shiiit, the off-load is gonna take a good hour ta two by itse'f. How much time we got 'til doors?" Eli knew he had a valid point. This one was gonna be tight.

"We got about twelve. We'll make it work, always do, right?" He knew he could get a smile out of him. Eli's gut tensed, and he could feel the heat rising up his collar.

Percy shook his head as he walked off, "Shiiit!"

Come hell or high water, Percy would make it happen for Eli. The difference between Eli and the rest of the suits was Eli had been in the trenches and did whatever it took to make things happen. He knew the business from the bottom up.

The dock door banged open. It was Dick, polished and grinning, as usual.

"Hey Eli, got your message. What can I do for you?"

"What can you do for me, well *Dick*," with a smart-ass tone, "you can start by getting these trucks outta my way. I got twenty men on the clock. It was supposed to be *my* dock from five this morning, but we been sittin' here for an hour doing nothing. That's for starters."

Dick was trying hard for damage control. Eli could almost see him tap dancing. "Let me see what the hold-up is, and I'll be right back."

Wise to the ways of the hotelier, Eli piped in, "I don't think so. Get on that little radio of yours and make it happen. I don't care whose trucks these are; get them off my dock, now!" Dick quickly got on the radio. "While you're at it, order two dozen Danish an' a pot of coffee an' have them bring that to the dock. Oh, *and* that's, of course, a *comp*."

"A comp?" Dick tried to look shocked. "I can't do that; I'll discount it thirty."

Eli looked at him with a cocky smile. "Sure you can; you do it all the time. I would *really* hate to tell my, or should I say, *our* client that y'all screwed up, an' that's why his event won't be on schedule. How much is he spending in your hotel?" Eli cocked his head.

"Okay, okay, you're killing me." Dick promptly got on the radio and ordered Danish and coffee. He knew Eli was well seasoned and couldn't be pushed around or intimidated. There was no point in arguing.

Although Percy was in the truck and couldn't hear a word of the conversation, he knew how it had gone down. Eli had made someone pay for the inconvenience and screw-up, and he also knew they'd be paying all day. Despite his shrewd business practices, everyone in town, venues, and suppliers liked him and held the highest respect for his abilities and accomplishments.

The next twenty minutes were fast-paced. Dick had tried to make small talk with Eli and smooth things over so that the rest of the day could proceed without a hitch and everyone would be happy—most of all, the client.

The first of his trucks pulled up to the dock. Percy watched intently; he knew what was coming next, and, like clockwork, Eli began unbuttoning his smartly starched shirt and then hung it on the corner of the crate where he'd put his suit jacket earlier. Percy just shook his head, sporting one of his ear-to-ear grins. Time was of the essence, and like the rest of his crew, Eli would begin the vicious off-load. He called out instructions, yelling over the roar of the engines, the blasting of some rap crap, and the general noise of the load-in beast.

It was going to take all men on deck. The procedure ran like a well-oiled machine, and in no time, they had the trucks off-loaded, and most of the equipment had made it into the ballroom. Eli grabbed his shirt and jacket off the crate and proceeded to the men's room for some freshening up. The rest of the day went smooth as silk; the client was thrilled, the hotel staff was happy, and Eli's guys got a good tip from the client—it was a win-win for all.

After schmoozing with the client for the first two hours of the party, Eli bid farewell and headed for the dock. It was desolate. He reached for a cigarette, and as he leaned into the flame of his lighter, out the corner of his eye, something caught his attention.

The ramp from the street into the dock was dark. Eli thought he had seen some kind of movement, but there was nothing. He decided to wait a few minutes as he had to pass that way to get to his car, and he really wasn't up for a mugging. It had been a long day, and he was dead tired. He ran his hand through his hair and continued looking in the direction of the entrance ramp. This time he was sure, even though it was difficult to detect, he could see a silhouette slowly moving in his direction.

He called out, "Hello? Hellooo?"

There was no response. The movement almost stopped when the person collapsed on the cold, dirty concrete. Eli tossed his cigarette and jumped off the dock, running to help. As he got closer, he saw that the victim was a small woman. She laid in a heap, trembling; her lace slip of a dress was torn almost entirely from her body.

"Okay dawlin', we gotta get you some help." He tried to remain calm, but someone had really put a beating on the girl.

He picked her up and headed for the dock. Her limp body hung across his arms like a rag doll. Just then, the hotel door opened; some of the banquet staff had come out for a quick smoke break. Eli called out to them. Two of them came to his assistance, and the other ran to the phone to call for help. He sat on the dock and held her in his arms, gently stroking her shoulder and whispering to her.

Eli looked down at the young woman; he figured she couldn't have been more than twenty years old. The left side of her face was swollen and bruised, and she had a few small splits in her lip crusted over with dried blood. She had shoulder-length hair matted in the back with blood. Someone had worked the girl over. Through the layers of dirt, grime, and dried blood, he could detect an innocence, almost child-like. Hell, his daughter was probably older. The more he thought about it, the angrier he became. Even though she was still Jane Doe to him, he wished he could get his hands on the bastard that beat her. She opened her eyes and tried to focus on him.

"Help's comin'. Hang in there." Her eyes rolled back, and her body seemed to go even limper. He shook her. "C'mon, heart, open your eyes."

It was only a matter of minutes before the place was swarming with the hotel G.M., security, and the boys in blue from the NOPD. Eli could hear the screech of the siren as the paramedics flew closer. Questions were flying in his direction, but he couldn't answer. All Eli could do was focus on her and hope that the paramedics got there soon. She seemed to be barely holding on.

The police tried to move her from his lap, but she clutched onto him. She opened her eyes slightly and gasped to him, "Sha, stay."

He felt compelled to follow her request. He tried to tell the police what happened from what he knew, but he couldn't take his attention away from her. His answers were a short series of quick blips, mostly "yes," "no," and "I dunno."

The paramedics arrived and, in a split second, had the situation under control. Eli stepped back and watched. His head was spinning; the whole thing seemed like some weird dream. The police took the opportunity to question him again.

"Like I tried to tell you. I don't *know* who the girl is or *what* happened." He felt numb. "I was standin' here, thought I saw something, waited a couple of minutes, and that's when I saw her." He felt a lump developing in his throat and found himself fighting back tears. "As soon as I realized it was a person, I ran to see if I could help; that's when we called you." He cleared his throat and said, "Look, I wish I could be of more help, but I can't an' to tell you the truth; I was on my way home when the whole thing happened. So, can I go now?"

The officer studied him as if looking for some hint that maybe he was somehow responsible. "You have some I.D.?"

Eli couldn't believe the whole thing. He kept thinking that the cops should be trying to find the guy who did the deed rather than harassing him. He dug in his wallet and pulled out his driver's license and a business card. The officer wrote the number next to Eli's name on his notepad.

As he wrote, he asked, "Mr. Rosen, is this a current address?"

"Yes, sir," he answered. He wanted to get out of there, and it seemed to be dragging on.

"And you are still employed by Class Act?" The officer was polite, but it was more than obvious he had a questioning eye.

"Yes, sir."Eli impatiently ran his hand through his hair.

"You said you were on the way to your car. Where are you parked?"

Eli pointed toward the ramp. "Last car on the right, the dark blue Volvo."

"We may need you for further questioning. What's a number that I can reach you at tonight?" As he called out the number, the officer wrote it on his pad, "and tomorrow?"

"I'll be at the office by 9 or 10; the number's on the card."

"Any imminent travel plans?" Eli shook his head no. "Okay, Mr. Rosen, you're free to go; we'll be in touch."

HOME AT LAST

He was totally numb the whole way home. His mind couldn't fathom what had just happened. There was a whirlwind of emotions playing through his head. Why were the police so intent on harassing him? Ideas bounced through his brain like a pinball game until they hit upon her face. In his mind's eye, he could clearly remember her face, every line, every detail.

Eli pulled up in the driveway of his Esplanade cottage. He had spent countless hours on the renovation, but he'd finally gotten it almost perfect. It was such a source of pride. In any case, it was his, paid in full. The soft glow of the television in the front room gave just enough light that he could navigate through the cottage toward the kitchen.

A voice whispered, beneath what appeared to be a heaped-up blanket on the sofa, "Things go okay? I was starting to worry because you're late. Your plate's in the fridge."

"You won't believe my night; everything went okay at the show, and the client was happy most of all. But after, wow. I'm still kinda punchy over the whole thing."

He sat on the sofa and told her a broad version of the sordid tale. She snuggled into him, wrapping her arms around his waist. As he unraveled the happenings of the evening, she pulled away, turned on a lamp, and looked at him. Blood and dirt smudged his shirt, and the left sleeve was almost completely soaked in blood.

"Look at you. Oh, my God. You're covered." Her voice started getting that panicky squeak he knew all too well.

"Rach, I'm okay. All right? The shirt's ruined, but with that, I can live. You should have seen the girl," he shook his head, "Someone did a real number on her." She could see his mind drifting. He looked tired and was obviously and understandably frazzled. "I gotta get these clothes off. I'll tell you everything in the mornin'; you need your sleep." He leaned forward in a slight attempt to stand.

"Sleep? Are you kidding me? I'll pour you some wine; it'll be waiting right here. I want all the details."

She watched as he lumbered up. He was a good man; he didn't deserve some of the rotten things that had happened to him. She smiled at him as he patted her head and gave her one of his infamous winks. Even though he was now 53 and had a little more salt than pepper in his hair, she still thought he was the most handsome man in the world. She always had.

"Oh, before I forget, Lee called. She wants you to call her. Dad, you really ought to give her a chance. I mean, you're not getting any younger, you know?"

As he walked down the hall, he called out, "Thanks, Rachel. What do I need with a woman in my life when I got you to nag me all the time?" he chuckled.

Eli couldn't help but think what a good job he'd done raising his kids. It really hadn't been that hard. Rachel and Alan were good kids, top students at Ben Franklin, and culturally active. He'd never had any trouble with either of them. After his wife did the Houdini on him and disappeared into thin air, he was left with a four and two-year-old and an enormous fear that he couldn't handle it alone.

His mother had begged him to come home to Miami, but he decided to forge ahead and do the best he could; that was all anyone could have asked from him.

He poked his head into Alan's room. At 15, he was already over six feet tall, and his feet dangled off the bed. Even though he had the body of a man, he was still a young boy inside. A trail of clothes littered the path to the bathroom. When he had added the second bathroom to the cottage, he thought it had been a good plan to connect his and Alan's room. That way, Rachel could have her own bathroom with all her feminine stuff, and she would undoubtedly keep it cleaner for company. He made his way through Alan's room into the already lighted bathroom.

As the bathroom door squeaked close, he faintly heard a mumbled voice call out, "G'night, Dad."

"Goodnight. See you in the morning. Go back to sleep."

It was good to be home, Eli thought, as he tossed his suit in the dry-cleaning basket and turned on the shower. Etched in his mind was the image of the girl's limp body, and the horrible scene rolled endlessly through his mind. Eli shook his head, trying to shake off the memory. He felt sure the paramedics had gotten there in time to save her. Maybe he'd hear more on the news.

The shower felt good on his worn body. He stretched his neck and shoulders, and his mind raced back again. Just that brief moment when she looked up at him, he felt the penetration of her teal-colored eyes. She was like an angel. He could picture her in a smart dress or suit, going out with friends to lunch. He wondered what her life was all about. Did she work? If so, where and what did she do? He fantasized, creating a storybook tale that had a nasty twist ending up with her beaten and fighting for her life in the basement loading area at the Magnolia Hotel.

Rachel was waiting, perched on the arm of the sofa. Not only had she prepared his wine, but she also had his plate warm and waiting on the coffee table. She was a good kid, he thought to himself.

"My heart, you need to get some shut-eye. I've told you everything there is to tell. Thanks for the wine and food." He closed his eyes, savoring the taste.

She slid down into the sofa. "Okay, sport, you can tell that to someone else, but that's not what your face is showing. You got some kinda look, and I'm not buying it's all about your ordeal. It looks to me like you got your mind on the girl." She gave him a smirky half-smile.

"Rach, you've been watching too much of those damn soaps!" he mussed her hair and shooed her to bed.

"Fine then, be that way!" she put on a pout, gave him a quick peck on the cheek, and headed back to her room.

He had a hard time getting to sleep. All he could think about was the girl. He tossed from one side to the other and finally gave up. Picking up the phone, he called the Medical Center. As suspected, they routed him from one person to the next, but eventually, he made some progress.

The surly voice on the other end answered his question. "Yeah, we admitted someone matching that description, but that's all I can tell ya unless you're family, which you ain't!"

"All I want to know is, do you know if she made it so far?" he was getting aggravated.

"Mista, the phone is ringing off the hook; I don't have no time to be answering your questions. You want to know, come down and find out," she hung up the phone.

He wasn't about to go down there. It would have to wait until morning. Sleep came upon him without warning, and he entered the strange realm of the dream world. Over and over, he relived the night's experience, each time changing the outcome. He had a feeling of guilt, like he should have done more. But what could he have done? The continuous roll of dreams terrorized his sleep.

He bolted upright in bed, his heart pounding complete with clammy hands and drenched in sweat. He got up and padded his way to the bathroom. The clock read 4:30. After using the bathroom, he forced himself back to bed, thinking he was ridiculous.

Talking to himself, he mumbled, "I have nothing to feel guilty about, nothing. Why in the hell am I feeling so damn guilty?" He had to shake this off; the day after the show was always a bitch. He climbed back in bed, but instead of drifting to sleep, he found himself watching the clock as it marched its way to 6:30, followed by the ever-present morning ritual of getting the kids up and out.

As usual, the three of them managed to get out on time, despite the everyday organized chaos. Though exhausted, Eli shook the thoughts of sleep from his head and navigated the streets of the Quarter on his way to work.

The daily transformation of the French Quarter would never cease to amaze him. The lure and enchantment of the nightlife, which wooed millions of people a year, vanished quickly as the sun peaked in its glory, announcing a new day. While hordes of visitors nestled in their beds were sleeping off the evening's libations, the worker bees, the actual soul of the city, would be out in force, preparing the way for the festivities to begin again. The morning was his favorite time, almost seemingly reserved for the locals. This was where the action was.

Between the street cleaners and delivery trucks, a few stragglers would aimlessly wander with that look of bewilderment—where had the magic gone? But to Eli, this was the real magic. The fact that these people had day-in and day-out, year-in and year-out, dressed their town in its finest regalia, readying it to greet its guests, spoke volumes that could only be described as love. These people loved their home.

Every trip Eli had taken reminded him of why he'd chosen New Orleans as his home so many years ago. There was no place on Earth like it, and it wasn't just the food or the architecture. *No*, he thought, *it was the people*. He would often tell his clients that this was the only place where one could wait for the bus and make a new best friend. These people loved life and lived it with more gusto. He would try to explain that the service wasn't slow; it's just that every dining experience was an event, not just for those visiting but even more so for the locals. The locals made New Orleans a dining extravaganza; through inheritance, their culinary expectations went beyond demanding and were most unforgiving. He turned into the parking garage.

"How you do, Mista Eli?" chimed the weathered old white guy that ran the parking garage.

"Can't complain, Salty."

"That's good. I hear you had yourself quite a night. Everyone talkin' 'bout it, cha know. Can't keep no secrets, not in N'awlins, anyway."

"I hear you." Eli grinned to himself. Salty's comment was so accurate.

There was no point in wondering if everyone in the office knew about the ordeal; he knew they did. Although Class Act had grown to be one of the largest event companies in the city, it still maintained a family atmosphere, which meant everyone was in everyone else's business.

"I seen you on TV this morning. That was something, huh? You did good, Eli, real good."

"Television? It was on the TV? What'd they say?" Eli was most curious; there might be more information to quell his curiosity.

"Just that some girl got beat up, and you were the one that found her an' all and then called the police. They said that as far as they knew, you didn't know the chick. But cha know how people like to talk, 'fore you know it, they'll have y'all as lovas or somethin'." The old guy chuckled.

"Yeah, well, I'm sure you'll nix that rumor, Salty if you hear it."

"Sure thing, Mista Eli."

By the time he made it to the office, his phone was buzzing.

He picked it up, "Eli Rosen."

He recognized the raspy voice of his cohort in crime. "Ya got my message last night?" I was callin' to see how your event went, but then over coffee and the mornin' news, whadda I see, but your mug. Jesus, Eli, you sure get yourself into it, you okay?"

"Shit, everyone's seen it but me." He read through a stack of messages.

The receptionist poked her head in and mouthed that he had a call.

"Got a call; I'll stop by your office after I'm done." He punched the blinking line. "Eli Rosen."

"Mista Rosen, hey, dis is Desiree, ya know da girl from las' night? I just wanted to say t'anks. You didn't have to do whatcha did, so t'anks. Das all. I'll let you get back to—"

He had been taken off-guard and quickly spoke, "W-wait."

"I'm sorry, I didn't mean ta both—"

He broke in, "Right, no, I mean you're not." She had a heavy Cajun accent which he found interesting. "I tried to check on you last night. Are you okay? I'm sorry, your name again?"

"Desiree, and yeah, I'm okay. A little bruised up an' I got some stitches in na backa my head an' on my cheek, but nuttin' I ain't lived t'ru before."

"You been released yet?"

"Nah, dey keepin me fa observation, but I can leave tomorrow if everythin's okay. Which it's gonna be. I just gotta figure where I go from here. Ma situation's a mess."

"Where you hail from, I can tell you're not completely home-grown. Thibodeaux? Raceland?"

"Kinda, you hear of Lockport? Dere, dat was home a long time ago. Mista Ro—"

"Please, Eli." He could feel his face flushing. *What was this?* "Since you'll be there tonight, you want some company?"

"Why?"

"I'll bring you something to eat. What ya say?"

"Whaddeva floats your boat. I guess I can see you tonight. It's room four twenny t'ree. You can't miss me; I'm da girl wit da black eye and busted mout'."

"I'll see you around six or so."

"Lata," she sounded confused but was rolling with it.

She was a total mystery to him, and why he was obsessed with her even perplexed him more. Maybe the oddity of it all was the lure. It was nearly impossible, but he turned his attention to work.

Somewhere mid-morning, Lee popped into his office. "Gee, Rosen, still on the phone? Thought you were gonna come see me." She sat in a chair in front of his desk, crossing her shapely legs.

"Sorry, I got involved in a million things, post-production, you know how that goes." He placed his hands on the desk in front of him and smiled. He could feel he was being distant. He really didn't want to offend her; they'd been friends and co-workers for too long. He knew she had other feelings, and things could have happened on several occasions, but he never allowed it. Still, they had the friendly banter that someone else might frown upon and may even deem as sexual harassment. It worked for them. No matter how hard he tried, he could not give her his full attention.

"What is it with you today? You're out there, even more n' usual, my friend." She re-crossed her legs.

"Last night was something; I guess I'm still in shock, that's all." He shuffled some papers around and pulled out the Profit and Loss form.

"You wanna buy me a drink after work and talk?"

"Not tonight, pal."

"Oh?" She pouted. It was the same routine he got whenever he didn't give in to her. Next, she would pop out of her chair and whisk out with her cute girlish figure and perfectly coiffed red hair.

As expected, that's just what she did, but then she turned at the door, smiled, and said, "Your loss."

He knew she would be a little pissy for a few hours, but by the following day, everything would be right as rain.

The afternoon seemed to drag on, and his constant checking of the clock only exaggerated the sluggish movement of time. He couldn't wait to see her; just the thought brought a tickle to his stomach, a feeling he hadn't had in over two decades. *What was it with the chick? It had to be the eyes; they were mesmerizing,* he pondered.

He was reeling. Sonny had never seen Manducci so mad. "Whaddaya mean ya tru her out? Boy, you are some kinda stupid. Ya betta find her dat's all I gotta say!" Manducci paced back and forth behind his desk and then turned with a cold stare. "Sonny, I can't cover ya ass on dis one. Ya on ya own."

"I'll find her; I'll find her. Don't you worry, Unc."

"I ain't da one dat should be worried, Sonny-boy! Now get the—"

"I'm outta here, boss." Sonny backed away with both hands raised.

Battered women occupied the other three beds in the room. Two were beaten by their pimp, and the other mugged for a fiver. Desiree had had her fill with the hospital, the incessant whining of her roommates, and the constant barrage of questions. It was nobody's business what happened to her, and she wished they would all shut up.

Eli had never been to the city Medical Center, and as far as he could tell, he never wanted to come back. If it hadn't been for his fixation on the girl, he would never have punished himself with the likes of a place so unsettling. It was downright scary. He finally made it to her room. With a handful of flowers and a bag from the bakery held tightly in his fist, he turned right into the room.

His memory had served him right. Desiree was all he had remembered. Her dark hair and olive complexion set off her pale bluish-green eyes.

"Hey," and all he could do was grin.

"Hello again." Her eyes danced with a sensual glisten. "Flowas for me, sha? How sweet. Pull up a chair an' take a load off." She pointed to a chair

He caught himself staring at her. "I hardly recognize you. Your injuries are nowhere as bad as they looked last night." He handed her the bag and pulled up the chair. He could feel all the eyes ogling him, wondering if he was the one that had put the hurt on her.

"Ooh, la, la." She pulled out an éclair. "How'd ya know, dese are my favorite, yeah."

"Yeah?" He smiled and could feel a blush in the making.

"You wouldn't be makin' fun of me now?" she put on an angry face.

"Nah, don't mind me; in fact, I rather like the accent."

"Dat's good cuz ain't much I can do aboud it. Talk dis way all my life."

All he could do was grin. He turned and nodded to the other three ladies in the room. They nodded back.

"You look nervous, Mista Rosen. Now, why ya all nervous? Bet ya neva been here before."

"Can't say as I have," he was still grinning like some stupid schoolboy.

They spent the better part of two hours getting acquainted, but ninety percent of the questions were coming from her. Eli wanted to ask her what happened but thought it would seem too personal. He stayed away from any mention of the night before. He told her he needed to leave and asked if she had found a place to stay. She said no, but she would work it out.

"You can stay with me until you find somewhere." What in the hell was he doing? He couldn't believe he had said that but now it was out there, and there was nothing he could do about it. He stood to leave. She touched his hand gingerly.

She didn't seem surprised or wary. "T'anks. You pick me up tomorra? Maybe durin' your lunch cuz, I don't wanna stay here any longa than I gotta."

"Sure thing." He nodded, still smiling.

"Ya a real nice man, Mista Rosen an' I t'ank ya fa all ya done. If I don't see ya tomorrow, no hawd feelins, okay?" Desiree shrugged her right shoulder and cocked her head to the side.

"You'll see me tomorrow, that you can count on." Where was this machismo coming from? It certainly wasn't his usual disposition. He made his way out of the jungle and safely to his car. He tried to process the whole encounter and couldn't believe he had asked her to stay at his place. How was he going to explain it to his kids?

Wasn't he always the one to tell them to be cautious, and here he was throwing caution to the wind. For all he knew, she could have been the one that came out on top. Maybe some poor fellow was lying in a pool of blood following some attack by this wild woman. He didn't know anything about her, yet he offered her a place in his home. He needed to have his head examined. The more he thought about it, the more he considered the out she gave him. She didn't expect him to show up; it was no big deal if he didn't, right? Wrong. He wouldn't have said it if he didn't mean it. He was a man of his word. His kids would have to understand, and if they didn't, too bad. The mental battle went on until he pulled into the driveway.

He could smell dinner on the stove as he came in.

"That you, Dad?"

"Yep, it's me. Rach, dinner smells great. How was your day?" Rachel was at the stove, so he spoke to her back and didn't have to look into her eyes.

"Okay, I guess. Lee just called minutes ago; she seemed surprised you hadn't gotten home yet. She wants you to call her."

"I've been at the hospital. I went to check on Desiree. Just to see how she was doing." He spoke as though it were a perfectly normal thing to do.

"*Desiree?* What kind of name is that, sounds like a hooker name." Rachel was none too pleased. She turned to face him.

"She's from the bayou country," he felt himself getting defensive.

"A coon-ass? Dad, those people are crazy. Stay away from her."

"Not funny; give it a rest, Rach."

She sensed his mood. "God, what crawled up you're a—"

He shocked himself as he cut her off. "Enough, Rachel, enough already." He instantly felt terrible and turned back into the kitchen. "I'm sorry, babe; I didn't mean to be so cranky."

She was pissed; he didn't blame her. She spoke with attitude, "Whatever, Dad." She continued to fix dinner. The conversation wasn't going well, and he hadn't even told her the news about their soon-to-be houseguest.

He stood looking at her.

"Yes?" She turned with her hand on her hip.

"I'm *really* sorry."

"Okay, I got that."

"Rach, there's also something I want to talk to you about," he stood looking at the back of her.

"Go ahead," she remained at the stove with her back to him.

"This is going to need your undivided attention."

She turned the stove down and sat at the table. "What's so important that you need my *undivided* attention?"

"Ya know how I told you I went to see the girl?"

Sarcastically she retorted, "*Desiree?*"

"Yeah, Desiree. Well, I kinda offered for her to stay here until she finds a place to stay. She has nowhere—"

She was appalled, "*You did what?*"

"She didn't have anywhere to go," Eli felt he had to make excuses, but he was the dad, and he shouldn't have to explain himself to anyone.

"Uh, like, that's what shelters are for; it's not like picking up a stray dog, Dad." She got up from the table. "What's wrong with you? I don't believe this." She turned to face him. "She's not staying in my room; you can forget that, so don't *even* ask!"

Silence fell upon the room. He didn't know what else to say. He knew she was right, and this was definitely atypical for him; he was always reserved. It was more than obvious the conversation between them was over. He left the room feeling like a dog retreating with his tail between his legs. He settled on the couch to call Lee.

"Hi, Rachel told me you called." He relaxed back, adjusting the pillows.

"Yeah, I did. You seemed especially odd today, odder than usual, I mean," Lee snickered. "No, in all seriousness, I worried about you, that's all."

"Hell, I'm okay, I guess. I think I must be going through some kinda mid-life crisis." He fell silent, reflecting on the situation. "I screwed up big this time. Rachel's pissed, really pissed." His voice started to drift.

"Whaddaya do, buy a Corvette or something? Hey, pal-y, don't get so down on ya'self. She'll get over whatever it is you did; she adores you, you know that."

"Nah, not this time. Rachel's right. Part of me wants one thing, yet the other part knows it's not the right thing."

Lee went quiet for a moment. "Well, pal-y whaddaya do that was so terrible?"

"Long story." He sighed.

"I'm listenin'."

He didn't know quite how to verbalize the whole thing; besides, he knew she was interested in more than a friendship, and that, in itself, would make things awkward, but there was no one else.

"Remember the thing by the loading dock?"

"Yeah, that was only, whatever, of course, I remember. So?"

"I went to see the girl at the hospital."

She interrupted, "Why?"

"I don't know, she called me at the office to thank me, and well, I felt bad for her."

"Okay, go on." He could hear the irritation in her voice.

"Well, when I got there and started talking to her, she's a kid with no direction. There's no one to care for her, nowhere to go—"

Interrupting again, she said, "Gawd, don't tell me ya didn't? Ya told the girl she could stay by you, at your house. Tell me ya didn't, Eli." There was no answer. "Yeah, I would say you've done it this time. You're right; you screwed up. And, pal-y, don't play that you felt sorry for the girl; you and I both know that dog don't hunt."

Once again, quiet from Eli's end. Lee continued, "I guess you don't have much to say. If it were me, I'd get her out soon as possible an', Eli, start thinkin' with the right head."

He got defensive. "It's *not* like that! You got that wrong. For cryin' out loud, she's not much older than Rachel."

"Maybe in age, my friend, but trust me, that chick's been around the block *more n' once*. She saw you comin', old boy."

Eli detected a trace of bitterness, a sharp edge. Exhausted by the mess of it all, he bid his farewell and said they would talk more the next day. By the time he got off the phone, Rachel had prepared the plates and had already begun eating.

"Looks great, Rach," he rubbed his stomach.

She cocked her head and just looked at him disgustedly.

Until Alan bounded in the door, there was complete silence at the table. His positive, upbeat demeanor crashed into the cold wall of his sister.

"What's up with you?" he looked to his dad. "What's wrong with her? PMS?"

She shot a look of daggers at him and left the room. "I did the cookin'; y'all do the cleanin'." Eli heard the slam of her bedroom door.

"What's up with her?" Alan wanted to know.

"She's mad at me, nothing to do with you. By the way, we're gonna have a houseguest for a coupla days, okay with you, sport?"

"Sure." That was the end of the discussion, and there were no more sarcastic comments, questions, or attitudes. He and Alan sat and watched the end of some mindless movie.

Morning came, and as promised, he arranged to have the afternoon off so he could pick her up from the hospital and get her settled. The loud clamoring and incessant whine of the somewhat questionable clientele lounging around the hospital were enough to drive him insane. The faster he could get her out, the better. She was waiting for him.

Desiree sat on the bed in the same dirt and blood-stained frock she wore the night of the incident. It was evident someone had tried to wash the stains out and pin the pieces back together, but it had been in vain for the most part. It was remarkable how fast she was healing; she looked a hundred percent better than the day before. *Youth,* he thought. She looked much younger than he remembered. Perhaps it was the absence of make-up and hair spray. He knocked on the open door.

"You showed?" she had a devilish twinkle in her eye, "I sorta t'ought dat ya might come fa me. But, like I tol' ya b'fore, sha, I don't need ya to do dis. I been takin' care of myself since I was a girl." She winked at him.

"You're still a girl," he had to remark and remind himself as he stood there completely self-conscious.

"Beg your pardon, how ol' ya t'ink I am, sir?"

"Old enough, already. Don't mind me. I'm just an old fart. But to me, *chere,* you are *still* a girl. It's a compliment."

"Well, fa ya information, I'm almos' twenny-four." She linked her arm in his as they left.

"Yeah, like I said before, you *are* a girl, *just a kid.*" He glanced down at her.

She smiled back at him, "Okay, chief, *whadeva.*"

She was tiny. Eli surmised that she might be five feet, but that would be tops. Everything about her was miniature and perfectly proportioned, except for the personality; she seemed most bold and outspoken, which was amplified by a sharp lace of sarcasm.

"Is there somewhere we need to go to pick up your clothes and personal stuff?" He asked nonchalantly.

She thought about his question and answered, "Nah, I'll handle dat, ya don't need ta get inta it, jus' in case. I'll get someone ta pick da stuff up. Lemme worry dat one."

"I don't mind." Perhaps by seeing where she lived and maybe even meeting the guy, he could start to understand her.

She patted his hand. "Trus' me, sha, you don't wanna go dere." She laughed to herself as the vision of Eli meeting up with Sonny played through her mind. It sure as hell wouldn't make for a pretty picture. Getting her stuff was going to be tricky, she thought. She wasn't sure how she'd get her things without someone seeing her and maybe even following her. She'd have to time it right.

"You need something to wear until you get your things." Eli pointed out.

"Ya know da Thrif' Store in Mid-City? If you can spot me five bucks, fa now, I can pick up a coupla t'ings."

"For five dollars? Are you kidding me? Five dollars doesn't even buy a barrette for my daughter. I tell you what, let me worry about today, okay? What size do you wear, if you don't mind me asking?" He navigated the streets, watching for early hour drunks or unobservant pedestrians.

"Extra-small." She answered with a slight smile.

"Right," he felt foolish—*that* he could have guessed.

They pulled into his driveway. He had already told Desiree about the kids, his work, his house, actually *all* about his life. But, he still knew nothing about her except that she wore an extra-small, which any dummy could have seen.

He walked her into the living room and turned on the television. It was time for the midday news, and like usual, there was some scandal regarding politics and a new casino. The newscaster was commenting on the licensing and, of course, litigious residents. The brouhaha went all the way to the governor's office. In the standard monotone commentator voice, the newscaster continued, "The governor's office has denied all allegations regarding a relationship between Anthony Manducci and the governor. They stated, 'the governor has at no time made any indication Mr. Manducci's casino would be pushed through without a vote.' An investigation is being launched to stop this type of false allegation in the future."

"What bull shi—the governor an' Manducci been frien's for years. I tell ya, sha, dose news people, dey so clueless. I guess dey get paid fa sayin' what dere bosses tell 'em but do dey really t'ink de people are so stupid ta believe all dose lies?"

"I didn't think you'd be so politically interested. Then again, I don't know much about you, do I?" He looked straight at her waiting for some response.

"Nuttin' too special ta know, sha," she ignored his question and continued to watch the news.

Eli left it alone and went in the back to call Lee.

"Lee Perrone, how can I help you?"

"Hi, got a big favor to ask you," his tone was humble.

"Shoot."

"I'd do it myself, but I don't know I'd get it right."

"What?" she was getting irritated.

"I need you to pass by some lady store and pick up a few things for me, well not *for* me. Anyway, coupla things extra-small."

"Eli, Rachel doesn't wear an extra-small," like he was stupid. That was the second time he was made to feel like a moron in one day.

"I know that. It's not for Rach—" he caught himself. There was an awkward silence coming from the other end.

"Yeah, I'll do it," she sounded disgusted. Suddenly Eli felt ashamed and wanted to say something, but there was nothing he could say to make it any better.

"I owe you."

"Whadeva. Hey sport, does this girl have *anything*?"

Sheepishly he answered no.

She sighed, "Okay, pal-y, I'll do my best."

Lee had been a good friend to him, and it seemed like she was constantly bailing him out. He felt guilty the relationship was so one-sided. He made a mental note he'd have to do something special for her.

He went back into the living room. Desiree made her way around the room, stopping to look at his assortment of framed photos. There were pictures of the kids from tiny tots up to the present day. She longingly looked at some of the three of them, especially one of his favorites from a summer vacation in the mountains.

"That was taken in Gatlinburg when the kids were younger."

"Dey look like good kids; you see dey momma much?"

"It's been years," changing the subject, "Make yourself at home. There's plenty in the fridge and," he opened the pantry, "as you can see, lots in here."

He heard the back door open.

"Hello?" It was Rachel. He wondered what she was doing home so early from school but decided to wait until they were alone. She came into the room like a ray of sunshine.

"I thought I'd come home a little early from school and see if you needed help." She walked right up to Desiree and put out her hand. "I'm Rachel, and you must be Desiree. My dad has told me all about you." Rachel stood straight and tall with a warm smile glued to her face.

There was a huge contrast between the two girls—Rachel was 5'7", towering over Desiree. Like her dad, she was tall and thin with a mass of dark hair. Despite the fact he knew she was angry about the houseguest, she managed to appear warm and hospitable.

Desiree smiled at the warm welcome. "It's good ta meet ya. He tol' me you were a beauty. He mus' keep a big bat by the door, hon, to keep de guys away, yeah?" Desiree talked with her hands which Eli found amusing.

"Not exactly, but thanks." Rachel threw a glance in her father's direction.

Idle chatter filled the rest of the afternoon, no one daring to broach the obvious curiosities.

Although seven-thirty in the evening, the avenue was still basked in the soft daylight as it filtered through the majestic branches of the oaks that lined the street. The sounds of traffic had begun to wind down, awaiting the setting of the sun. Alan had returned home and was as pleasant and exciting as any teenage boy might be. He retreated to his room and the comforts of his TV and games.

The chime of the doorbell was a welcomed interruption. Standing at the door with an armful of bags stood Lee. She had covered all the bases as the bags were from a local department store and the corner drugstore. He suspected she had gotten everything from deodorant and lingerie to clothing appropriate for an evening of elegant dining. Eli quickly relieved her of the shopping bags and put them on the dining table.

Without hesitation, Lee sat on the couch next to Desiree.

"You look so much better than when I saw you on the tube the other morning. What on Earth happened?" There it was. Lee had asked the question they had all been dying to ask. "Let me take a look at you." She adjusted herself to get a better look. "I don't think you'll scar. Who did this?" Lee kept shaking her head. "I know you're gonna press charges; this guy needs to be put away. Someone needs to dance on his face like he did you."

Desiree just sat there; she didn't know what to say. She was hoping someone would bail her out, but they all sat there waiting to hear; there was no way out. She put her hand to the side of her face, delicately tracing her cuts as though this would help her to explain. "Not much ta tell, really. I got in a fight with ma boyfrien', Sonny, and well, dis is his handiwork. He's a real gem, lemme tell ya."

Lee wanted the details, the whole uncensored story, but it would wait. In her brief few minutes at Eli's, they had learned more than he had in two days of conversation.

"I detect some Coon Ass?" Lee asked as she got up and poured herself a glass of wine. Eli glanced at her as if to say back off the questions; she merely raised her eyebrows and gave him a curt little smile. If he wasn't gonna find out who she was and what her story was, she certainly had no qualms.

"Lockport." Desiree didn't quite know what to make of this stranger.

Lee shook her head, saying, "Don't think I know anyone from Lockport. So when'd you move to the big city?"

"Ten or so years ago. I don't mean to soun' rude, Miss?" Desiree looked like an animal trapped in a cage.

"I'm sorry, it's Lee. Lee Perrone."

Desiree continued, "Miss Perrone, I'm awful tired, and it's been a long day," she looked at Eli. "Where you want me ta bunk up?"

ELI'S
WORLD

It was so still and peacefully silent. Desiree could hear the beating of her own heart as it seemed to keep time with an old grandfather clock down the hall. These new surroundings were a dramatic contrast to her tiny apartment on Burgundy. Eli's home was clean, quaint, and smelled of fresh bread and all the food things one might expect to find in a fairy tale house, while her dingy little place smelled of stale beer, cat piss and was, all in all, nothing much better than a hole in a dark, cracked and peeling wall.

She wanted entrance into Eli's world, away from the likes of Sonny Ramone. She had often admired the couples she would see touring the French Quarter. They strolled the street with utter amazement in their eyes at the decadence allowed to run rampant in plain view for all to see. While she and her group of degenerate friends would laugh at their innocence as though it were a bad thing, inwardly, she envied the purity and respected their disdain for the life she was thrown into from the very beginning. Right from the start, her life had little to no potential.

Born out of wedlock to a rebellious fifteen-year-old, she'd had it hard. She had been taken by the state and placed with her grandfather in Lockport, where life was somewhat normal. Although he tried, he was seldom home. Making his living on a shrimp boat equated to long peculiar hours and little home time; hence when her mother showed up demanding the child, he put up little fight. She was immediately torn from the country and dumped in New Orleans to be raised by bartenders, street mongers, or anyone who would agree to watch her while her mother worked the streets and fed her heroin habit. Time took its toll, and after a fatal overdose, Desiree had to make her way fending for herself. Had it not been for Simone, she would still be on the streets or perhaps even dead.

Simone was actually Simon when they first met. Desiree saw him as an easy target. She scoped him out like a lioness stalking her prey and watched as he walked down Bourbon Street, peering in through the open doors of the vast array of strip clubs. He was interested in some play, so she approached him. He wasn't as easy as she had thought. In fact, this nice-looking black man was in the midst of his own metamorphosis. It wasn't long after their first meeting, those ten years ago, that Simon, a city planner out of Chicago, became Simone LaFleur, one of the hottest transvestite acts in the Quarter. Nonetheless, Simone gave the girl a helping hand and got her off the streets and on the stage as a dancer.

The perversity of mankind never ceased to amaze her. Due to her tiny stature, although fourteen, she could have easily passed for ten, which seemed better for some clientele who thought the younger, the better. She hadn't been at the club for more than a couple of months when she met the owner's nephew, Sonny, a wiseguy in training. The two of them hit it off.

At first, Sonny was a nice guy and treated her like a princess, but with time, he became increasingly consumed with the need to impress his uncle. She couldn't help but notice that Sonny's personality would drastically change whenever Manducci was on the scene. He'd become demoralizing, crude, and spiteful toward her. It only worsened over their years together, as nothing he did seemed to put him in favor with his uncle. He would always be some second-rate wannabe wiseguy.

It was no wonder he jumped at the call from Manducci with such exuberance. It was the call he'd been waiting for his whole life. The message came loud and clear—this was important. It was his first shot at something big. Manducci wanted him to deliver a message to the governor that he, Manducci, wanted in the game or else. If the threat didn't work, he was to take care of the problem. Sonny, in his over-eagerness, made the mistake of responding. "Ya wan' me to whack the gov, no problem, Uncle Tony." End of call.

She couldn't believe it, and in step with her outspoken personality, she put her two cents in, "Sonny, wha's da madda wit choo, boy? Ya gonna get caught, ya uncle's only gettin' ya to do dis cuz he knows dat whoeva does dis, fa sure is gonna be toast. Dis ain't no step in da business. I know dat's what ya thinkin', don't tell me ya dat stupid." She didn't even see it coming.

Before she knew anything, he smashed her in the back of the head with a bottle, and as she started to fall, the massive beating ensued. He pounded her with years of stored-up rage, making him completely merciless. His finale punctuated the brutality of the encounter as he literally picked her up and tossed her out of the apartment and onto the street. Only through the grace of God did she stumble into the right place, finding a safe haven in the life of Eli Rosen. Yeah, she wanted in; she wanted in bad.

Desiree faded in and out of sleep, waiting for five. She figured Simone would be home by then. The magic hour had arrived, so she called.

From the other end of the call came an obviously annoyed voice, "Yaaaiiis, and it better be good."

She tried to whisper so as not to wake her host. "Simone, it's me."

"Oh, my Gawd, Desiree, I been so scar't. Where y'at? All I heard wuz that the bastard threw your ass out on the street."

"Yeah, he tr'u me out, alright. But not 'til he cracked open my head, busted my mout' an' put a couple whoppa bruises on ma face. Girl, you should see me. I look like I been a few rounds in da boxin' ring, yeah."

She told Simone the whole story about Sonny and the Manducci phone call, the terrible beating, being thrown out, and then the blessing she literally stumbled into.

"Don't know why I went for Canal; all I can t'ink is Gawd walked me right inta Eli's arms. Ya know, sha, dis horrible t'ing might jus' be da bes' t'ing to happen ta me, ya know? It's fate, dat's what it is, fate." Simone listened intently. "An' now I'm at his place fa the time bein'. Look, I got a favor to aks ya, sha. I need my stuff, an' I can't go back dere, ya t'ink ya might be able ta do it if not, it's okay. Dis Eli dude bought me some t'ings to wear."

"I'll try, but no promises, princess. I sure as hell don't need any bruises. Course he'd have a helluva time bitch slappin' me around. Sista, it's been a while since I've had any machismo, but I'd enjoy kickin' his ass. If that was all there was to it, no problem. My concern is that he thinks he's the deal and's been flashin' a piece like some gangsta. I'm surprised he hasn't shot himself with the damn thing."

They chatted a little longer until Desiree heard a symphony of alarms go off. "Gotta go, be cool, ma sha."

"W-wait, Desiree, how do I get in touch with you?"

"I'll call ya," and she quickly hung up. In the back, she could hear Eli prodding the kids to hurry and get ready for school.

Rachel whispered to her dad, "You gonna let her stay here all day by herself? How do you know she won't steal all our stuff?" She threw a glance of concern at him.

Slipping into his jacket, "You think you might be overreacting just a little bit."

"No, do you ever think it might be you, Dad, underreacting?" shrugging her shoulders with hands upturned.

"Rach, what do you want me to do? I can't very well take her to the office with me. Gimme a break."

In an *I told you so* voice, she sarcastically retorted, "Shoulda thought about that before offering her to stay here, big guy." She swished out of the room with a smug demeanor.

Eli had to give it some thought, but maybe that's just what he would do; he'd take her to the office. After all, everyone had been complaining there wasn't enough support staff. All that could happen was they'd say no. He could afford to pay her for a day's work if the company wasn't willing. The next thing was to find out if she would be interested. Maybe she already had a job; once again, he found himself with the realization he knew almost nothing about her.

He wasn't sure of how to broach the subject; he figured he'd come right out with it. Lumbering down the hall, he called out, "Desiree, is there someplace you gotta be this morning?"

"For why?" She looked surprised by the question with raised eyebrows.

He continued, "Like do you have work you need to get to or something?" Rachel had been right; he certainly could not leave her alone in their home.

"No, m'ami, my works kinda on holt til I heal up. Wit' my job, a girl's gotta look her best. Why ya got somethin' ya want me ta do fa ya?"

That was the perfect opening for him to ask her just what it was she did, but he had that horrible feeling in his gut that said he probably didn't want to know.

"I tell ya wha', sha, I'll fix da dinna. Ya know us coon ass can do some serious cookin' an' we're good in na kitchen, too." She winked at him and gave a girlish giggle.

It took him a moment, but he caught on yet still maintained a baffled look on his face.

"Hello, you still dare? I tell ya, dis mornin' ya one sandwich short of a picnic, ma frien'."

Eli put a couple of pieces of bread in the toaster. "Sorry, just a little foggy. I haven't had my morning coffee, and it's showing. If you have nothing to do, I thought you might want to come to my office do a little filing, typing, clerical stuff and pick up a coupla bucks while you're at it." The toast popped up. He handed a piece to her with a warm smile.

"T'anks fa da offa, but I got some stuff I gotta take care of today. You make dat offa tomorra, yeah? Den, sha, I say yes." She answered with a spunky attitude.

"Do I need to drop you off somewhere?" He was hoping she would get the message; however, he hadn't made it clear so far.

"Nah, I'm gonna walk," she smiled at him, but he couldn't help thinking she looked like a schoolgirl.

He dug in his wallet for one of his cards, handed it to her, and told her she was welcome to come by when she finished her errands. If not, he'd be home around five-thirty and looked forward to seeing her then.

"How long til y'all leave?" He couldn't get over how tiny she was, and the tee shirt he had given her to sleep in swallowed her miniature frame. "It'll only take me a minute to get ready. Man, you're crazy. I can't believe all de shit Miss Lee brung. You see dem all? Damn."

His belly flopped when he heard her refer to Lee as "Miss." She probably wanted to call him "Pops," as he was a heck of a lot older than Lee.

"Desiree, word of advice, *whatever* you do, don't call her Miss Lee. I shudder at the thought of her reaction," he chuckled. "Just don't do that."

"Sha, is she ya woman?" She raised one eyebrow.

The question startled him, "My woman?" he smiled, shaking his head. "Nah, she's just a good friend, that's all. Now get ready; time is tickin'." He waved her off.

"Shame, y'all make a han'some couple." She grabbed one of the outfits from the back and proceeded to the bathroom to change. Within the next twenty minutes, they were dressed and heading out the door. He watched her in his rearview mirror as he pulled away. It was apparent she felt more than comfortable on the street. Desiree moved down the avenue like she owned it. He watched her until she turned down the corner and disappeared from sight.

Eli had to admit that even though she didn't want to do it, Lee had done a thorough job with the shopping. Everything seemed to fit the girl perfectly. He couldn't help but think how different she came across; she took on a more healthy and wholesome appeal which was a dramatic contrast to their first encounter. He preferred her without heavy make-up and hairspray. Granted, he thought, she was not at her best when he saw her for the first time; nonetheless, he preferred her with a more conservative look.

Desiree walked briskly, focusing straight ahead and avoiding eye contact with the people she passed. Block after block, she walked until she came to one of many brick corridors off the street and turned. She went past two windows to the door and lightly tapped. She waited a minute and started to tap again just as the door opened.

Simone quickly ushered her in, whispering, "Now I know you crazy, Desiree. What in the hell are you doin' wanderin' the streets? Ya think someone's not gonna see you and tell ol' lover boy? Damn girlfriend, I thought you'd be smarter than that." Simone tied the sash of her robe.

"It's nice ta see ya too, Simone. How da hell have ya been? Ya t'ink ya could give me a betta hello dan dat, no? I know what I'm doin', don't ya worry. Got a cup o' coffee fa your bes' girlfrien'?"

Desiree followed her into the small shoebox kitchen, perching herself on the counter. She watched as Simone poured two cups of her tasty dark roast coffee; the aroma was delicious. Her long thin brown arms had the look of soft velvet complemented by perfectly tapered fingers and meticulously painted nails that matched her silky pink robe.

"You realize, chickadee, this is the second time you've woken me today, and *you know LaFleur* does *not* like to be woken from her precious beauty sleep. Not for nothing, dearie." She flipped her long braids over her shoulder and put her hand on her hip with a made for the theatre, *Miss Bitch* attitude. "So, talk to me, what's the deal, but before we get into that, what is it with this new look? It just ain't you, girl." Her voice took on a higher pitch, "Not that it looks bad, don't get me wrong, I just neva saw you like Kid College, all I'm sayin'."

Just as they started to settle down into a conversation, the phone rang. Simone exclaimed, "Shiiit, has the whole fucking world los' they minds?"

Desiree found great humor in Simone's antics; one thing was for sure when Simon came out, he *really* came out, right down to the finger-snapping, arm flailing, show-stopping dramatics. She was the highest essence of the term *queen*.

"Yaiiis?" she listened, "Sonny, what you callin' me for, she's your girlfriend, not mine? How the fuck I'm supposed to know where Desiree's at?" she once again listened. "Boy, I don't care who told you what; you gotta lot of nerve calling me so fucking early in the day. That's your problem, stud, now adios!" she ended the call.

Simone turned and looked at Desiree with seriousness and worry. "What did I tell ya? Your boyfrien' says someone seen you out on the street and he wants to know where you at. I tell ya, girl, you need to get away and *stay away*. He's not playing." Simone took a long sip of her coffee, looking Desiree in the eyes. She was worried, no doubt.

"Just where in da hell ya t'ink I should go? Dere is nowhere fa me." Desiree looked at her with sorrowful, pleading eyes.

"What about your new sugar daddy? It sounds like the best thing that could happen, like a once-in-a-lifetime chance to get *out*. Get your ass off the street for good." With a throaty laugh, she shot Desiree a look, "Make an honest woman of you, Des."

"Ya real funny, ma frien'. What I should do, sleep on a damn sofa the rest of my life? Not fa me, sha. B'sides he's in his fifties or somethin'." Desiree sitting on the counter, made her eye level with Simone.

"Listen to yourself. Girl, someone might think you some uptown lady." Mocking her, Simone put on airs, "Pardon moi, I almost forgot we only fuck under fifties. What's with it? I mean, is the guy like butt ugly or something? If so, just close your eyes; I can't believe your shit. The guy gives you a place to sleep an' buys you clothes. You think it's just cause he's nice? Hello, get a grip! B'sides, who do you think you are a fucking princess?"

"You goddit all wrong. Eli's jus' nice. I t'ink he looks at me like a daughter or something. He ain't made no move yet, an' I don't see none comin'. Dey diff'rent kinda people. He made me toast dis mornin'." She sipped on the coffee.

"He a man, Desiree? If so, then eventually, he'll be lookin' for the sweet stuff."

They argued for a while, and then both gave it up, knowing neither would change the other's opinion. Desiree told Simone about Eli, his family, and all the beautiful trimmings that went with the package.

"When I tell ya he's a good man, an' I mean it, but I gotta get out of dere soon. Someone spots me an' brings da shit ta his kids or something; I can't have dat. Mebbe I jus' need to go make my peace wit' Sonny." She hopped down off the counter.

Simone interrupted, "Or maybe you should put a gun to your head and pull the trigger. Just stay away, Desiree. Disappear into Mister Eli's world. You clean up good. Hell, you can do it."

"I don't know, sha. I gotta t'ink dis one tru'. Sides, girl, what I'm gonna do wit'out you?" She made her way to the door.

"No, this way, dearie. Get on out of here with ya bad self before ol' Sonny Ramone comes banging on my door."

Simone let her out through the bathroom window, leading her to the street behind and giving her a better chance of getting away unnoticed.

A block down from Simone's, a seedy-looking character stood with a cell phone to his ear as he watched the apartment.

"I don't care what the fucking faggot she-man told you; I saw Desiree go into his place. Yeah, I'm sure it was her." He was quiet for a few minutes,

"Yeah, she's still in there. I ain't seen her come out, not yet." He held the phone away from his ear; anyone passing by could have heard every word Sonny said. "Okay, Sonny, I'll be waitin' right here for you." The conversation was over.

Ten minutes later, an old beat-up black Trans Am pulled up. Sonny got out of the car with two of his sidekicks. He told one of them to stay with the car and snapped his fingers at the guy with the cell phone. The three men made their way to Simone's apartment. Sonny banged on the door.

"Hey, I know you in there with your faggoty ass, lemme in."

Simone opened the door, still in her pink silk robe and slippers to match. She had a sarcastic, bothered sneer on her face.

"Just what do you gentlemen want?" she put on a snide grin.

"Simone, stay outta this. Be a good little fag an' send Desiree out." He leaned on the doorframe with one hand.

Simone pursed her lips and batted her eyes. "Sonny, *boy, you so cleva*, only Desiree, as I told you before, ain't here. I don't know where she's at, but if I hear from her, I'll be sure to tell her to give you a call. So, *ta-ta*, now."

She started to close the door when Sonny pushed it back open. "Think I'll have a look-see for myself," and tried to push through.

As he started to pass her, she pulled a small gun out of her robe pocket and put it to the back of his head. "I don't think so, mutha-fucka. Now just turn yourself around and get the fuck out of here, an' we'll be cool."

Sonny turned with an icy stare. He said not a word and left, but she knew in her heart of hearts she had crossed the line. He'd get even, eventually.

Desiree navigated the Quarter through alleys and courtyards, bringing her right to the fancy glass doors of Class Act. She felt conspicuous and awkward, but she had nowhere else to turn. She held her head high and entered. Luckily, the receptionist was away from her post, which Desiree took advantage of and began her hunt for Eli.

As she made her way down the hallway, she quickly glanced in, hoping to find Eli's familiar face, but office after office was held by yet another beautiful professional woman or man. They all had the look of success about them that Desiree desperately wanted. As she walked past one of the offices, she nearly bumped into Lee as she was coming out.

"Whoa, that was close. Looking for Eli, I take it?" she turned and pointed, "Two more doors down on the right."

There was an awkward silence; she felt like she should have told Lee hello, but to say it after the fact would sound stupid. She just said thanks and headed for Eli's office.

She poked her head around the corner to find him with a phone to his ear. He gestured for her to enter and sit. It was apparent he had been on the phone for some time, and it appeared he wouldn't be getting off anytime soon. She used the time and flipped through one of the magazines on his desk. She never really understood what he did, even though he had told her the first afternoon in the hospital. The magazine made it perfectly clear. Each page took her from one theme party to another. Eli began snapping his fingers at her and pointing to the page. She read the bi-lines next to the picture. "The guests of Abguard 'let the good times roll' in their very own Mardi Gras Mayhem while sampling the tantalizing tidbits of the Big Easy. The entire gala evening was created by renowned designer Eli Rosen of Class Act, New Orleans, LA."

The party in the picture looked festive, and it seemed the guests were having the time of their life. She wasn't surprised he was known in his field; he had that "in the know" kind of demeanor. She gave him two thumb's up. After another twenty minutes, he was off the phone.

"Sorry about that," he apologized.

"You can t'row me a pawty anytime you like, sha. You done good, yeah."

"Yeah?" he smiled.

"Yeah, "she smiled back at him.

"What choo been up to, sha?" he said, teasing her with a poor imitation of a Cajun accent.

"Oh, nuttin' much, tryin' ta fin' a few frien's."

Apparently, she had no intention of telling him anything else; he moved on to other subjects.

"Since you came by, is it fair to assume you might be interested in some work around here?"

"Depen's on what ya pay, now dudn't it?" She gave him a quick smirk.

"Cheeky little thing, aren't you?" He could feel his eyes glistening. He rocked back in his chair.

"Hell, Eli, I'm jus' playin'. You don't gotta pay me anyt'ing. You give me food" She held up her fingers, counting the things he had done for her. "An' a place ta sleep, an' clothes, and hell, le's face it, saved my life. Dis is you on dis han'. An' me ta you, ya see any fingers up on dis otha han'? No. Like I said, ya ain't gotta pay me nuttin'."

She was such a live wire he found her most fascinating and wanted to know more.

He called one of the Production Assistants, introduced her to Desiree, and instructed her to show his new assistant the ropes. "She's totally green." The two women left his office, and he went to Lee's.

"Hey, pal-y, what can I do for you?" Lee looked up from the file she was working on, and while she didn't say it, there was tension in the air.

"Nothin' just stopped by to say hey; besides, we haven't gone to lunch in a while. Thought maybe—" Eli started to enter her office but stopped short.

"You gotta be kidding." She slung daggers from her eyes. "I'm up to my ass in alligators; besides, I don't know if I would want to go to lunch with you anyway; I might get sick to my stomach. I see your young friend came to visit. Take *her* to lunch." She cocked her head, but her eyes said it all.

"Gimme a break. The girl's not here for lunch. I told her I needed some clerical work and figured I could kill two birds with one stone. Get some help an' the girl can get some money and move out." He leaned on the door frame, then moved in and sat in front of her desk.

"Eli, you kill me, you really kill me." She looked down at her work.

He was frustrated. "Dammit Lee, whaddya want from me? I'm getting sick of the cold shoulder an' pissy attitude when you *do* speak to me." With tense, squinting eyes, he shook his head.

"I want you to get back to work; that's what I want. You seem to forget you *happen to work for me.*" As though confirming in her own mind. "That's precisely what I want. We've got shows coming up, and then you'll be on vacation the following week, or have you forgotten that it's that time again, the old visit to Miami with Mims and Pops?"

He got up; she had pissed him off—more than anything, he hated that she was right. Since his last show, the night Desiree stumbled into his life, he'd been so ensconced in *her* mystery life he'd put his own on hold. Determined, he returned to his desk and pulled the files on the upcoming events. Not only had Lee been right about the work thing, but he had also forgotten about the trip to his parents. He had gotten behind on everything; it was time to get back on track.

The Golden Lady was nothing more than your average sleazy topless bar that, along with a dozen others, littered the streets of the French Quarter. Although defined as a gentlemen's club, there wasn't even a trace of anyone one might refer to as a gentleman. The only thing that stepped it up was the transvestite act, which *was* the draw and brought in good money and some class.

Sonny and his pair of thugs sat at one of the grimy tables in the corner of the room, waiting for the inevitable phone call and ass reaming from Manducci.

"Sonny, how long's he gonna wait outside her place? I bet the second we left outta there, he booked. He ain't got no loyalty. He's just a two-time punk. You want me to wait? She's gotta come out sooner or later."

"Nah, stay here with me for now. You got a smoke?"

Hours passed, and the three hung around shooting off their mouths, smoking cigarette after cigarette. The tension mounted, and the phone call finally came. The bartender motioned to Sonny with his hand over the phone. "Some guy won't give me a name." Sonny was relieved it wasn't Manducci.

Sonny took the phone, "Yeah, stay put; I'm comin'." He hung up the phone and turned toward the table, "Let's go."

Sonny tore down the street, whipping corners, nearly hitting a few tourists along the way. He screeched up to his contact with the phone standing across the street from Simone's apartment. The four men made their way across the street and down the alley. With one on the lookout, the other three jimmied the door, gaining entry to the apartment. Sonny flew in like a madman searching every closet, hamper, and cabinet. There was no sign of Desiree. He had to rethink the whole thing again. He plopped on the sofa running his hand over the velveteen slipcover. Two of the men sat with him.

"Only thing I can think, Sonny, is she musta gone out a winda."

"If so, she'd still come out through the alley, and you woulda seen her. There's only three windas, and they all off the alley." Sonny was at his wit's end.

The third man rounded the corner. "No, they ain't. There's a really small winda ova the tub. It's one of them frosty ones. Come see what you think. I dunno if she could fit."

Sonny got up and made his way to the bathroom.

"Oh, yeeaaahh, she could fit. In fact, she did fit," pointing to a smudged print on the windowsill. Sonny smashed the mirror over the sink with his fist, going into a wild rage. Simone had bottles of every shape and size filled with perfumes and makeup. He jumped up on the counter and began trashing everything. He slammed bottles to the floor and against the walls; splintered shards of glass flew across the tiny bathroom. Streams of obscenities blasted from his mouth with each kick and crash. He jumped down and moved through the other rooms leaving a wake of destruction behind. His cohorts jumped into the frenzy, and within a few short minutes, Simone's once tidy apartment had been transformed into something more along the lines of a war zone. They left with a feeling of demented satisfaction.

The stagnant summer heat felt like a heavy blanket making the short stroll from Central Grocery almost unbearable. Dripping with perspiration and an armful of groceries, Simone made her way home. As she rounded the corner of the alley leading to her apartment, she saw her door was ajar. Simone put the bags of groceries down and stealthfully approached the door. Gently she pushed it open and peered in. Nothing could have prepared her for the disaster she was going to face. Almost dazed, she wandered from the living room to the bedroom, the bath, and the kitchen. There was nothing she could say; she felt paralyzed. In all the years she had lived in her apartment, not once had she ever had any problem.

She felt it was too coincidental following her confrontation with Sonny. It was perplexing why some people thought they could get away with this kind of behavior without consequences. Maybe someone else might be too scared to call the police, but she wasn't. After searching for a few minutes, she found her phone at the bottom of her purse.

The officer she spoke with told her not to touch anything but to leave things just as she had found them, and they were dispatching someone right away. At first, she may have been a little scared, but after seeing all her things smashed, her feelings melted into grief, and the more she looked around, the more that feeling passed onto anger.

Talking to the walls, she began to rant. "They have played with the wrong mutha fucker. This time Sonny done crossed the line, and he has no idea what's comin' his way."

A loud rap on the door followed by a gruff-sounding voice, "NOPD," broke her thoughts. She ushered the police officer in, "You got one helluva mess here." As he studied the room, he wiped the dripping sweat from his brow with an old dingy handkerchief. "This how you found it?"

"Well, I certainly didn't do this myself!" She blinked hard, followed by a tilt of the head and exaggerated raised eyebrows.

"No, uh, ma'am, uh," he wasn't sure if he should address the victim as ma'am or sir but decided to leave it at that. "I was referring to whether you had moved anything. It'd be perfectly natural to wanna start putting things away. That's what I meant."

"Put things away? Shiiit, everything is trashed; he trashed it all."

"*He*?" the officer asked. "You think you know who did this?"

"Think? No, honey, I know! This," and she waved her hand with a flick of the wrist, "is the handiwork of Sonny Ramone, he and his moronic sidekicks. That's who done this, and Mista, he's easy to find because he bounces at The Golden Lady."

"He did this with you here?" the officer asked.

"Hello, no." Her lips curled in disgust.

"How do you know it was him?"

"He an' I had it out already today; that's how I know. B'sides I can smell his cheap nasty cologne; it stunk the place up." She twisted her face, turning her nose up. "Ya smell it? Go on over and pick him up. Bring his sorry ass—"

"We gotta first make sure it was him."

"Are you listening to me, hellooo? I told you, I *know* it was him."

"Look, just cause you an' your friend had a disagreement—"

"*Excuse me?* Mista, he ain't no friend of mine. He's nothing more than a two-time losin' street punk that thinks he's all *that*." She was getting worked up.

"What y'all get into it about?" He made his way further into the apartment, scanning the destruction.

She was fit to be tied, "his girlfrien'," Simone was getting the distinct impression this joker wasn't taking her seriously.

"An' her name might be?" He half-smiled as he asked.

"Desiree DuBose."

"Why'd he harass you over his girlfriend? It don't make no sense." This was a routine call, and he didn't have the time to get in the middle of a love triangle.

"I guess he thought I'd know where she was. He came by here lookin' for her an' when I told him she wasn't here, he busted through the door an' said he'd come look for hisself an' I said, 'No, he wasn't' and showed him the door." The officer went through all the motions of listening to her, but Simone could tell his mind was elsewhere. "Excuse me, sir, you gettin' all this?"

"I'm trying to place the name," he answered.

"I wouldn't be at all surprised if he was one of y'all frequent flyers."

"Not him. *Her.*"

"Desiree?"

"Yeah."

"Well, honey, it was all over the news. Desiree's the chick beat all up, almos' on death's doorstep when some businessman found her, you know, at that hotel off of—"

"Just the other night, that's right." It was starting to twig in his mind.

"Who do you think put the hurt on her?" She put her hand on her hip and flipped her hair back. "You got it, Sonny. He was her boyfrien' 'til she heard him on the phone with Mr. Manducci—"

He interrupted, "As in Anthony Manducci?" He mopped his forehead again.

"That's the one. Sonny works as a bouncer for him at his club." She hoped he was starting to listen a bit closer.

As though starting to see the picture, he nodded, "Right, The Golden Lady." He pulled out his phone and made a call. Quickly he sketched the story he'd just heard from Simone. He put his hand over the mouthpiece, "You know where Desiree's at now?" Simone wasn't sure whether to tell him and decided to talk to Desiree first. She gracefully turned up her palms and shrugged her shoulders.

Upon completing his phone call, he asked if she thought she might hear from the girl again.

"I'm sure. We close, like sisters. But I gotta ask you, what are y'all going to do about all of this?" she dramatically swept her arms, motioning to the disaster around them.

"Unfortunately, there's not much I can do unless we find someone who saw him come in here. I doubt he'll tell us he did this, so it's your word against his until we can match a fingerprint, and that's not likely anytime soon. I hate to tell you." She was disheartened and afraid.

"What if he comes after me? What then? He's crazy like that; he might even shoot my ass. I need some protection. Ain't your motto, "to serve and protect? I want to see some protection." She pointed her finger at him.

"I can get you a restrainin' order so he can't come aroun' here." The detective continued to scribble on his pad.

"Mista, you an' I both know that ain't worth the paper it's written on," she looked down, feeling defeated.

"I tell ya what. I'll go talk to him an' see what I can get out of him. But, if I was you, I'd tell my good friend Desiree she better file some sort of complaint so we can get him off the street. When's the last time you talked to her?"

Simone was hesitant but conceded, "She stopped over early in the mornin'," she quickly added, "But I don't know where she's at now."

There was no doubt summer had arrived. After leaving Simone's, he headed for the club. He felt confident nothing would come from it, but a promise was a promise.

The Golden Lady, to look at, was no different from any other Bourbon Street strip joint, dark and dingy with a pungent odor of stale beer and nasty body funk. There were a few men perched at the bar. They reminded him more of fixtures than people.

He scanned the room, noticing the barkeep was on the phone, and there was a table with three sleazy-looking males. A loud whine followed by a startling bang reverberated through the air as the door of the men's room slammed shut. The piece of work coming from the can had to be Sonny Ramone. He chuckled to himself; Simone couldn't have described him any better. He was definitely a two-time punk that thought he was the deal.

As the detective walked in, he flashed his shield toward the bar, "Hello, boys."

Sonny had made it to the table with his three compadres, and the four of them stared as the detective came over.

He plopped his meaty hand on Sonny's shoulder, "How ya doin', Sonny?"

Sonny moved from under his hand with attitude while pushing his chair back and posturing to his feet, "I know you?"

"Nah, not yet. I'm looking for your girlfriend, Desiree. You know where she's at?"

With a smart-ass grin and a shrug of his shoulders, he coyly answered, "What's it to ya?"

"Name's Duncan MacFarland, NOPD, an' it ain't none of ya business, smart ass."

"I ditched the bitch; she ain't my woman no more. You want her; you find her." He turned his back to the officer and sat back down, showboating for his friends.

"Oh, Sonny-boy, not that easy. You see, you was the last one seen with her, and we have it she might have met with some foul play after leaving the hospital. We know it was you that put her there in the first place, ma man." He put his hand on the back of Sonny's neck and squeezed hard as he leaned over to deliver his message. In a loud threatening whisper, "Ya see, it really chaps my ass to hear of no good scumballs like you beatin' on women. I take it very personal, if ya catch my drift. Oh, an' no need to keep lookin' behind yourself because I'll be there every time waiting for you to fuck up." He addressed the table. "You boys better think twice who ya hang with, cuz I'm gonna be on the sombitch like white on rice." With a sarcastic smile, he said, "Now you boys have a good day, ya hear?"

The table fell silent as the pudgy middle-aged detective strolled out of the club.

OH, THE POSSIBILITIES

Desiree took to the job like she'd been doing it all her life. She could easily get used to these new surroundings and desperately hoped they would become her new reality. Time flew by, and before she knew it, Eli was knocking on the war room door, ready to go for the day.

It was evident Desiree had enjoyed the experience. The entire ride back to the house, she chattered with animated descriptions of her grand time at the office.

"Am I to take it you'll be back again tomorrow?" he asked.

"Hell yeah, if y'all have me. Ya got some good people workin' in ya place. Everyone's so frien'ly. Took me right in, yeah—dey t'ought I was doin' some intern somet'ing. Course dey had ta tell me what dat was," and she laughed, "but I tol' dem 'hell no.' I wadn't in school. Wished I was. Course when dey foun' out how ol' I was, dey realized I was no intern."

By the time they got to Eli's, Rachel had started dinner. Uninvited and despite the cold shoulder, Desiree jumped in to assist with the meal. At first, it was most unwelcome, but Desiree's personality made it hard for Rachel to stay cold. It was hard to keep from laughing at some of the coon-ass expressions. Desiree went on and on about the day at the office.

"I worked at Dad's last summer for a few weeks, and you can have it. I guess it's not my cup of tea. I certainly didn't have fun. *Boooooring!*"

Desiree looked up at Rachel and winked with a nod. "Anyt'ing can be fun, sha. It's all aboud what ya make of it, ya know. Me, I'm just grateful ta ya daddy *an all y'all* fa whacha done fa me." She spoke sincerely to Rachel; she knew it had been harder on the girl than Alan.

The evening rolled on. Desiree waited for the silence of slumber before she placed the call to Simone at the club. It was only ten-thirty, and her show usually didn't start until eleven. She called the back line to avoid having to yell to be heard and felt confident Sonny would be up at the front door. There would be no risk of him answering. The phone rang several times with no answer. She was about to give up when one of the dancers picked up. "Lemme speak ta LaFleur."

"She ain't here tonight, but I can leave a message for her," the girl offered.

Desiree hung up as her stomach twisted in knots; it was unlike Simone to miss work. Simone may have missed a total of five days in the ten years she had known her. Come hell or high water Simone always said she owed it to her fans to perform. Desiree tried her apartment. The machine picked up.

"If you're there, sha, pick up."

She picked up, "Desiree, don't call me here no more. Call my cell, girl."

"What's wrong, Simone?"

"Like I told ya, Desiree, someone saw you on the street, got word to Sonny, an' now he's come an' fucked my place up. He trashed all my stuff. Trashed, do you hear me? I told ya the boy's crazy. I got a name ya gotta call. It's a guy with NOPD."

"NOPD? You called da police? Oh, my Gawd, why ya done dat?"

"Des, you oughta see ma place, girl. There is nothing left; everything is all torn up. I had to do something; I really thought they'd arrest him an' put his ass off the street. Shit, I'm scare't he's gonna come up in my face with a gun. The cop said the only way we can get him off the street is fa you to press charges against him; then they can do something. For the both of us, ya gotta talk to him."

"Me an' da police don't get along so well. I don't know whad I'm gonna do; I gotta t'ink dis one t'rough, m'ami. I'll get back wit ya tomorra; ya gonna go inta work?"

Simone was angry, not to mention deeply hurt by Desiree's insensitivity to her situation. She felt betrayed. "Oh, I see how it works, now—you gotcha self a safe place, and screw ol' Simone. Girl, I got nowhere to run that Sonny can't find me. Please, talk to the police. You don't gotta tell 'em where you are."

"I dunno, give me da numba, jus' in case. I gotta t'ink it ova. It's not aboud you, Simone, you know betta dan dat. Dere's nuttin' I wouldn't do fa you, 'cept dis is de police, sha. Whad guarantee do I got dat dey'll pick him up. Gawd, dat's all I need fa dem to harass him an' den turn him a-loose. Lawd, have mercy. Dis one helluva fix we in."

"Tell me." Simone read off the number and the name.

"Duncan MacFarland? Now whad kinda name is dat; I aks you. We gonna put our lives in na han's of some f'in Scotsman? I talk witcha tomorra. Lata, ma girl."

Neither of them slept very well.

An uncomfortable atmosphere was brewing in the club, and there was almost a wall of silence that appeared when Anthony Manducci arrived. He was preceded by two of his goons, both in dark suits that seemed two sizes too small and conspicuous dark glasses. They looked like they belonged in some Chicago gangster movie. Manducci made his appearance with a bosomy platinum blonde draped on his arm. The sight would have been none too pleasing to Mrs. Manducci, who was probably home with the kids and the nanny. As per usual, Sonny glued himself to his uncle's coat tail, offering streams of overly sickening compliments. Manducci took little or no interest in anything Sonny had to say, but then he never did. Manducci deposited the girl at a stage-side table, and the entourage proceeded to the back office.

It wasn't until the group had settled in that Manducci spoke. "It's been brought to my attention that the DuBose girl's out the hospital and on the street. I also got word that our main act, The Golden Lady, ain't at work because some two-bit hoodlums trashed her place." He looked straight at Sonny.

"Whoever did this stupid thing must have their head up their stupid fuckin' ass. See now, we got the law nosin' in our business and that I don't need. I tell you what I'm gonna have to do now. I'm gonna give Miss LaFleur my word that I will replace all her things and that this most unfortunate circumstance was surely a mistake, and I will personally guarantee she and her things will be safe. Do you know what that means, fellas? That means I'm gonna have to give Miss LaFleur a personal bodyguard. Like it or not, the fairy brings in a lot of dough, and as far as I'm concerned, no one, and I mean no one fucks with the fairy." He signaled for everyone to leave but Sonny.

He grabbed Sonny by the collar, "Sit."

Sonny obeyed. Manducci sat behind the desk, put his feet up, and lit a cigar. Clouds of gray smoke billowed from his mouth. His cold, empty stare sent shivers up Sonny's spine. There was no life behind his eyes, no emotion, just a dark frozen void.

"I don't know what I'm gonna do wit you. First, ya beat up the girl; then ya trash the fairy's apartment. You not right in the head? You must have some kinda death wish. I try hard to keep low-key under the radar. I don't want no one nosin' in my business. The cops and me we stay out of each other's way. Ya know why they leave me alone? It's cuz I take care of my own business; no loose ends, if you catch my drift. There's never nothin' for them to investigate. But you? You leave them one big fuckin' mess and that, boy, opens the door for them to start nosin' in my affairs. That's it, Sonny, your goose done been cooked. Outta here."

"But, Unc—"

Manducci put his hand up in silence and walked out of the door.

Sonny grabbed his arm, pleading, "Don't do dis. Uncle Tony, c'mon."

Manducci turned and looked at him with disgust. "Ain't you got no cahonnas, boy? You make me sick, beggin' like a little girl." He stopped for a minute, and then as though he had some sort of revelation, he spoke. "I got a job for you. You gonna be the fairy's bodyguard and at her beck and call. Sissy boy like you oughta get along real nice with the fairy."

That was the icing on the cake; Sonny had all the insults he would take. "You want me outta here; you got it. I'm outta here. No one, not even you, is gonna talk to Sonny Ramone like dat." Sonny stormed past Manducci.

It didn't take long for Desiree to fit into the Rosen's day-to-day routine. She was like a sponge absorbing everything in her surroundings and in no time felt like one of the family. Friday evening rolled around, and the four of them, Eli, Desiree, Rachel, and Alan, went for an early supper at Port of Call. She was always fearful of being spotted by someone from her other life; she felt hesitant to go out on family outings. Her greatest fear was not for herself but for Eli and the kids. If recognized, her presence would be like a magnet for trouble. The Miami trip was coming up fast, and dinner was filled with great stories about the kids' Mims and Pops. She figured she would have plenty of time to straighten out the mess with Sonny while her new family was on vacation.

"Des, you ought to see the beach by my grandparents' house. Every night after dinner, we all go for a walk on the beach; it's really cool." Rachel added, "There's a lot to do for people our age."

Eli piped in, "*Y'all's age?* Rach, Desiree is *a lot* older than you."

"Really? Whad ya sayin' there; ma frien' you insultin'me? I wonda if you're ma frien'." Everyone at the table had a good laugh, "On dat note, I'm gonna take dese old bones back home and get in da showa."

"That isn't what I meant." He put his hands flat on the table and looked apologetically at her.

"Don't start ya crawfishin', Eli. We all heard wha' ya said," she gave Rachel a wink.

Eli watched as she got up from the table; she made him feel like a kid again.

Alan interrupted his thoughts, "Dad, this year, we won't need to get a house sitter when we go to Miami. Desiree will be there."

"Dad," Rachel jumped in the conversation, "I thought she could go with us to Pops and Mims. She can stay with me; I know Mims and Pops won't mind."

Eli had to think about that one. He didn't want to give anyone the wrong idea, "Rach, she may not want to go. Not everyone likes to visit old people. That was the end of the issue, or so he thought.

Simone wasn't sure if she wanted to go to work or not. The ordeal had shaken her, but she didn't want to disappoint the people who had come to see her show. It had become quite the attraction. With a deep breath, she put her a brave foot forward, grabbed her purse, locked the door, and made her way to the club.

Midway down the block, a long black limousine cruised slowly. She paid little to no attention as there had been countless times visitors would slow to gawk and snap photos. All the attention ever did was add a little more wiggle to her walk; that way, they'd get the full effect. She could hear as the window glided down. She looked over with the sexiest smile she could muster. To her surprise, it was Manducci, the man himself. She stopped dead in her tracks, figuring if he had wanted to kill her, it'd already happened.

"Good evening, Miss LaFleur." He had an icy smile.

"An' to you too, Mr. Manducci. Coming to see the show tonight?" She asked with a slight quiver.

"Not tonight, dawlin', but I did want to talk to you and apologize for the mess my nephew caused you. Get in; I'll give you a ride to the club."

A bit nervous, she climbed in.

"Dawlin', I really wished you woulda called me. I can get way more done for you than the cops; you oughta know that by now. Let me know how much it'll be to replace your things and consider it done. Tell me, you always walk to work? Simone, you know you bring a pretty penny into the club."

"Well, yaaiis, sir, it's only a couple of blocks. When it's raining, I catch me a cab so's not to mess my hair. Since I'm an entertainer, the cabbies usually don't charge me," she patted her hair.

"I think I'd feel better if my golden lady wuz picked up and brought home. That way, I'm protectin' my interest." The look in his eyes was intense, even scary.

"Whateva you want, Mr. Manducci, you da bossman." She giggled nervously.

"Done. How much you figure in damages? Ten grand, fifteen, twenty?"

She nervously giggled again, "Oh no, sir, maybe a thousand or two. It would do just fine. I could replace all that was broke, yes sir, that would take care of everything."

"I'll split the difference and call it fifteen. Okay, wit' you?" He took her hand.

She stammered, "I'm not sure what to say, sir."

"Done."

The car pulled up in front of the club. A crowd was already forming outside; Manducci ordered one of his men to escort his "Golden Lady" to her dressing room.

Simone loved the attention but was wary of the price she would eventually have to pay. The show was at hand, and it was time to put her personal life on hold and get on with business. As usual, she'd start the show with her amazing Diana Ross, then go to Tina Turner as the crowd's heat grew, then an outstanding Whitney, and finally what the people had come to see, the Golden Lady, Miss Simone LaFleur. She fingered through the rack of splashy gowns organizing her costume, headpiece, or wig and the jewelry for each change. She sat at the dressing table, studying her face and trying to push the previous day's horror from her mind. Her thoughts were interrupted by a knock on the door.

"Miss LaFleur, it's Mac; you decent?"

She called out, "Suga, I'm never decent; that's why they come to see LaFleur, don't cha know?" She gave a throaty laugh.

She opened the door, and he entered in the same worn-out-looking jacket and stained tie he'd worn the last time she'd seen him. She shook her head from side to side.

"Ain't you got no otha jacket and tie. Look at you; you're a mess." Simone straightened his tie. "What's this?" she pointed to a series of minor stains, "lunch?"

"Everybody's a critic. Enough with the compliments, Miss LaFleur. I jus' stopped to tell ya I talked to ya frien' Sonny. Don't know what good it'll do, but I wanted to let ya know."

She warmly smiled at him, "Thank you for stoppin' in. I appreciate it. Wanna stay for the show? I can get ya a great seat." She sat down and glanced at him in the reflection. For a brief moment, she went back to Simon, the city planner from Chicago. There wasn't the usual exaggerated femininity in her voice. "Mac, I know you said you couldn't do much, and I'm grateful you spoke with Sonny.

"Truth be told, my place needed a facelift. From what I've heard, Mr. Ramone has screwed the pooch. He's pissed the wrong people off. This whole thing is going to go away, and life will go on." Back to her stage presence, "Now, dawlin' thanks for tryin', and I hope ya make the show," she batted her eyelashes at him, still speaking with him through her reflection. "This girl's gotta get ready, so unless you wanna see it all, you better take your leave, or you gonna get more than you bargained for. The show?"

"Thanks for the invite, but I gotta decline. By the way, ya heard from ya girl yet?"

"I gave her ya number, baby. She ain't called you yet, I take it?" she shook her head. "Doesn't come as a surprise, Desiree is on Desiree time, she neva gets back quick, but she may call you, then again, she may not. Get along now, or you may see something you don't wanna see, or maybe ya do."

He chuckled, "Don't butter my bread on that side." He was out the door.

Saturday mornings at the Rosen residence were quiet and low-key. One by one, the members of the household would groggily pad into the kitchen for their caffeine jump-start or orange juice rush. There were the typical morning greetings, but that was about it. There was no idle conversation or small talk. It was quiet, cozy, and comfortable. The gentle hum of the ceiling fan was most relaxing, and the slight stir of air generated was barely enough to ruffle the corner of the newspaper.

Splashed on the front page was a large picture of the Governor with his arm around the shoulder of Anthony Manducci. Heading read, "Gov. and Manducci, No Relationship?" Both men had hearty smiles, and it was obvious they knew each other well.

While the Governor's office referenced an impending investigation in an earlier interview, they had been beaten to the punch by one scrappy young journalist. The article explained that while a picture may say a thousand words, campaign contributions and the like could write volumes. With much digging, he linked a series of contributions via an intricate weave of shell companies, ultimately landing on the Manducci name.

"This is so typical, Louisiana politics at its finest," he tossed the paper on the coffee table in disgust.

"I tried to tell ya, sha. Dem two dey t'ick as t'eives."

Eli seized the opportunity, "How's a little country coon-ass, like yourself, know they are thick as thieves?"

"Oh, ma frien', I jus' know, I hear talk." She winked at him with a quirky smile.

He was going to push it, "and where do you hear this talk?"

"Here and dere, ya know?" She fiddled with her phone, trying not to look at him, but it was useless.

Emphatically he looked directly in her face, "No, Desiree, I don't know, tell me. I'm all ears." His demeanor was stoic, not his typical easy-going attitude.

She sat silently, hoping he'd back off like he usually did when she avoided his prying, but not this time. He sat there, waiting.

"Can't a girl have some secrets, no? I tell ya sha. Ya wanna know? I really didn't eva want ya to know," she was still stalling, hoping he'd say to let it go, but no such luck. He sat there still waiting. "Okay, you win. I used to dance at da Golden Lady; ya know, da gentlemen's club. Mr. Manducci owns it. I seen him an' his boy, the gov together in da club. I figure dem mus' be frien's, right? Dey always seemed real chummy. Does dat answer to ya satisfaction?"

Eli felt terrible, ashamed that he had pushed her, yet somehow relieved to know something about her. There was still so much more to know about her, and this provided the perfect entry.

"I've never been there, but I hear the show, the one with the transvestite, is supposed to be excellent. I've had many clients tell me how marvelous they thought she was, and if you didn't know better, you'd swear she was a woman." He sipped his coffee.

"She's a woman, alright. She's jus' trapped in da wrong body, sha."

"You know what I mean. You know her well, I take it?" He reached and grabbed the newspaper again.

"Yeah, sha, ya might say we're t'ick as t'ieves. I swear da questions dey jus' keep on comin'." She flashed her eyes and made it clear storytime was over.

Just at that moment, Alan emerged from his room. He looked at Desiree, "So, you comin'?"

Confused, everyone sat silent. Alan asked again. "Desiree, you comin'?"

"Where to, ma man?"

Figuring he stepped in it, he tried to offset the blunder. "Nevermind, I don't know what I was talking about."

"No, ami, I t'ink maybe you do," she looked at Eli, "Whad adventure ya got planned fa dis soon ta be hot an' sticky day?" She folded her legs underneath her.

The paper rustled in his hands as he turned the page. He looked up, "Today? Nothing I know of, but I think Alan must be talking about the Miami trip."

"So, Alan," she jokingly flirted, "You invitin' me, sha? I don't t'ink ya dad would go fa dat. He might t'ink I'm a smidge too ol' fa ya, now," she winked at Eli.

Alan turned bright red, "No, I, that's not, I, no, I mean—"

"Chill, little man, I'm playin' jus' givin' ya a hard time," she snickered, "Gotcha." She pointed at him.

Playfully, he pushed her over on the sofa onto her side; it made her laugh.

"Alan, you too easy, sha. Jus' foolin' wit' ya. Ta answer ya question, I don't know if I'll be goin', dis is da firs' I heard, 'sides I got a real job now an' ma boss, ooh la la, he's a real slave driva. Can I get back ta ya?"

As the noon hour began to roll around, the crew, one by one, readied themselves for the day. Rachel and Alan left to rendezvous with their friends, leaving Eli and Desiree alone for the afternoon.

"You got some good kids, Eli. Alan is too funny; I neva knew someone could blush so bright. I know he's jus' bein' a kid; I took his invite wit' a grain—"

Eli interrupted, "The invitation is real, but I don't know if you'd want to go to Miami; I don't know how much fun it would be. If you don't want to go, that's certainly understandable. You're welcome to stay here if you want; it's up to you." Eli, still with the newspaper in hand, hadn't taken his eyes off the television during the whole conversation. He was engrossed in the sports program. When he spoke, his voice seemed to trail off.

"Oh, my Gawd, your ent'usiasm overwhelms me, ma frien'. Both offas sound so, what is da word, *invigoratin'*. I can hardly decide. You really know how ta finesse da women. Eli, no wonda ya ain't got no woman."

Still not taking his eyes off the screen, he responded, "It's because I don't want a woman, not that I can't get a woman. Who needs them anyway? All they do is complain and run up the credit cards. This time he looked over and gave her a smart-ass smile. "I forgot, they're also good at gabbin' at the wrong time during a ballgame." He gave her a broad smile.

"Excuse da hell outta me. I'm startin' to see jus' whad a sexist pig you are. Nex' you'll be aksin' I bring ya slippas an' ya food." She kicked her sock foot from underneath her playfully.

"I'm glad you said that," she did a double-take. "No, seriously, I gotta go down to the market for some vegetables; you wanna take a walk?" He folded the paper.

"Who me? Wit' you?" She paused, "I guess since dere's nuttin else ta do, I s'pose I'll go."

Her quick sarcasm was contagious; he loved how he felt when she was around. He caught himself looking at her a little too long. He wondered if she had any idea he had fallen hard for her and lived out his fantasies in the far reaches of his mind. He wanted to tell her, desperately taking her in his arms and holding her like there was no tomorrow.

"Sha, wha' aboud ya precious game, huh? If you go now, ya might miss somet'in' an' we couldn't have dat, no, no. I'll go ta da market, and you stay here an' hold down na game. I'm expectin' ya ta tell me play by play what I miss, ya hear?" She popped up and dressed.

After she emerged in shorts, tee, and tennis shoes, he continued to argue for a few minutes but had to give in to her hard-headed way. She stuck the money he handed her deep into her pocket and went out.

The midday heat was stifling. On the way to the market, she replayed the morning, going over and over the family banter; she loved being a part of it all. Sometimes she would think of Eli and all he had done for her. The feelings of gratitude had even turned into curiosity. She had never seen him with a woman; it was all about his kids and work. She wondered if he ever dated. She wondered how he felt about her. Did he view her as just some kid, or did he look at her as a woman? If so, he had never exposed his thoughts.

Her mind rambled as she passed block upon block. Just as she got within sight of the flea market, screeching tires zapped her from her daydream world tossing her into a ring of hell. She looked up. He looked greasier, for some reason, than she remembered, and she found herself questioning how she had ever fallen for him.

"Looky, looky, where y'at Desiree? Why ain't ya come round?" She walked around his car and continued to the French Market. He inched up, almost touching her; she didn't stop but did turn her head with glaring eyes in his direction. She kept going. The door of the car slammed; she could feel him behind her. Did she dare make a scene? She knew it would do one of two things, either piss him off in the extreme, and he'd nab her butt, tossing her into his car, never to be seen again, or the attention could possibly scare him off, and he would retreat to the rock he had slithered from under. It was worth a try.

She screamed for him to leave her alone in a loud frightened voice. "I said, leave me alone, creep." She could see people turning around to catch a glimpse of the action.

"Shuddup Desiree, I'm warnin' you, shuddup."

Desiree had to go for it; she started to pull from his grasp, screaming for help. By this time, vendors had come out; one picked up a bat and ran toward Sonny. "You want some, Mista? I got something for you right here," he waved the bat. Sonny had just grabbed her arm but let go and turned back to his car.

He hissed at her, "Another day, bitch an' ya mine, all mine."

She heard his car as it peeled away. The man with the bat had made it to her asking if she was alright and could he call someone. She thanked him but said she was okay. It only took a minute, and a crowd had formed around her. A few people were calling out for someone to call the police.

Desiree knew she had to get out of Dodge in a hurry, but the crowd wouldn't let her.

It seemed only a few seconds when two cop cars and an unmarked pulled up. The five officers descended upon her. The last one to her was an older guy, overweight and almost slovenly. He locked eyes with her.

"I got this one, boys; y'all go on."

The four officers were more than delighted to return to their squad cars and the easy patrol of the Quarter. If anything could be said about cruising the Quarter, there was always more than an eyeful of gawking available.

"You sure are a sight for sore eyes, Desiree."

"I know you?" she was a bit put out that he knew who she was but couldn't place him. She had lucked out and never been arrested, but one could say she had no real fondness for the police. She'd heard her fair share of horror stories about girls beat up or bullied into sexual favors by the boys in blue. Most of them, she figured, were on the take, anyway; why bother with respect.

"No dawlin', you don't know me, but I sure as hell know who you are. Yes indeedy, in fact, we share a mutual friend, Miss Simone LaFleur." He had a warm smile.

"Oh yeah? An', jus' how do ya know Simone? Ya sure as hell don't look like y'all would travel in da same circles." She cocked her head with a sassy grin.

He wiped his brow, "What do they say; looks can be deceivin'?"

She stood silent for a moment sizing him up, "Whad ya want wit' me?"

"I wanna talk to you about your friend, Sonny Ramone. From what I gather, you and him's not on the best of terms right now. According to Miss LaFleur, it seems he's the one that put you in the hospital and then trashed her place. Boy, you shoulda seen her home, whew, what a mess. You got some time to talk?"

"Now?" Desiree asked.

"Why you got something better to do? If it was me, I'd wanna see that slimeball behind bars, but hey, that's me. Simone don't feel safe, and there's nothing we can do about it; it's a he-said-she-said thing, but what he did to you that is a whole different arena. All ya gotta do is press charges."

She no more wanted to talk with this guy than fly to the moon, but she also knew she wouldn't be safe trying to walk back to Eli's. "I tell ya whad, sha; I'll give ya a few minutes in exchange fa a ride. Part of dis deal is dat any future meetin's are on ma terms. I don't want no one ta know we talked. Because whetha ya want ta admit it or not, ya can't keep me safe, much as ya t'ink ya can. Oh, an' make no mistake, there *will be no* testifyin' from dis li'l chick. You on ya own once I give ya da info. But firs' I gotta make groceries, stroll along wit' me or wait in da car, it's up ta you."

What a pistol rolled through his mind. He couldn't believe this tiny girl could possess such a tough attitude. "Ya know, I can't promise all that, but I give you my word; I'll do the best I can, providing you play it straight with me. Deal?" At least he was honest with her.

"I dunno," she had to think it through. "Are ya comin'?" she made her way through the market. She had always loved shopping at the French Market; so much to see. The produce was always good, and the people were colorful. She picked up a few items to bring back to Eli's.

"Ya know, Simone told me aboud ya. You're dat Mac guy, Mac Mac something. Your momma couldn't come up wit' anyt'ing more original. It'd be like namin' me Des Desiree," she laughed.

"The name's Duncan MacFarland. Only my friends call me Mac, and from what I can tell, we ain't friends yet," he turned on a sarcastic grin, "or are we?"

"Mista, I wanna help, long as it don't interfere wit' ma new life. Ya see, I kinda stumbled into a chance fa a new life an' nuttin's gonna get in da way. Dese people, da ones I'm staying by, are good people. Dey don't know nuttin' an' dat's how it's gonna stay. Ya got dat, or am I goin' too fast fa ya?"

"You always so charmin'?" he found her quite amusing.

She grinned, "Only ta ma frien's. You ma frien', Mac MacFarland?"

"I suppose I am, Dizzy Des. I suppose I am."

They walked back to his car. She confirmed the story told to him by Simone and elaborated on her relationship with Sonny.

"Is it safe to assume he is the one who grabbed you just now?" he asked.

"Yeah." She sadly nodded.

"You realize the sooner we pick him up, the safer you're gonna be?" She pointed for him to pull over.

They talked about their next meeting. Desiree suggested lunchtime on Monday; she should be able to break away. She got ready to get out of the car and turned to him. "I'm gonna stay on da neutral groun' while ya pull off. I don't want no one knowin' where I'm at. Dat's all I need someone nosin' around aksin' questions." Mac nodded. She crossed to the neutral ground, waited for him to pull away, crossed the street, and slipped down the driveway.

Still glued to the TV, Eli broke his gaze and briefly looked at her, "You were gone a long time; everything okay?"

"Yeah, I did a little lookin' at da Flea Market. Ya can get some good deals dere sometimes, ya know?" She put the produce in the sink to wash.

"Can't say as I do; I've never been there," talking over his shoulder. "I go to Central, and sometimes the veggie stands at the French Market, but not the caps and stuff."

"An' ya live so close," she shook her head. "Ya min' if I use da telephone in Rachel's room?"

He intently looked at the game, "Gotta new beau?"

"Oh, yeah, lookin' like dis? Right." She kept walking.

"Huh? Everything healed up, almost. You look good." He seemed shocked by her comment; he thought she was exotically beautiful.

Desiree stopped, turned, and looked at him. "It's not dat. Look at me; I look like I'm ten wit' dis new look y'all give me."

"You look healthy, not like—" He decided it was best to leave it there.

"Like whad, you sayin' I look bad b'fore." She put her hand on her hip. "Ya neva saw me, how can ya say dat? Brotha, I tell you, yeah, dere were many men dat liked whad dey saw. Didn't see no school girl lookin' t'ing, no sir, whad dey seen was a sexy petite woman."

"Desiree, go make your call."

"You gonna sit dere an' tell me I can't look sexy?" she was getting a little offended, not to mention her feelings hurt.

He chose not to say anything else. How could he possibly tell her not only did he think she was beautiful, but in his mind, he had been preoccupied with the thought of knowing her in a more intimate and different way? She was obviously offended even though playful, but there was nothing he could say without revealing his feelings. He didn't comment on her huffy disposition and hoped it would pass fast.

She went to the back, hoping to get Simone on the phone. It felt like weeks since she had spoken to her.

The phone rang only a couple of times. "Yaaiis?"

"Simone, it's me. Wanted to let ya know I talked ta the Mac guy you tol' me aboud."

"Shiiit, girl, I shoulda called you. The way it all worked out, ya didn't need to talk to him after all. Things have gotten *bizarre*." Her voice went up a couple of octaves. "You wouldn't believe it even if I told you."

"Like whad?" she had piqued Desiree's curiosity.

"For starters, Sonny don't work for the big man no more. Manducci's all up in his face on accounta throwing you out and trashing my place. He says I am his money maker and gave me a car and driver to go to work."

"Get outta here."

"Really, and get this, I think, not for sure, but I think he's put a hit on Sonny.

"No way. Oh my Gawd, Sonny knows dis?"

"Girl, I dunno, and I don't care. That little piss ant tore my place up good. Course, big daddy Manducci's given me enough scratch to get my place *all* fixed up."

"Ya betta watch y'self. Somet'ing stinks aboud de whole t'ing."

"Honey, the man just realized I was the star and is treating me like he shoulda all along. I'm not too worried. Hell, I'm just gonna enjoy it while it lasts."

Desiree changed the subject; Simone was obviously too into the hype to look at it sensibly. "Guess who ran inta me t'day, like almos' really? Sonny. Sha, he had dis look on his face. I know fa sure, he woulda kilt me. So I did like da commercial says, an' yelled an' ran. I wadn't fast enough; he got hold of my arm. Sure enough, some big bruisa from da flea market comes at him wit' a bat. You shoulda seen him; he nearly crapped himself. But it's not ova, sha. He's still comin' fa me; I won't jus' get ma ass kicked; it'll be da numba. Lights out."

"Maybe you should come back to the club and get some Manducci protection. Tell him all about what Sonny done ya. Don't be surprised when the skank nasty winds up being fished out of the river."

"Nah, I'm likin' dis new life fa da mos' part. I gotta go, but b'fore, answer me one t'ing. Ya t'ink I'm sexy?"

"Whaddaya talkin' bout? You know you are. Girlfrien' you always had men coming after you. Why did Sonny say ya not? F' him."

"T'anks I'll see ya soon. You take care, sha. Watch y'self, now."

CLASS ACT AND ALL THAT

Monday mornings were a drag, but with one week remaining in school, Desiree was getting a kick out of the kids' anticipation for summer. With all that had been going down, she thought it might be a good idea to take Eli up on the Miami offer. She hoped things would settle down while they were gone. Despite all that had happened between her and Sonny, she felt bad for him if what Simone had said was true; he didn't have much time left on the earth.

Even though he had mistreated her at times, there were other times when things were better than great. She missed those great times. The Rosen house provided a sense of belonging, being a part of something, something good, but all in all, she still felt alone in many ways and knew the fairytale wouldn't go on forever. They'd eventually find out she was no more than a scuzzy little street rat. Oh, they'd understand it hadn't been all her fault, then they'd feel sorry for her; she'd never be able to deal with the pity.

The Rosen's were good people, and they'd try not to make her feel uncomfortable; that's just how they were, but they'd never be able to look at her the same way, especially Eli. Then again, she didn't know how he looked at her. After his comment, it was more than obvious; he didn't look at her *that* way.

Things were a-buzz at Class Act Events. They always were on show days. Desiree was gearing up for the event, going through the file, making sure all contracts, checks, and the like were in order. Her concentration was interrupted by the phone.

"This is Desiree. How may I help you?"

"Dizzy Des, this is Mac. You forgot me or somethin'?"

"Oh, Jeez, we gotta make it fa anotha day. I got a big event tonight. You jus' caught me; I was headin' out da door, fa real."

"Where ya gonna be at?" he pried.

"Marriott, why?"

"What ballroom?"

"Oh, no way, friend. Gimme a break," just then, Eli showed up at the war room door.

"Wrap it up; we gotta go now," she waved at him and mouthed, "I'm tryin'."

"Look, I gotta go; we'll have ta do dis tomorra or da nex' day, sha. See ya." She didn't wait for a response; she just hung up.

"On the phone with your new beau again?" he teased.

"Right, som'tin' like dat." She had to put it all behind her and focus on the matter at hand. Eli had entrusted the coordination of the show to her, and she was determined it would be letter-perfect. There was no way she wanted to disappoint him; he'd given her one hell of a chance, which did more for her self-esteem than anyone would ever know. It was almost like a rite of passage.

She had everything together and got up. Eli put his arms around her and hugged her tight, "Where y'at, girl? Calm down, don't be so intense;

it's not like we got any babies dyin' here, ya know. It's just a freakin' party, and it'll go smooth as silk. You'll see." She mustered a smile.

As they rode to the hotel, Eli threw question after question at her regarding the show. She had all the answers. He pulled into the garage and looked into her eyes with an air of complete and total confidence. "Desiree, you got it all covered; now relax. If you aren't relaxed, the client won't be relaxed, so just roll with it, understand?"

She saluted him, "yes, sir!"

Eli moved through the hotel with such grace and polish. She admired him and was proud, not to mention thankful, to be his right-hand man, so to speak. He introduced her to everyone he talked to, giving her credit for the show. For once in her life, she felt important, like she counted, like she did something of value.

Desiree closely observed as Eli interacted with the crew, then the hotel people. He treated everyone from the highest honcho to the dishwasher with the same respect and dignity. She tried to emulate him; she desperately wanted to be like him. She watched as others around them seemed to flutter here and there in a state of panic while Eli rolled with the flow, taking it all in stride. He brought calm to the waters.

He told Desiree he was heading back to the office, and she was to stay on site. He reiterated the most important thing to remember. "I'm close as a phone call. Something comes up an' ya not sure, call me; otherwise, go with the flow. Whatever you do, girl, don't panic." He put his arm around her and squeezed, "You've done good on this one, babe. I better watch my step, or you'll be taking my job." He kissed the top of her head, released her, and headed for the door. He moved with such sleekness she felt a twinge in her stomach. Maybe it was nerves, and then again, perhaps it wasn't.

She loved having the crew come up to her, looking to her for guidance.

She felt empowered. Her first call to the hotel electrician was unnerving, but it wasn't long before it became old hat, and she wielded the power with authority and grace. There was no mistaking she was Eli's prodigy.

Desiree had her head buried in the file as she studied one vendor's contracts and didn't hear him walking up.

"I betcha didn't have no lunch," the detective was standing right next to her.

To say she was startled would have been a gross understatement. She grabbed her chest. "Oh, my Gawd, you almos' gave me a heart attack. Don't ya do dat again."

"I hope ya like roast beef po-boys." Mac handed her the bag, "I figured you for a Barq's kinda girl, am I right?" He grabbed a chair and pulled it closer to her so they could talk.

"Don't get me wrong, sha, dis is real nice an' don't t'ink I don't appreciate it, an all, but I'm at work, an' I sure don't need no one gossiping me out a good job." She looked at him.

"Yeah, I get it; say I'm your Uncle Mac. I wanna know what's going on, Desiree. I want to make sure you know Sonny's not giving up; he's afta you like a hound dog on a nutra-rat. He's gonna kill you if he gets his hands on you again. You do know that, don't ya? An' there's not a damn thing we can do if ya don't come forward and make an official complaint."

She sat silently, taking slow bites from the sloppy po-boy.

"I'm serious now. Think about it; Sonny's got mighty long arms being Manducci's nephew." His brows furrowed with concern.

"Where ya get dis san'wich. It's good," she put it down for a second. "I know you are lookin' out fa me, and ya prob'ly right. If he could, he'd sure as hell kill me; he promised me dat, but wha' he doesn't know is Manducci's done put a hit on him. My sources are pretty good, too. Once he fin' out, he gonna be on na run an' gettin' outta N'awlins, sha." She glanced around the ballroom.

"Desiree, maybe it's true, maybe it ain't. But let's just say, for grins, it's so. You honestly think Manducci's gonna let you off knowin' what you know 'bout him and our good governor? With his finger, he drew a line across his throat. "I don't think so."

One of the crew started walking her way. She looked directly into Mac's eyes, speaking loud enough that people might hear. "T'ank you so much, Uncle Mac fa da sandwich. Gotta get back ta work, now, I know ya understan'," she leaned over and kissed his cheek, "tell Auntie I said hey an' we'll get together mebbe lata in da week or nex' week, yeah?" She got up and walked toward her crew.

He couldn't help it; she made him smile. He shook his head as he shoved all the trash back in the brown bag and left. Mac went completely unnoticed.

With everything in place and two hours until doors, the client was ready for the walk-through. Desiree paced back and forth, constantly glancing at the entrance. She couldn't believe he wouldn't show. He couldn't possibly expect her to do the walk-through alone. The door opened, and her heart sunk; it was the client. Hand outstretched, Desiree walked up to her.

"Hello, I'm—" the client interjected.

"You are just as cute as he said you were. Your ears must have been ringing because all your boss could say was how great you were, and he kept you under lock and key. You were one of your company's hidden talents." The client appeared unruffled that Eli wasn't there.

"Nice of him ta say. Did he happen ta mention when he might be here?" She kept calm but could feel her heart rate picking up and her throat tightening.

Just then, the doors flung open; he spread his arms. "Looks like someone's gonna have a helluva party in here tonight. It looks great!" He walked up to the client and gave her a kiss on the cheek, "What I tell you, is she good or is she good? She's the best." He was all smiles and gave Desiree a wink.

She watched his every move as he schmoozed the client for the next hour. He made it look easy. She busied herself, ensuring the food stations were perfect; the band stayed out of the food and drink lines and *away* from the guests. After about another half-hour, the party went into auto-drive, and there was nothing left for them to do.

He stepped up to her, "All's well with the client, so it looks like we are *outta* here, and there is nothing left to do." She felt like a child, almost having to run to keep up with his long strides. "Ya eat yet?"

"Not since lunch an' dat was jus' a coupla bites, who had time to eat?" She answered with gaspy words.

"How about we catch a bite at Mr. B's?" He realized she was having difficulty keeping up with him and slowed the pace to suit her.

"Big money, boss, your treat?" she teased.

"Of course, my treat. You deserve it; great job tonight."

The beginning of dinner went well as they hashed and re-hashed the show, the load-in, and the client, but once all had been said many times over, the conversation waned, and an awkward silence rolled in like an early morning fog. Neither one knowing where the comfortable limits of conversations were drawn.

Eli broke the ice, "You know, I woulda neva thought you to be a homebody. I woulda pegged you for a party girl." He gazed at her as he took a sip of wine.

"T'ings change, ma frien'. I used ta go out lots, but I neva really liked it much; it was jus' somet'in' ta do. It was much betta dan sittin' in da crap hole apartment." Her lips turned up into a sweet smile.

"I've meant to tell you, feel free to come and go as you please, or if you want to have a friend come over to the house, you are more than welcome. I want you to feel completely comfortable until you get your own—" He didn't want to finish the sentence. Did he ever want her to move out?

"I been workin' on dat, ya know, getting' ma own place. Shouldn't be too much longa." She felt uncomfortable, so she straightened her napkin in her lap as any excuse not to have to look him in the eye. She never wanted to leave the comfort of his home and family. She felt like she belonged.

Eli became fidgety, "I'm not rushing you at all. That is not at all what I meant. I want you to feel 100% comfortable and at home." He didn't want her to leave, not at all. It went through his head. He shouldn't have opened the discussion. Looking at her, he tried to will her to look him in the eyes. Her exotic teal-colored eyes were beautiful and most sensual.

"I know, I know, sha. I can't stay with you for the rest of my life, and I'm gonna need ta leave at some point. As it is, I know the people in ya office t'ink dere's somet'in' goin' on b'tween us. I tell dem quickly dat dey barkin up da wrong tree. I mean a guy like you, all sophisticated, a man aboud da worl' don't need no girl like me, but I can tell some don't believe it." She swirled the wine around in the glass, looking at it, trying to avoid eye contact. She knew her feelings were hiding just below the surface and would come roaring out if she gazed into his eyes.

Eli lounged back into the chair with an almost amused look on his face. "*Really?* They think we're an item?" He chuckled. "Now, why would they think a pretty young woman like you would go for this over-the-hill—"

She interrupted, "Over-the-hill? Shit, Eli. Lots of dem women look at ya, don't be so naive." He started to blush.

He quickly responded. "Yeah, right. Most of them are way too young," she glared at him, "No kiddin', they say stuff? Like what kinda stuff?"

She laughed, "Oh, jus' girl trash." She paused, and then a devilish twinkle sparked in her eyes, "Dey aks me how you were, ya know?" She rocked her head from side to side

"How I am? I'd pretty much say I'm the same at home as I'm at the office. Ya think? You see both sides." He took a bigger sip of the wine.

"No, *Eli* dey wanna know," she wrinkled her nose as though a bit embarrassed, "how you are *in da bed.*"

"Oh." It then became his turn to be completely embarrassed. He was dumbfounded; he couldn't believe the people in his office would actually theorize about his love life. In all truth, there wasn't anything to theorize about.

"I tol' dem," she held up both hands, indicating a length.

"*You said what?*" Eli's eyes widened as he leaned forward in the chair.

She couldn't hold back the laughter. "Ya shoulda seen ya face. I'm jus' yankin' ya chain, but dey do aks, sha. Dey don't believe we not, well, lovas." Her face had turned a little pink.

His face felt warm; he could feel it glowing from embarrassment. There was absolutely nothing he could say to come back. He was greatly relieved when the waiter brought the check; it couldn't have been timed any better. It provided the perfect out for a change of subject.

"Dinner good? After all the work you've put in on this show, I thought it might be a nice end to the evening for you." It crossed his mind. Did she think of him as a father figure, big brother, or friend?

She beamed, "It did go good, didn't it?"

"The best. Desiree, everyone in town will know your name in no time, don't be surprised if you start getting calls and offers from other companies. It happens all the time. Most people in this business jump from place to place like it was no big thing. Me, I like to get to one place and stay. Call me boring, but that's how I roll." He paid the check, and they headed out.

The conversation went easy on the way back to the house. Eli could talk forever about the business, which was fine for Desiree; she loved listening and learning, especially from him. He was the man to learn the biz from, and his passion was contagious. He gave every ounce he had into it, despite the long hours, the intensity of unnerving deadlines, and the demand for a profitable show. As they said in the business, you're only as good as your last show. He never seemed flustered or overwrought. He took his own advice and rolled with the flow.

By the time they got home, everyone was asleep. Rachel and Alan were in the throes of finals and seemed to handle this precarious time of the school year with maturity and good sense. There wasn't any last-minute cramming or sleepless nights. Eli had taught them well, and their efforts were reflected, as always, in their grades. They each carried the highest honors and grade point averages in their classes. Although Rachel had decided to stay in New Orleans for college, she had multiple colleges interested even though she was only in eleventh grade. It was her choice, and she chose Tulane.

Desiree knew the next few days were going to be filled with post-event procedures and then readying for the trip to Miami; she was most anxious to get away and excited to meet his parents from all descriptions.

His police unit, while unmarked, certainly did not blend with the automobiles driven by Joe Public. Anyone with half a brain could spot him from a mile away, so there was no point in pretending he wasn't five-o. He suspected he had rounded the same corner more than fifty times that morning, but he was determined to catch Sonny coming out of his apartment. He could only hope that giving Sonny a heads-up about the hit may get his attention. Maybe he'd cop a plea or even go state's evidence if he was as close to Manducci as was speculated. None of his crimes were near the gravity of his uncles, but that remained to be seen.

Mac knew Sonny had a super-inflated opinion of himself and the reality of his importance in the family business. In all actuality, he was no more than a wanna-be wiseguy. He pulled his unit into a parking spot across the street from Sonny's to wait and eat his brown bag lunch of a tuna salad sandwich and six chocolate chip cookies, his Tuesday lunch. He'd taken the last bite of his sandwich when Sonny exited the apartment.

Mac slowly pulled into the street and leaned over to the passenger side window, "Hey, Son-ny!"

"Jeez, what the hell you want now? Bizniz so slow you gotta hassle me or what, you got a crush on me, Detective?" He took a long drag on his cigarette.

"Nah, you're not my type, Sonny-boy. But I would like a minute of your valuable time. I'd even say it was in your best interest, padna."

"Let's get one thing straight, my padna, you ain't." He got in the passenger seat. "Stinks up in here; you ever clean this thing? It's disgustin', now what you got to tell me, old man?"

"For starters, seems like your Uncle Tony has had his fill of ya, if you know what I mean?"Mac looked straight ahead.

"He call you up an' tell you that personally, I don't think so, Detective," he was smug.

"The way I hear it—" Mac began and looked him dead in the eye.

"Oh, yeah, where ya hear it from, this I gotta hear." He was too cocky for words.

"Let's just say; I was talking to a mutual friend of ours who seemed a little worried about you and thought you should know. I'm sure we could work somethin' out for your protection if you tell us what we might want to know about your uncle and some of his business."

He turned to Mac, "I don't think we got any mutual friends, to tell you the truth, and as for the other stuff, I got no idea what you're talking about. I can protect myself better than you, for sure. Looks like we done all the talkin' we gonna do, mista *po-liceman*."

"Have it your way; nex' time I see you, it'll probably be in a body bag, but your choice, right?"

Sonny got out of the car, "Whatever."

Mac had his fill of the two-time loser wanna-be wiseguy, his thirty-year stint was almost over, and soon it would be "see ya lata alligator." He and the missus would be mountain bound, but enough of that; there were still a couple of chocolate chip cookies to deal with; he wasted no time.

Before getting into his car, Sonny checked all around. It didn't look to him as if anyone had messed with his precious toy. Sliding in, he adjusted the mirror and spent the next minute or so combing his greasy black hair. It's not that he was bad-looking, one may even argue to the contrary, but he had a cheap, trashy way about him, offsetting any physical attributes he may have possessed.

He revved his engine and burned his tires as he took off in his typical style. Even though he didn't let on, the idea of his uncle being after him was downright rattling and terrifying. As he put the fire to his cigarette, he couldn't help but notice the distinct tremble in his hands. He needed to talk to someone in the know to find out what was really going on. He dialed his lookout's cell.

"What's up, ma man? What do you mean, who is this? Boy, you better lay the pipe down." The person on the other end said he didn't know him, didn't wanna know him, and he didn't think dead men talked. Sonny went ballistic. "What the fuck you talkin' about, paisan? We go too far back for you to treat me like this. Too far back."

Suddenly there was another voice on the phone, "You've never been too bright, have you, boy? You just thought, *ooh, I'll just have me some fun with this little nigga fagot.*" In a deep raspy voice, she laughed, "Tell me, Sonny, who's the little scar't bitch now?" She waited a millisecond, and then in a dramatic femme voice, she said, "Seeee, yaaa!"

There was no place to go to get away. All his people were on the Manducci payroll. Over and over, he replayed the words he had with his uncle. He still couldn't believe he had opened his big mouth; what was he thinking? It was too late now. There was no going back. The more he thought about it. The more the idea of going state's evidence didn't seem too bad.

Sonny shook the thought from his mind and decided to try a few phone calls; maybe someone might put him up until he could take care of Desiree and then get word back to his uncle that he had cleaned up the mess he'd created. It might just put him back in good graces, and Manducci would call off his dogs. The imminent situation was finding refuge, then he'd find her; the rest would be a piece of cake.

He tried three more phone calls; the first two strongly resembled the initial call. The word was out, and no one wanted to speak to him. He was a pariah. Finally, he caught a break; although this was his last choice and not really where he wanted to be, he had to humble himself and accept the offer of safe harbor. It meant going back to the old neighborhood.

Mid-City, by Jeff Davis and Banks, had been, at one time, primarily middle class, but had long since decayed, although it looked like there might be some restoration in the works. Block after block of run-down shotgun houses lined the street. Occasionally, one might happen upon a well-maintained home, but it was few and far between.

He pulled up in front of a small powder blue double. The cracked cement steps led to a visibly sagging porch that almost had a look warning treachery with each step. To the side of the house was an old wooden ramp, also in great disrepair. A torn screened door was ajar and creaked with the slightest breeze created by cars flying down Banks Street.

A voice yelled from inside, "That you, Sonny?" He heard the wheels whine against the wooden floor as his friend came to the door. "I thought I heard that old car of yours. How the hell have you been, it's been what two years?"

Sonny was shocked to see his old friend, it had been much longer than two years, but he wasn't gonna say anything.

"How's it hanging, Busta?" The name hardly seemed appropriate anymore. Once six foot plus and well over two-fifty, he had wasted away to a mere shadow of the person he had been. The transformation was appalling.

It had been ten years since the tragic night, which looking back, may have been the pivotal point in all of their lives, marking the end of carefree kid years and the beginning of a poisoned adult existence.

They had been a couple of kids, up to no good, stealing a few beers from the back of a storage shed to a neighborhood bar. Having been robbed at gunpoint on two occasions, the owner walked on the edge of crazy as a result of the two previous encounters. Upon hearing the noise from the shed, the owner grabbed his gun, raced out of the door, and fired. Sonny and one of the boys got away, but Busta took one in the spine, which condemned him to a wheelchair for life.

"Nuttin' much goin' on around here. I gotta tell you I heard through the grapevine about your *sit-u-ation*. When you asked if you could stay by my house, I was nervous agreein', but we been through too much for me to hang you out to dry. It's not any of my business, but I also heard what you done to your old lady and, telling it like it is, you were wrong, so wrong. I know you know that. We weren't raised like that, boy. I think my old man would kill my ass if he ever heard of me putting my hands on any woman, no matter what. You fucked up, ma man. Wanted to give you a heads-up about the girl because my pops don't know nothing about that. If he did, your ass wouldn't be staying here, for sure. Also, he's gonna lay out some advice about the whole Manducci thing. Do both of us a favor and just *agree*, alright?" He pulled out a cigarette.

"Yeah, sure thing, whateva you say. Speaking of, how is old man Salty? Still working the parking garage?" Sonny did his best at friendly banter, but he sucked.

"Yeah, you know him; he'll be there until the day he croaks," he rolled to the window. "Might want to get your car off the street, pull it around to the back; there's room in the shed. You can travel with me in the crip-mobile. All's I really do is drop off the old man to work and then pick him up; oh, and once a week, he has a card game with his Navy buds, at least the ones that are still kicking. He's lost a couple just this year. Those old guys get wild with them cards; you'll see for yourself; the game's tonight." He lit his smoke.

Sonny took the advice and pulled his car off the street and around to the backyard shed. The two men reminisced over a joint and a hand of cards. Before long, it was time to retrieve Salty from work.

They had stayed at the office unusually late, but Eli said it was best to finish all post-show figures and final billing while it was still fresh in memory. Everyone else had gone home for the night when they printed the final profit and loss report. They took their stuff, locked up, and headed for the parking garage. Salty had Eli's car ready to go.

"Mister Eli, y'all here late tonight. Ya got some big fancy party ya throwing or something?" While older than dirt, Salty still worked hard and had all his faculties.

"No, just winding things up from last night's gig." Eli nodded with a smile.

Salty was eyeing Desiree. "I know I've seen you here, miss, but I neva got your name, dawlin'."

Joking with him, Eli blurted out, "You gotta be kidding? Salty, you're losing your touch." He turned to Desiree and, with great animation, introduced the man. "My old pal here knows everyone that's anyone in this city. If you want to know something, just ask old Salty. He's got the breaking news before any of the news stations," he looked over at Salty and winked. "Without further ado, may I present the lovely Desiree DuBose, the best dang assistant I've ever had, and that is no lie."

Desiree put out her hand, "Good to meet ya."

Just then, a van pulled up; Salty waved to the driver. "Well, folks, looks like my ride is here. I swear, that boy gets later and later. I guess I'll see you two in the morning. Y'all have a good night."

Desiree finished putting her stuff in the backseat, and she and Eli took off, waving goodbye to Salty as they passed the van.

It was an awkward vehicle to get into, but Salty climbed in after a few grunts and groans. "I swear to Gawd, Busta, this vehicle of yours is getting harder and harder to get in. We're gonna have to get you something closer to the ground. He turned to view the passenger in the back seat, "Would you look at what the cat drug in, Sonny Ramone? I ain't seen you since you two was kids. What you been up to?" The old man asked with a set jaw and skeptical eyes.

"Oh nuttin' much, Mista Salty, just hanging with my boys, ya know. Who's the big shot in the Volvo? He looks familiar, but I can't place him. Maybe he's come to the club," Sonny saw Desiree clear as day with another man, and it infuriated him.

"I doubt you know him. Name's Eli Rosen; he's a big wig with one of the companies in the building. You mighta seen his picture in the paper. He's one of the nicest people you ever wanna meet. He always has time to say hello, not like a lot of them. Nah, not him; he's a regular guy, like us." Patting Busta on the shoulder, "You okay, kid? You're all clammed up."

"Yes, sir, I'm fine. Do we gotta pick up something for your card game?"

Sonny stewed in the back of the van as the father-son team went over their day with each other. He couldn't believe his luck. Who woulda thought he'd see Desiree so soon, plus where she'd been keeping herself? Pangs of jealousy twinged in his stomach; he felt she hadn't given it too much time to find another old man. He bet that proper stick up his ass, Eli Rosen, was having his knob polished like it hadn't been before. One thing he could say about Desiree, she knew how to please a man and then some.

Getting to her was going to be tricky, but he could follow her for a few days, get her routine down, and then, pop, he'd grab her. He'd have to get her quick and dispose of any evidence. Then, he could march proudly back to his uncle and be in again. He played it over and, before long, felt a smug feeling of accomplishment as though he'd already committed the deed. He snapped back to the here and now as the old man's hand slapped his knee.

"You alive back there?"

"Yeah, why?" he was still in the fantasy he'd created in his mind.

"Cuz I asked what you were doing for work, now that you ain't with your uncle?" he was already frustrated by Sonny.

"Right now, nothing. I guess you could say I'm checking out my options."

"I got one for your hip pocket. I still got connections on the river. I'm sure I could get you on a boat if you think you might need to get away in a hurry. You know you've never been my favorite person, but you're a young man, and a stint on a boat might grow you a set and teach you about real work." He patted Sonny's knee.

"Thanks, Mista Salty; I'll chew on it and let you know. Me and boats, I'm not so sure." That was something to think about, Sonny pondered. In fact, it just might be the perfect move. He could make the hit, send word to Manducci that he'd taken care of business, and he'd also arranged to be away for a while, long enough to let all the dust settle. His uncle was bound to admire his thoroughness. Who knows, he thought, where it might land him in the business.

She drummed her long, tapered fingernails as she sat by the phone. Simone was reveling in the stardom. Manducci had spared no expense in making her life far more enjoyable. The bodyguard, limo at her disposal, apartment facelift, and salary increase all came together, creating a brand-new attitude. There was no doubt about it; she was meant to be a diva; she did it well.

Finally, the phone rang. There was no mistaking the agitation in her voice. "Where *are* you? I've been waiting forever, dearie. You know I don't like keeping Mr. Manducci waiting." She listened to whatever excuse he was spitting out but cut him off, "*Whatever*, just make it snappy."

She put the phone down, gathered her purse and hat, and waited by the door. Celebrity had certainly gone to her head, and other than Manducci, no one else received any token of kindness or respect. She was out of control.

Trying to break the Mafioso image, Manducci had taken on some civic causes, and it was just that kind of occasion he had requested her appearance. She knew he'd probably be miffed she was late but also knew he'd play it as part of the celebrity diva personality for his guests. She knew he would deal with her later.

All heads turned as she made her entrance. It was an entrance even Hollywood would have been proud to claim. Her tall, slender figure was perfect for her dramatic ensemble, completed by a designer hat. Manducci greeted her with a warm and ingratiating smile. Under his breath, loud enough for only her to hear, he made mention of his disappointment in her tardiness. Equally as mute, she answered it was the driver, and had he been on time, she was ready and would have been well on time. He nodded.

Simone made the rounds with all the guests, most of them commenting on her fabulous outfit and the show. They were exuberant in saying she was their favorite act and amazing talent.

Even Manducci's wife commented she had never been to the show and would have to get Tony to take her to see it; Simone doubted quite seriously about that coming to pass as he rarely exposed her to the world, at least his world. She loved the money and the beautiful things it would provide, and he needed the once debutante to clean up his image. She had provided him with an acceptable circle of friends outside his usual criminal element, entrance into some of the stuffier social clubs where most Italians could not gain entry, and a picture-perfect home life complete with two children and a dog.

Simone found it most amusing; it reminded her of her previous life where everything was a pretense for Simon, the City Planner. If only his colleagues could see him now.

Manducci made his way toward her. Upon reaching earshot to her and only her, he inquired, "I hear you heard from a friend of ours?"

Simone looked perplexed, "a friend?"

"Yeah, a friend looking for a place to stay?" He surveyed the room with a pasted smile.

She nodded and smiled, "*That* friend, yes, sir, I did."

"Know where he's staying at?"

"No, sir. I don't, sorry." Holding the smile of the night, she slowly moved her head back and forth.

"I want you to do me a favor. The next time he calls, and I know he will. Tell him you've arranged for a place for him to stay that's safe. Tell him since everything worked out well for you because of y'all's little problem, you have decided to let bygones be bygones."

"What if he doesn't call?" there was worry in her voice.

"I don't think that'll come up, but if you don't hear from him in the next week, call me."

"Yes, indeed, sir, consider it done," and she nodded.

She got a sickening knot in her stomach, the thought of setting someone up to be killed wasn't something she thought she could do, but she also knew in no uncertain terms she could not go against Manducci. It'd be like signing her own death warrant.

In some ways, she wished she could still be Simon, the City Planner. All his worries involved keeping his alter life a secret, nothing quite as final as murder. She'd get the word out through the boys running the back of the club that she was looking for Sonny; maybe one of them would steer her to him. Before calling Manducci, she'd warn him; she'd have to. She knew a hit was in the planning and had felt it was Sonny's problem; he brought it on himself. What he did to Desiree and to her, the punk deserved whatever he got, but she didn't want to be involved; that wasn't part of the deal, or had it been?

It had been days since she had spoken to Desiree. She made a mental note she would call her before the show. She missed her.

ALL ON THE
STREET

It was countdown for the Miami trip, and everyone in the house was getting excited. They would leave right after the kids' last exam. Desiree had never been on vacation before, let alone a family vacation, and she was just as thrilled, if not more, than the kids. She had heard a great deal about their grandparents and felt like she already knew them. Just as she was anxious to meet them, they were eager to meet her.

Desiree imagined they thought there was something more between her and Eli and hoped they wouldn't be too disappointed when they finally met her and realized the relationship was nothing more than platonic. She knew through conversations with Rachel her grandparents, particularly her grandmother, yearned for Eli to find a wife and mother for them, even though they were nearly grown.

Rachel had described her grandmother as doting to the extreme and very opinionated; however, she said she would always begin her loving advice with, "Not that I'm one to meddle."

Desiree and Rachel were back in the bedroom planning their travel attire.

"Rach, dat's da one. You look hot. Your dad's gonna have a fit when he sees how grown you look." She wore a short black skirt sitting on her hips just below her navel with a pink knit halter and black sandals.

Eli poked his head in the room, "You got a call, and *what* have you done with my sweet little girl?"

"Dad!"

"Don't like, no? You say I got a phone call?" that was most curious. This was the first phone call she'd received since she'd been living with Eli and his family, and she couldn't imagine who would be on the other end of the phone. She had made it a point to stay incognito. As she walked up the hallway, a large knot began twisting in her gut as a shadow of fear and anxiety crept over her. She picked up the phone but was hesitant to answer.

She swallowed hard. "Dis is Desiree," she cleared the lump in her throat again.

The voice on the other end of the phone mocked her, "Dis is Desiree? Dis is Simone." There was silence.

"Girl, you too good to talk to me? I thought I betta give you a call. Things are starting to brew around here, and there is so much I gotta tell ya. I'm getting scared, *real* scared, and you should be too."

Eli entered the room, making it hard for her to talk. She kept her voice non-committal yet friendly, "Ya don't say? So, what ya been up ta, sha?"

Simone was perplexed by Desiree's casual reaction to what she had told her, "You don't get it, do you? Oh, I see how it is; you think you're safe cause you got this whole 'nother life—"

Desiree interrupted, "No, not at all, dat's no trouble at all. How's da family?"

She finally twigged, "Someone's in the room, that's it?" She understood.

"Yeah, work's jus' fine, busy, ya know?" She had been as subtle as she could be.

"Since ya can't talk, just listen. I told you how Manducci set me up good. Ya know, I knew things were too damn good to be true. That mutha fucka wants me to set Sonny up for him. Not that I give two hearty shits about no Mista Sonny Ramone, but girl, I don't want to be involved in getting him dead, ya know? If I have anything to do with that, then guess who'll be next on the list? He'll be sure not to leave anyone around who gets involved." Her voice raised, and Desiree could hear the fear with the wavering of each word. "I'm so scared, Desiree. I can't win. If I don't do what he asks, I'm done; if I get him Sonny, then I'm done for, too. Girl, I don't know what to do; I'm just scared to my bones. I got a bad feelin about all this. Thing is, I still gotta act all peachy with him, like nothin's wrong."

Desiree felt helpless; she could do or say nothing since Eli was only a few feet away. There was very little she could say to console her. She'd have to be vague but hoped Simone would pick up on what she was trying to say but couldn't. "How's all the family in Chicago, dey keepin' well?"

"Chicago? What? You saying go back to Chicago?"

"Yeah, I heard dat too. Dem late, middle a da night flights, dey call 'em red eyes. Dey go real cheap, yeah."

"I don't know, shit. The thought of going back to a fake life."

"Boy-ee, dat sure would be livin'," she responded as though commenting on some wonderful suggestion.

"Ya ain't walked in my shoes, girlfriend. It was no kinda living, but I'll think about it. I'd still be drawin 'breath, but shit, I'm sure Manducci's arms reach Chicago with no problem."

"But, mebbe not fa Simon, t'ink aboud it, ma frien'. Promise me dat."

"Sure thing, dawlin'. Don't wanna keep in this secret code; you got some time we could get together?"

"I'm pretty jammed. Can ya come by da office tomorra? Mebbe we go fa a quick lunch? Ya don't need ta dress up; jeans'll be jus' fine."

"I hear ya, but all I got is good clothes, you know that, but I'll do my best."

"Do whad ya can, but keep it simple, girl, goddit? I'll be lookin' fa ya aroun' noon? Lata, ma frien'."

As much as Desiree thought Eli was probably eavesdropping and curious about her conversation, he was deep into his own thoughts and was oblivious to anything Desiree might have been saying. She figured she'd clear the air before he started with the twenty questions game he loved to play.

"Looks like I'm havin' lunch wit' ma girl, Simone."

Eli continued to look through the hoard of food in the pantry, "They say crunch food is nervous food; you heard that before?"

"Whad?" he could say the strangest things sometimes. "Eli, whad you say?"

"You know, like chips, pretzels, crunch food. They say people eat that kinda food when they're nervous."

"I'm not nervous; why ya sayin' dat?" Desiree put her hand on her hip.

"I didn't say you were; it's just one of those random thoughts." He had both arms on the doorframe of the pantry.

"Good, cuz I ain't got nothin' ta be nervous aboud."

Eli looked over at her, bewildered. "Sometimes, Desiree, I don't know about you. Somebody dropped you on your head when you were a baby?" As though finding gold, he exclaimed, "Triscuits and Pimento, that's the ticket." He seemed enthralled with his find. "So, you say something about lunch?"

Rather outdone, she sarcastically retorted, "Yes, I said I was havin' lunch wit' ma frien', Simone."

"Sounds great," and that was the end of the conversation. Desiree figured she had made more of his hanging around than was necessary. She didn't need to be so paranoid, after all.

Simone tried on outfit after outfit, and no matter what she put on, nothing seemed to be working. Desiree had been specific in telling her to tone it down. There wasn't anything in her wardrobe that could be classified as corporate casual. She dug deeper into her closet and found a pair of tapered black pants. They would have to do; she coupled them with a white blouse, and to avoid looking like wait staff, she tied an animal print scarf around her neck, finishing the look with gold earrings and bracelets. She grabbed her purse and was out the door.

She had seen the office building many times but had never been inside. Behind the reception center sat a cute young girl with a smile that would put any toothpaste model to shame. Her bubbly personality went right along with a head full of natural curls.

"Good morning; how can I help you?" she was as sweet as possible.

"Would you be so kind as to let Desiree know that Simone is here? We have a lunch appointment."

"Certainly, I would be happy to." She rang Desiree, who must have sent the message to direct Simone back to the war room. The girl came from behind the desk and animatedly gave the directions as she pointed to the left and then right. Simone followed the instructions, making sure not to sashay too much as she made her way down the hallway. She tried to come across with what she felt was a corporate demeanor; it had been so long since her life in the business world. No one paid too much attention anyway. When she rounded the corner, she saw Desiree busily crunching numbers on a calculator at her desk. Everything stopped when she saw Simone.

"Look at ya, ma frien'. Oh, my Gawd, it's great to see ya, sha." She hugged her neck tight. "Le's get goin' b'fore ma phone rings again." She latched onto Simone's arm, and the two women headed down the hall. Just as they were about to round the corner, they heard someone loudly clear their throat. She turned around, praying the whole time it wasn't Eli. He was supposed to be in some executive pow-wow. She figured the coast would be clear. Wrong!

Simone turned as well and flashed one of her most charming smiles. "You must be Eli; Desiree has told me so much about you, suga; I feel like I know you."

Eli was dumbfounded at first, but then his eyes lit up, "I don't believe it; I take it you are *the* Simone LaFleur?"

"In the flesh, dearie," she put out her hand.

"I gotta admit I haven't seen your show yet, but from what everyone tells me, it's great. I'm gonna make a point of coming to see it when we get back from vacation." He tried to act nonchalant, but Desiree could tell he was excited as a kid seeing Santa in the department store.

"I guess I can forgive you, but you really do need to see it. Just tell ol' priss here, and she'll call and get you free tickets with stage-front seating. Hate to be rude, but I'm strapped for time and need a little girl talk with my friend here; I promise to have her back in an hour." She smiled, winked and turned to head down the hall. She reversed for a second and put her hand out, "It was truly a pleasure to meet you, and I can't thank you enough for all you've done for my Desiree." She stared him directly in the eyes. Desiree had never seen Simone so serious and straight; it was almost eerie.

The two women walked down the block and ducked into a quaint salad and sandwich shop, where they chose the most secluded table in the place.

"Girl, I been going over and over your suggestion. I don't want to go back to Chicago, but I been thinking I could make a break for the big-time like New York or Vegas."

"Sha, whad makes ya t'ink he wouldn't get ya dere? Da whole point of leavin' is ta get away, get a new life, ya know, one ya might actually be able ta live. When da chips are down, dat's when you go home. Whad ya need is ta go back ta Chicago, live like a man, just fa a bit til da heat is completely off ya. Mebbe give it a year, then come up with a new stage name an' go fa da big-time in New York or Vegas. I betcha could fin' somet'in' in a casina. You have ta give it time, real time, Simone. I know it's gonna be hard, yeah, but ya gotta do it."

Simone sulked through the rest of lunch but, by the end, promised Desiree she'd think about it, and yes, it made sense, much as she hated to admit it.

"When ya gonna make ya move?" Desiree took a bite of her sandwich.

"Girl, I don't know, and besides, I didn't say I was gonna move; I said I would think about it. There's a lot to think about. I got to get my stuff ready. I can't just pick up and go."

"Just sayin, pack a few t'ings don't make no fan farewell, keep it low key an' poof vanish. You don't need ta make it knowledge to no one. Ya watch ya back. When I get back, I'll help ya get outta here, but if ya t'ink, t'ings are too hot den go fa Gawd's sake. Leave ya shit an' go, ya goddit? I love ya wit' all my heart." They got up from the table, headed out the door, and Desiree hugged Simone's neck tightly.

"You goin' somewhere I don't know about?" Simone raised an eyebrow in curiosity.

"I t'ought I tol' ya aboud da trip wit' Eli ta Miami. No? No big deal, ma frien', just a family *va-ca-tion*." She primped herself in the reflection of the window. "Dis'll be ma firs', hell whad I'm talkin' aboud? I neva even had a family?"

"Excuse me, Miss Thing, what am I chopped liver? I been more of a momma to you than that bitch that birthed your scrawny ass. You probably given me more labor pains, to boot." They hugged again, warning each other to take care and that they'd meet up when Desiree got home. "By the way, your Mista Eli Rosen is pretty easy on the eyes, and he must think special of you to bring you with his family. I'd maybe give that a second thought, ma girl."

Simone thought about what Desiree had said the whole way back to her apartment, and she was right; like it or not, there would have to be identity *and career* changes. She felt a lump forming in her throat and knew it would be only minutes until the tears would begin to fall. Her bottom lip began to quiver. She loved her profession and didn't want to change, but she also knew that even if she moved to New York, she could never go back on stage with her act. The show would have to be completely different, *not*

just the name. Tears were streaming down her face when she reached her apartment. She needed a good cry, it always made things seem a bit clearer once the drama reached its finale and all had been recollected.

After a couple of good cry hours and a box of tissues, she felt better. She began seeing things with a clearer head. She had decided that Desiree was right, maybe not about Chicago, but about Simon. She had to bring him back and return Simone to the closet for a while.

As she readied herself for work, she began to map out everything. She had managed to save over thirty thousand dollars over the years, and surely it was enough to get a new life started. She had to pick a place that would be gay-friendly and had a better-than-average economy and the potential for employment. She had left Chicago on a good note and felt confident she would be able to get a few recommendation letters; hell, someone might even know of a job opening. Her mind spun, and the faster it went, the more clearly the whole plan came together. Since she wouldn't need women's clothing, she didn't have too much to pack. When the night of the grand exodus came, she'd finish her show with one hell of a finale, accept the company of one of the many offers she had received for the evening and entertain her guest at one of the cozy, intimate hotels in the Quarter.

Earlier in the morning, she would have already done some manly shopping, and with bags in hand, she'd check into a hotel as a missus awaiting her mister. She'd leave the butch attire in the room and exit to her apartment on the sly.

She had kept her accounts open from her previous life. She'd transfer all she had into those old accounts, reserve the room and buy a plane ticket on an old credit card. She patted herself on the back for having the foresight to maintain those old accounts. More than once, she had considered closing everything which would complete the Simon chapter, thank goodness she never acted on those thoughts.

The complete life change was becoming more palatable. The question now was when should she make the run? She'd make the decision when

Desiree returned. The loud ring of her doorbell pierced the silence of her tiny apartment and the consumed inner sanctums of her mind. Peering out of the window, she could see Manducci's long black car. Although the windows were too dark, it was impossible to see into the vehicle; she knew he was there.

"Commmmm-ing, hold on, dearie," she called as the bell rang again. Like a dark wall of gloom, the driver stood statue-like at the door with not even the slightest indication he had any intention of leaving until the door opened.

She cracked the door, "Yaaiis?" smiling at the monstrous man.

"Mr. Manducci wants a word with you, now." His monotone voice sounded completely lifeless, giving her the creeps.

"Give me a second to get dressed."

"He don't like to be kept waiting; make it quick." He had the personality of a rock; if she couldn't get someone to smile, then there was a malfunction inside the other person—no soul.

She put on her clothes from the lunch date, hit the lipstick, and headed to his car. She was all tied up inside. The door opened, and he beckoned her in.

"How's ma girl, t'day?" He watched her with his pasted-on smile.

"Just fine, Mr. Manducci."

"Ya heard from our friend yet?" He raised his eyebrows, and she could see his pulse rage in his reddening neck.

"No, sir, but I did put the word out. I'm sure he'll be in touch with you soon." Her hands were visibly shaking, and the more she tried to stop them, the worse the shaking became. She knew Manducci had noticed her apprehension, which made her even more nervous.

"You make sure you let me know when the son of a bitch calls."

"Yes, yes, sir, I'll be sure to call you first thing." She interrupted herself with a nervous giggle. "You know I'll be calling you just as soon as I hear from him. That's a promise." She could feel the nervous rambling coming on. "Is there anything else you need from me? If not, I gotta get myself ready for the show tonight, and it takes me a while." Trying to lighten the moment, she said, "Perfection doesn't come easy."

He looked at her and smiled. One couldn't really call it a smile; it was more like a chilling calculated grin that made a shiver run down her spine.

He didn't hear the alarm clock ring or even the two of them moving about in the small shotgun double. When he finally picked his head up and focused his eyes, he could see the cable box, and it was already two o'clock in the afternoon. He called out to see if anyone was home.

"In the kitchen, sleepin' beauty. You want some grub?"

He shuffled into the kitchen. "Nah, I think I'll grab a sandwich or somethin'."

Sonny didn't want any company but could hardly turn Busta down when he asked if he could go and suggested they go in his van and keep Sonny's car out of sight. Sonny had hoped this pal thing wouldn't be an everyday occurrence. He'd have to find some way to ditch Busta; otherwise, he'd never be able to execute his plan. Salty had been right about the card game, and his old river friends were more than happy to reveal their findings. Through networking they had come through, they located a ship leaving port in a week or so, which flagged urgency to his plans. Perhaps he thought he could use Busta's presence to his advantage.

The two took to the road navigating their way to the closest Micky Ds. "For all ya done for me, let me pay for your sandwich, and while we're at it, get something for your old man. We ain't got no place to be, so we might as well drop it off with him."

None the wiser, Busta thought it would be a good idea and remarked on Sonny being a real stand-up guy. *Whatever*, he thought.

Eli was full of questions when Desiree returned from her lunch with Simone. "Ya know, sha, I neva pegged ya fa a groupie."

"Yeah, right, like I'm a groupie," he was a bit put off.

"Since I been back, all you've talked about is Simone dis and Simone dat." She turned to face him as she walked to her desk.

"Curious, but never mind. Because Simone is as important in your life as she is, I thought it'd be fun to get to know her. Not trying to be nosy." He went back into his office.

"Good."

She returned to her work, but her heart was hardly there. She felt an impending doom and was worried about Simone. She should have never asked her to stay until she returned home. She picked up the phone and called her.

After five rings, Simone picked up, "Hellloo?"

"Hey, chickadee. Good to see ya at lunch. Been t'inkin' ma frien', mebbe ya betta cut out b'fore I get back."

"I'm ahead of ya, dawlin'. The bossman came by just a few minutes ago, and I got the clear picture things were moving a lot faster than I'd thought." She told Desiree her plan, and while she had wanted to wait a few weeks, at least until Des had come home from Miami, she had pushed things forward and was leaving that night with the assurance she would leave word at the office of her whereabouts. "It may take me a few weeks to get myself together once I get there, but don't worry, I will call you with all my info. Until then, I love ya, baby, and keep yourself safe. They're still looking for you."

It wasn't her style to cry, but Desiree felt empty pangs in her stomach. Feelings she had never felt before. She quickly got up and made her way to Eli's office. As usual, he was on the phone. She entered, closed the door, and took a seat. Upon seeing the tears, Eli turned and hurriedly got off the phone.

"What's wrong, kiddo?"

"I'm upset, dat's all. I needed a place away from everybody ta gatha ma t'oughts." Eli handed her a tissue, then got up and rested against the corner of his desk.

"Anything I can do to help?" His eyes looked sad and sincere, like he genuinely wanted to help.

She shook her head no. "It's a long story, sha, an' ya really don't wanna know. Trus' me," she wiped her eyes.

"But if I can—"

She cut him off, "You can't," she looked distraught and done, which broke his heart. He wanted to help but didn't know much about her world and wasn't sure he wanted to. He much rather her in his than he in hers.

The two sat silent for a few moments, "Mebbe ya can. Ya drive me somewhere an' wait while I run in wit' *no questions?*" He rocked his head slightly back and forth in thought.

"Tall order this no questions thing, but if it's that important, I'll try."

They quickly made their way to the parking lot and into the car. As rushed as they were, they took no notice of the van following them. Desiree gave directions, and there was a pensiveness in the car that could be cut with a knife.

"One thing, Desiree, you not doin' anything illegal, like selling drugs or something?"

She glared over at him with a look that more than answered the question, punctuating it with a look of disbelief. How could he be so ignorant? "I had to ask; sorry didn't mean to offend or imply." He put his hands up in surrender. She instructed him to pull over and hopped out of the car. She banged on Simone's door.

Simone was obviously annoyed by the profuse knocking, but upon seeing her friend, quickly opened the door and ushered her in, "Are you *crazy*, Desiree?"

"I had to see ya b'fore ya lef'." She held her like a scared child clutching her mother.

"Girl, you gonna break my neck. It's not like ya not gonna see me soon. Now get a grip."

"Simone, I love you so much, sha. I'm gonna miss ya." Her eyes were tearful.

"I'm gonna miss you too, but you gotta get yourself outta here. Now shoo, I'll call, I promise." Simone kissed her cheek.

Desiree gathered herself together, wiping her eyes and trying to shake off the nauseating pit in her stomach. She heard the door close behind her as she made her way to Eli. Out of nowhere, she was thrown against the brick wall. Her world spun from the force of her head hitting the wall. It all happened so fast that she was down before Eli could get out of the car. Sonny pinned her with his knee on her back and yanked her hair thrusting her head back. She felt the icy coldness of the knife against her throat.

Eli wailed from the innermost center of his soul, "Nooo!" As if in slow motion, Sonny turned in time to feel the full impact of Eli's size fourteen into his face, which bounced him off Desiree, but Sonny scrambled to his feet, wielding a knife in the air for an attack upon Eli. For such a tall man, Eli had the agility of a lightweight prizefighter and managed to sidestep the attack. Busta pulled into the street and laid on the horn, "Sonny, get in, get in, get in!" The van door swung wide, and Sonny jumped in as the van squealed away.

Eli stared as the van rounded the corner. The adrenalin raced in his heart. There was no way he would comprehend what had just happened; it was all such a blur. One thing was for sure; there was nothing malfunctioning in his survival instinct. Wasting no time, he scooped Desiree up and put her in the car, checking her for any blood. "You okay, huh? You okay?"

"Oh, my Gawd, Eli. I'm so sorry." She continued apologizing amidst a steady stream of tears and bursts of anger. "I can't believe it, that sorry sack of shit."

In record time, they made it to his house. There was little he could say, and his heart pounded out of control. The whole thing ran through his mind like a loop of a never-ending nightmare. His body was trying to process, to no avail, wondering if life would return to normal.

He opened the Jack Daniels and swigged straight from the bottle, then reached for his cigarettes, something he never did at home, but this day was like none other he'd ever had, either. He held up the Jack offering Desiree a straight hit from the bottle, as well. She declined but sat on the arm of the couch, her face flushed and wet from tears. Eli could feel his heart ever so slightly slowing down. He took another swig which caused a choke-like cough.

He looked over at his pathetic little friend and made his way to her. Clutching her in his arms, he wished he could take it all away. He led her around the sofa and lay down, reaching out and pulling her close. She nestled in his arms where she felt protected and loved, yes, loved. An hour went by without a word; they lay in silence. It wasn't awkward or heavy, more along the lines of a healing, comforting hush. They knew something had changed in their relationship, but neither would be willing to discuss it, so they just lay entrusted in each other's arms.

Just about the time they started to stir. Rachel and Alan returned home. They were more than rambunctious with one day left until vacation—Miami bound.

Looking at Desiree, Rachel could plainly see something was or had been wrong, "You okay?" She crouched down so they were eye to eye.

"Yeah, I'm alright, how 'boud da exam? Did good, yeah?"

"Yeah, it was hard, but I think I did okay." She stroked Desiree's arm.

There were no more questions about any suggested strangeness, and it was just as well. If anything romantic were to ever develop between Eli and herself, it would more than likely get real sticky in the house, and she was pretty sure she could kiss her closeness with Rachel goodbye.

After a quick cold-cut dinner, the kids went to their rooms to prepare for their last day of exams, leaving Eli and Desiree alone again. "Desiree, I'm calling the police, your friend pushed things too far, and someone coulda gotten hurt, big time. So, I'm calling." He was matter-of-fact.

She begged him not to call, but her pleas were ignored.

"Since ya gonna call anyway, aks fa Detective Mac MacFarland."

He looked up at her as he dialed the phone; he hesitated, then said, "I don't wanna know." The voice on the other end said they would page him. In a matter of minutes, the phone rang; it was Mac.

Desiree grabbed the phone, "Lemme talk."

"Mac, Dis is—"

He cut her off, "I know who it is. What ya got for me?"

"We gotta meet," she looked at Eli for confirmation, "Here." She rattled off the address and hung up.

Almost wringing her hands, "B'fore he gets here, I owe ya an explanation." She told him about the night Sonny had beaten her, the close encounter on the way to the French Market, the trashing of Simone's, and then the events of the day. Eli held onto her every word yet had a bewildered look on his face as though he was seeing her for the first time. He couldn't believe she had held all of this from him. Part of him was pissed, and yet another part admired her courage and strength.

"So dat ma frien' is da whole story on how I come to know Mac an' all the info you may wanna know, or mebbe not wanna know, but it is what it is. I can't tell ya how sorry I am dat I hid all dis from ya, but I didn't want ya ta get involved, ya know? Ya hate me now?" Her bottom lip quivered as a single tear trickled down her face.

He shook his head, "No, I don't hate you, Desiree; I can't say I'm not pissed you didn't tell me all this before."

The knock on the door interrupted his comments. Mac wasn't at all what he had pictured. What he saw was an overweight middle-aged man whose clothes looked a size too small. Eli couldn't help but notice the distinct sparkle in the man's eyes, which was a dead giveaway to the shrewd intuitive intelligence held inside. While far from the picture of perfect fitness, Mac created a calm in the wake of all the craziness; he was most commanding.

The two men hit it off, both were straight shooters, and while Mac was a little less polished than Eli, someone somewhere in his life had given him lessons in social graces. Eli admired his ability to read between the lines. He could see the genuine fondness he had for Desiree, and it was more than obvious the admiration was along the paternal lines.

Desiree began to ramble, starting the story mid-way through, then trying to back up. How Mac could have gotten anything from the blubbering mish-mash she delivered was beyond him, but he did.

He demonstratively pointed a finger. "What'd I tell ya, missy? I told ya straight out the scumball was gonna get ya, and what happens? He coulda killed the only friend you got. You lucky, this man here didn't say fuck this and leave you to get your throat slit." He stood for a few minutes looking out of the window onto the avenue. Through frustration and disgust, he clutched his lower jaw, which contorted his lips, and gently shook his head from side to side. "So," his voice dripping in sarcasm, "You gonna go for it *this time*, or you gonna let the bum go scot-free?"

"Ya know, ya ain't gonna be able to make anyt'in' stick an' he'll be out in no time runnin' me down, again." She pleaded.

He looked at Eli, then back at Desiree. He couldn't believe his ears, "Why are you gonna tell me this shit if you ain't gonna charge him? I know good and well your friend here's gonna make a move, so like it or not, your name will come up here and there."

Still punchy from the events of the day, Eli had finally had his fill and broke, "You gotta be kidding me, Desiree? You're gonna talk, oh yeah, you're gonna talk, alright. You're gonna try to get him for the whole enchilada, from the beating to the assault at the French Market to today's melee. Hell, you oughta throw in stalking as well. It is more than obvious that's what the creeps been doing." He turned to Mac, "She's gonna do whatever you want her to do. You got my word."

Desiree's back was up, "You don't own me an' you sure as hell ain't gonna tell me whad I gotta do. Where ya get off t'inkin ya can tell me anyt'in'? It's ma fuckin' life." Her jaw clenched and set, tensing her body.

"Got news for ya dawlin', the day you moved in here, guess what? Your life became my business, especially since it put my kids at risk. Had I known what I know now—"

She cut him off, "Whad? You'd neva let me step foot in ya house?" The tears welled up in her eyes.

Mac jumped in, "Hey, hey, the two of you, don't be sayin' anything ya can't take back."

"Sonny, you must be out cha eva lovin' mind! What the hell you going after that skirt like that? You been smoking too much of the wacky weed, padna. You betta get a grip, or you're gonna be out with me, goddit? My old man hears about your adventures, and you may already be out."

Sonny put his foot on the dashboard and looked over at Busta. "How the fuck he's gonna hear? Sometimes I worry about you, boy. And that chick, *that*, paisan, is my ex ol' lady. She's nothing but one big-mouth bitch. And what goes down between her and me, that's my business."

He glared at Sonny. "You drug my ass into it, remember, by crashin' on my couch and riding with me? Hell, I don't want no trouble, so don't be bringin it around. I got my own shit to deal with and sure as hell don't need yours." He slammed his fist on the steering wheel.

"Okay, okay, I gotcha. Only one more favor, I need to drive by the club. Me, I can't go in the place, but you, ya think you could go in and get one of my ol' boys to come out to the car?"

"Jesus, Sonny, didn't I just tell you to cut it out." Busta spit out the open window. "Fuck me. You gonna get me in some bad shit. I can feel it."

Sonny put his lighter to his cigarette and drew in a deep drag. "I gotta know what my uncle is up to, cover my back. Shit, maybe he already knows I'm hold up in your house. Think about it that could be *det-ri-ment-al* to one's health, if ya know what I mean. What about your old man? You wouldn't want nothing to happen to him. If we knew ahead, we could prepare. If I was you, I'd wanna know." He was such a manipulative son-of-a-bitch.

"Whatever, Sonny. You too fuckin' much. By the way, *paisan*, Manducci knows you hold up with me? Consider yourself out; I'm not playing. I'm not getting my old man into any of your crap, *capiche?*"

"Yeah, yeah, I got it." Sonny sat back smoking his cigarette while his mind went a million miles an hour with ways to manipulate the situation.

Busta maneuvered his big boxy van through the narrow streets of the Quarter with little or no trouble. In some cases, he only had an inch or two to spare on either side; nonetheless, they made it without incident. Well-practiced in the art of getting out of the van, it was only moments before Sonny saw the back of his wheels turn into the club.

The minutes dragged on, and he began to wonder if Busta had any luck finding one of the boys. Sure enough, ten minutes later, two of the boys emerged from the club, looked around, scoping the street for Manducci informants, then made their way to the van.

"Ya padna says you wanna talk?" One of the guys asked.

"Yeah, what's going down here? Anything happening I should know about, any kind of warning?"

The two chuckled and shook their heads in disbelief. "What? You crazy? You goin' down, brotha, that's what's going down." They gave him a snarky grin.

"That so?" Sonny got cocky. "You get a message to my uncle, I righted my wrong, and I'm gonna lay real low, like outta the country low, at least for a while until everything settles. Then, I'm coming back, and he and me can bury the hatchet once and for all. I know I done wrong b'fore, but this time," he drew his fingers to his mouth, kissed the tips, and flicked the air with attitude, "will be perfection."

The timing was perfect just as he made his grand acclaim; Busta rolled out of the club, "And now my driver's here, boys. Make sure you give my message to Manducci."

"Whatever, Sonny, ain't gonna make no difference anyway, you just a dead man walking, with a lot of ifs, gonnas, and maybes, that's all." They laughed as they strutted back into the club like a couple of peacocks.

Sonny looked over at Busta, "Fuck 'em."

All the while, Busta was thinking, *no, Sonny, it's gonna be fuck you!*

Simone was unaware of the attack that had just happened in front of her apartment. She was consumed with her plan of escape. Everything was in place now; all she needed to do was execute her masterpiece. By the time anyone realized she had flown the coop, she'd have dumped Simone and resurrected Simon, and the trail would come to a cold dead end.

Ready for work, she called her driver, grabbed her bag, gave one quick glance over her shoulder, and headed out the door. This was it; there was no looking back. A lump was developing in the back of her throat, but she cleared it away and thought to herself she would give the best performance ever, and no one would be the wiser.

She waltzed into the club like the celebrity she was, with an even more exaggerated swish to her hip-swinging strut. Head held high; she was the star! The place was packed, which always made the show better. Like any other evening, she went straight to her dressing room. The fresh scent of flowers filtered from the tiny room. She wondered which one of her fans had sent the token of affection.

While there were regulars, there would be a mystery bouquet at least twice a week. It was one of those nights. She loved the intrigue of anonymity. It was easy to solve the puzzle, all it took was one call to the florist, and she knew them all. She knew them well enough to call them on their cell. Simone dialed the number and began the inquiry.

"Well, Suga, what do you mean you can't tell me? Of course, you can. You always do." The voice on the other end said he couldn't tell her because they didn't have a delivery for her that day. "You sure? Okay, thanks anyway, dawlin'." She made a mental note to ask the day manager about the person with the flowers. She knew they had come from Floral Perfection; she could easily spy their work, anywhere, anytime, as it was the best in the city. Whoever the fan was, they had spent a bundle on the arrangement. Too bad, she thought, she'd never be able to thank them personally.

With a twirl of her chair, she faced her wardrobe. It was a magnificent view. Her gowns shimmered with sequins, satin, velvet, and all kinds of jewel, feather, and fur enhancements. Her collection of wigs, hats, and props was ideal. The rack of clothes and accessories sparkled more than a ten-carat diamond. These were some of the things she'd miss the most. She'd have to pull out all the stops for this farewell performance.

SHATTERED SCHEMES AND MIAMI DREAMS

Returning the house to its usual pace of peace was no easy task that evening at the Rosen residence. The usually quiet, sublime family home enveloped by all that was good and loving had been transformed into a likeness one might refer to as a spot on the Jerry Springer show. It took strong negotiation, but Mac finally calmed things down. Burning with fiery anger, the conversation reached a level of calamity and raucousness. Bedroom doors flung open, and the two kids flew to the front scared, startled, and completely confused.

They agreed both Eli and Desiree would meet Mac at the station house to file a report against Mr. Sonny Ramone the following morning.

The family needed the Florida getaway more than ever. Mac assured them Sonny would have been incarcerated and no longer a threat by the time they returned from Miami. In her heart of hearts, Desiree had trouble believing Mac's assurance. She wasn't quite sure he understood the way the game was played.

Somehow she didn't think Manducci would let it go once Sonny was out of the picture. Then, too, the question remained, who would get to

Sonny first, Mac or Manducci? Either way didn't matter; what did matter was her safe haven was no longer secure, and once again, she was an open target. What made it worse was Eli and the kids now played into the picture; she knew she'd have to make some decisions when they returned from Miami.

With all the splash, sizzle, and drama of a Los Vegas show, so too was this last hurrah performance for Simone LaFleur. She sparkled and shimmered as she commandeered the stage rendering the audience spellbound. At first, she couldn't tell which fan was tossing single long stem roses after each number, but it was from one of the tables in the front.

Given the obvious persuasion of the two closest tables, she surmised the party to her right must hold the answer to the question at hand. There were three men, all exhibiting feminine mannerisms. The two older men seemed to be an item leaving the younger man the probable choice. She blew him a kiss to test the water, and he bit.

He stood and tossed an armful of flowers onto the stage. The darkness of the room, coupled with the bright stage lights, made it difficult to see her admirer. She only knew that he had a head full of long flowing blond hair. From her perspective, he seemed to have a soft angelic presence, but that could have been wishing rather than reality.

Directly before the finale, she sent one of the backstage crew members to invite the young man on her behalf for after-show cocktails in her dressing room. Simone performed the last act to perfection, strutting back and forth across the stage, dramatizing every movement. She was hotter than hot, and the audience was just as reactionary. Whistles, cheers, and wild applause begged for more.

She stood center stage and dropped her head, her woven locks dramatically framing her face. Slowly she raised her head, flaunting one of her too-good-to-be-true smiles. Her eyes sparkled, and the crowd went wild; she wanted to hold this moment forever as the exhilaration was intoxicating. The time had come, and in her deep sultry voice, she exclaimed with all the fire of her passion for the stage and her fans, "Thank you, I love you all!" she disappeared off stage.

Five minutes later, a knock came on her door. "Yaaaiiisss?" She dramatically thrust the door open. Before her stood one of the most beautiful men she had ever seen, he had pulled his thick mane into a sleek ponytail which revealed a strikingly handsome face. Something in his coloring suggested there might have been some coffee in the cream at one time in his lineage. He was gorgeous.

He bowed from the waist, gently took her hand, and kissed it with an ever-so-soft touch of his lips, "Enchante."

"Oh, my Gawd, Suga, you know how to knock a girl off her feet. Honey, you're just as pretty as those flowers of yours."

He stood and smiled at her but remained in the doorway, "Am I correct in assuming the message I received was from you? If not, I'm truly sorry for the intrusion."

"I can tell you're not from these parts, are ya? *Indeed I did* send the message, and excuse my rudeness, do come *in*." Bodaciously, she waved him inside.

His graceful, sophisticated gait hinted at aristocracy; if not, then definitely blue blood in one way or another. He sure as hell wasn't somebody's homeboy. He remained standing at the foot of her chaise lounge. She sat at the mirror, watching him in the reflection, "Dawlin', you gonna have a seat, or what?"

He sat, admiring her reflection. "Your performance was flawless, perfection from every angle. I've never seen anything quite like it. Miss LaFleur, you are indeed a treasure, and I am most flattered you chose me to share in your private time. We should get you on a European tour. You left me breathless." His smile was warm with smoldering sensual heat.

"Oh, believe me, dearie, the pleasure is all mine." She returned the smile through her reflection. "Why don't we go get ourselves a little nightcap somewhere a bit more," she batted her eyes seductively, "*private*. What do you think? Are you game?"

His air of self-confidence and elegant demeanor was most charming, but nothing would ever compare to the glimpse of a naughty boy twinkle she caught when she suggested the change of venue.

She took his hands as he stood up. He was a good four or five inches taller than she, and Simone was every bit of six foot one in her heels, making him maybe six-five. She locked her arm in his and led the way out. She could feel his body heat through his clothes. "We have a night ahead of us!" her heart was pounding as the temperature began to rise.

He patted her hand in the bend of his arm, "My car should be waiting outside if you like."

Simone's eyes glistened, "So is mine. Yours can take us to breakfast in the morning if you survive the heat of LaFleur. Excuse my presumption; perhaps you have plans for later this evening."

"Can't wait for the challenge, mademoiselle. I'm sure I'll be more than *up* to it." Again he flashed a quick devilish grin. As they walked out onto the street, both cars were waiting. He signaled his driver, and the sleek black stretch silently glided away.

In all actuality, had it been a different night, she would have jumped at the offer to take his car, but she wanted one of Manducci's boys to see her leave with the young man. Too bad, she thought, it was going to all end that night; this new friend was showing so much promise.

She led the way through the hotel to her room. Although not the largest suite in the place, the room was elegant beyond words. She draped herself across the loveseat. Taking off his jacket, he made his way to the wet bar, all the while watching her watch him. "Dawlin', there's some vodka in the—" Before she could finish, he had retrieved the bottle and poured the libation over ice, added three olives and a touch of the juice.

She was flabbergasted, "I see you've done your homework. Ooh, you precious thing, get your sexy self on over here."

He had a seductive roll to his walk. He knelt, slipped off her evening shoes, and kissed the inside of her foot, ever so gracefully caressing it with his hands. "Think I'll start here and work my way up, that is, if you don't mind." He pleasured her to ecstasy. Rolling in the back of her mind was a small voice echoing, "This may be the one."

She had thoughts of telling this man all about her plan; maybe they could run away together and live happily ever after. These dreamy thoughts heightened the sensations of her pleasure. Simone slowly sat up and kneeled on the floor. Seductively she began to undo his pants. She could already feel the heat radiating from beneath his clothing.

She coyly looked up at him. "Now, you just hold on, Suga, and let Simone take you places you've *neva* been."

She was beyond practiced; he groaned with delight as he clutched her hair. The intensity mounted. Just as she was getting to the peak of her performance, she had a warm sensation trickling down her neck. The room began to sway; she reached for her throat only to come back with a handful of blood. Total confusion and bewilderment enveloped her mind as the energy poured out of her body. She collapsed and gazed through a thick groggy blur; she could see his eyes. They still had that devilish twinkle.

"Don't take it personally, Simone. I *really* did *love* your show."

He stood up, fastened his trousers, and left. In a pool of her blood, she lay still and watched as the door closed behind him. The room grew dim.

Parking was always difficult at the airport, but it was worse than usual for some reason, which made the kids nervous.

"I told you we shoulda left earlier, Dad." Alan seemed to be the most concerned about the closeness of time.

"We're okay, sport. Plenty of time," his dad reassured.

Desiree was just plain excited at the idea of leaving; the actual trip itself was lagniappe. "Sha, I'm sure ya daddy's gonna get us where we need to be at, getcha drawers out of a knot." She squeezed his hand out of excitement.

Rachel remained quiet and had since the episode the prior evening. There was a definite coolness to her voice, and it seemed to Desiree this shield would be up for some time, maybe even forever. She wanted to talk about it, but the opportunity had not presented itself. She was hoping they might have some time once they settled in Miami.

They made their way onto the airplane with only minutes to spare and quickly settled in their seats. Rachel and Eli's seats were across the aisle a few rows in front of hers and Alan's. All she could see was an occasional glimpse of Rachel's mass of dark curls. She could tell Eli and Rachel were talking but couldn't see their faces.

She wondered what they were talking about; perhaps they wished they hadn't extended the invitation to join them on their family vacation, but she couldn't have been farther from the truth.

"Rach, you okay? You been so quiet all day." He coaxed her to talk.

"I can't help but think about last night. I mean, ya know the stuff about Desiree and that creep. It's hard to picture her having a different life. I can't imagine what she must have gone through. She's such a good person and doesn't deserve any of it." Eli patted her hand.

"I know what you mean," he sounded sad.

"I feel bad for her like I don't know what to say. Do I say, God, Desiree, you had a horrible life? Ya see, what do I do? I feel like maybe she doesn't wanna be friends anymore or something. Can you talk to her for me?" She put her head on his shoulder.

"You talk to her yourself. She knows she's had it rough; just let her know it doesn't have anything to do with how you feel for her. Let her know you like having her as a friend and don't want to lose it. I think she'll appreciate it a lot more coming from you, agree?" He kissed the top of her head.

By the time the captain announced their approach to Miami, all four of them were ready to get off the plane, each with a different reason. Not only was Desiree anxious to talk with Rachel, but the thought of meeting his parents was a whole other deal. She leaned up and across the aisle, pulling at Eli's sleeve.

"Sha, I got *gargantua* butterflies in ma stomach, mebbe I should get ma ass on da nex' plane and fly back to N'awlins." She bit half her bottom lip.

"You'll do fine; what's the expression? Oh yeah, getcha drawers out of a knot," he laughed, trying to take her edge off.

"For me, ma frien', *it's panties,* not drawers, *just fa ya information!*" She tried to swat his shoulder but couldn't quite reach it.

Alan grabbed the back of her belt and tugged her back into her seat. "Shhh, Desiree, get a grip; it's only Mims and Pops. Nothing, I promise, to be nervous about, I swear to you. Just smile and agree with them; oh yeah, and they're die-hard Republicans. They get offended with wisecracks about their party, but don't worry; they're gonna love you."

They landed and taxied in. It was a mad scramble to get off the plane and to the awaiting people at the end of the concourse. Mims called out from the back of the crowd waiting for their loved ones. She nudged the lady next to her. "Oh, there he is. Would you get a look at my Elijah? He's a big businessman in New Orleans. Does very well for himself." The woman merely smiled back at her.

Eli navigated his group through the crowd. Rachel and Alan picked up the pace as they moved closer to the couple.

As if exclaiming to the whole world, Mims put her arms out to Rachel. "Would you look at this, Pops? Our Rachel is almost a grown woman. I would've never recognized her. Just look at what a beauty she is." Rachel hugged her.

Pops mumbled under his breath and sighed the occasional, "sheesh!"

"And Alan, you look just like your father when he was a boy. You're growing to be quite a looker, aren't you?" His mother was proud of her family and wanted the world to know.

Eli tried to usher them along, "The two of you look great, Mom. We can catch up on the drive to the house, but right now, we better make our way to baggage claim before—"

Mims cut in, "Aren't you the mister big shot? Can't even give your own mother a kiss before it's rush, rush, rush. Elijah Rosen." She was shuffling along.

"Leave him alone, already. The boy's right. Sheesh, if you don't watch them like a hawk, who knows what'll happen. You read it every day in the paper; this one's stealing that, and then who knows where the luggage turns up? And you better believe that's after they've thrown your bags here and there. Maybe even opened them, and who knows what they could've done to your things," he shook his head as if he already knew the answers to all of his postulates. "Yes, sir, you read about it every day." He went on as if pondering the state of airline criminal activity throughout the world. He shook his head, making a face of total disgust. "Like they think we don't know what they do."

She had seen pictures of the infamous couple, but nothing could have prepared her for the reality of the two of them. They epitomized the stereotypical Jewish parents; the perfect image of Mims would have been a pot of chicken soup on legs, and Pops was aggravated by anything and everything and managed to come up with some of the most astounding complaints. She found it hard to keep from laughing; they were hilarious. Eli ushered them to baggage claim as though he didn't hear the drivel. When they got there, the luggage was already stacked on a trolley. All bags accounted for, despite Pops' trepidation.

Other than a brief introduction, no one had said anything to Desiree, although she could feel Mims scoping her up and down. She sensed her trying to read the relationship. Eli took hold of the trolley and started to make his way to the parking garage.

Mims shrieked as though stuck with a pin, "Elijah, what are you doing? Leave the cart be." She flagged a skycap and turned to Desiree, "What he thinks he's a teenager, now? You'd think the boy's never traveled. We used to take nice trips," she looked over at Pops, "Tell her, tell her how nice it used to be when our Elijah was just a boy and the trips, oh my, beautiful."

"They were nice," he confirmed in exasperation. He walked alongside Eli, who smiled at his dad, shrugging his shoulders.

"I understand you work at the same company as our Elijah." Mims, with eyes like a hawk, watched Desiree.

"Yes, ma'am, I sure do. In fac', he's ma bossman." Desiree gently and nervously smiled.

Eli graciously tipped the skycap, and before long, they were on the interstate, driving along with the rest of the crazed freeway drivers. Mims continued to grill Desiree with question after question. Occasionally she would throw a comment to Rachel or Alan, but it wouldn't be long before she was back to Desiree.

"And in what part of the city do you live?" Silence fell upon the entire car, yet Mims' facial expression had not changed since the end of her question. She didn't acknowledge the pause everyone else was so nervously feeling, and it was apparent she expected an answer.

Desiree cleared her throat. "I actually had a place in da Quarta, Mrs. Rosen, but afta dere was some problems, fa safety I had ta move out. Eli was kind enough ta offa me a place on his sofa on accounta he t'ought it was too dangerous, bein' a young girl an' livin' alone amidst the nastiness. Dere had been some scary situations right in my own block."

Eli couldn't believe it, she pulled it off without a bat of an eye, and his mom could say nothing other than a word of praise. There it was, out in the open and clear; there was no shacking up or anything smacking of impropriety.

The Rosen's house was quite impressive, hardly what Desiree had expected. It was a one-story home that seemed to ramble forever. The entire back of the house was floor-to-ceiling glass overlooking a spacious deck and the Atlantic Ocean. The house was inviting and airy. It was hard to visualize only two old people lived in such a place. Some of the doors were wide open, allowing for an almost euphoric breeze.

"Y'all's place is somet'in' else, Mrs. Rosen. I gotta keep pinchin' myse'f ta make sure I ain't died an' gone ta heaven." Desiree's eyes were wide open as she looked around the beauty.

Alan took her arm and brought her out onto the deck. She leaned against the railing and let the ocean breeze blow through her hair. It was glorious. She couldn't for the life of her figure why Eli had not taken his parents up on the offer to move in with them. She could feel someone approaching from behind; she figured it was Eli.

"I can't believe you lef' dis paradise fa grungy old N'awlins, ya sick in da head, boy?" She looked up at him.

He stood next to her and looked out at the ocean, "As they say, great place, but don't wanna live here." He smiled down at her creating an electric buzz between them.

"I say, you some kinda crazy, yeah?" she raised an eyebrow with an ear-to-ear flirty smile.

"Yeah? Tell me again when it's time to leave. You'll be begging for home." The three stood silently basking in the bliss of the warmth of the sun and the crash of waves upon the shore. It couldn't have been more relaxing or intoxicating.

Ever so quietly, Rachel slipped in next to Desiree and put her arms around her, "You still my best friend?"

Desiree smiled, "I was beginnin' ta wonda, sha, if ma deodorant wadn't doin' da trick. Yes, we're tight, tighta dan eva, ma frien'." She took a deep breath and audibly sighed.

"Want to go for a walk on the beach? Scope out the local talent? Leave your shoes here." Rachel grabbed Desiree's hand and pulled.

The sand was hot, and despite the intense heat, Desiree had to squiggle her toes in it. This was the first time she had ever been to the beach, Grand

Isle didn't count, and she wanted to take it all in. Rachel pulled her toward the water. "My feet are burning; come on."

The feeling of being at the beach was exhilarating; it was as though her soul was being restored. She loved her new life; perhaps there was a God after all.

"Des, I know I been acting weird and all. I just kinda freaked out, I mean, I knew you had some problems in the past, but I guess I never knew or really understood, and not that I do now, because I don't. I want to say that I don't care what was in the past. Forgive?"

"Mais oui, b'sides, dere's nuttin ta forgive, ma frien'. I wished I hadn't had the kinda life I had, but I did an' dat's dat." As the girls walked down the beach, Rachel was keen to point out every decent-looking guy. Desiree found it almost humorous. "Sha ya gotta be a lot more picky. I ain't seen nuttin ya dad would approve of, an I can't say I'd blame him." She lightly chucked Rachel on the shoulder.

"You gotta be kidding; a bunch of those guys were hot; I make it a point to find a guy every visit to Mims' and Pops', ya know, summer fling? Vacation boyfriend? You gonna tell me you never had a holiday romance? It's great cause you know it's only for the time you're here. Love 'em and leave 'em."

"Can't say as I've ever had a holiday romance. I guess cuz I neva been on holiday." They both had a good laugh. "Ya smart aboud it, huh? Ya know, protection?" Desiree stopped her and looked into her face, decidedly serious.

"Oh my God, no, you got it wrong. It's not like ya do *it* or anything; the most that's ever happened is some heavy kissing." Rachel thought Desiree's assumption was hysterical. "Hell. I'm still a virgin." The conversation waned as Desiree's mind drifted; she couldn't even remember being a virgin. The slight difference in their age suddenly grew into a mammoth divide. "I assume you've been with someone before. Everyone I know has. I guess I'll just be a late bloomer." They kept walking.

"Ya be jus' dat, Rach. Ain't nuttin wrong wit' late bloomin'. I wisht someone woulda cared fa me ta be a late blooma, but, dat girlfrien' is a whole 'nother story." On that note, they turned back toward the house.

Pops had trapped Alan. Every visit since he was small, he and Pops would start their own chess tournament, not as though it was Alan's idea, but if it made the old guy happy, and it did, he was a willing competitor.

The girls were off on their beach adventure, giving Eli time to join his mom in the kitchen. She loved to feed people and deemed it one of her most important responsibilities handed down by God. The visit to Miami always resulted in a gain of five pounds, if not ten. "You don't look well, Elijah. You look like something is bothering you."

He went to shake his head. "Don't argue with your mother. God gives mothers an extra sense to know when something's wrong with their children and I smell something wrong. I can always tell." She kept nodding as though each nod represented some Divine confirmation known only by God and mothers. "What's the story with the girl? You know you've always been one to befriend the underdog, even if it wasn't the best for you. Remember the first time—"

Eli interrupted, "Ma, I'm fine. I promise. I'd tell you if something was wrong."

"And your job still going well?" She was old school; she carried on the linguistic challenges of her parents by pronouncing a hard "g" at the end of an ing word meant to be silent.

"Yes, Ma, job's fine." He grabbed a glass from the cabinet and a bottle of water.

"And Lee? She's such a nice girl, settled with a good job. She'd make a good wife for you, I sometimes think of her in my prayers raising those children alone, but what, look at you. You did a fine job with your two. Now, what about the girl?"

"Nothing about the girl, already." He abruptly turned his head toward his mom.

"What now? It's wrong for me to ask my own son a few questions? You want I should stop, then fine; I'll stop." She clammed up, and he felt guilty, which was all part of the mother plan.

"Aw, Ma. It's just like she told you in the car. She was in an abusive relationship and had no place to turn."

"And her family, she couldn't turn there?"

"Evidently not; I truly haven't grilled her on her family. She never mentions them. Hell, I don't know if they're even alive."

"Hmm. Okay, for now. She's a looker, isn't she?"

Eli choked on his coffee, "What?" He thought she had said hooker and nearly choked to death.

"What? What? She's very nice looking, don't you think?"

"She's alright." He was non-committal.

"You sleeping with her?"

Again, he nearly choked. "Ma warn me before you ask such a question; what're you doing, trying to kill me here?"

"Elijah, I just asked a simple question. What you think I'm stupid now? I know a lot more than either you or your father have ever given me credit for; I plainly don't tell and keep my thoughts to myself. You're still a good-looking man; many a woman would like to have you, Elijah Rosen. And don't try to tell me for one second you don't find her attractive. I see how you look at each other like you're trying to hide something. A mother knows and sees these things."

He felt saved by Alan and Pops when they came looking for lunch. He put his arm around Eli. "Your mother, she fixes lunch like it was dinner, every day, same thing. I tell her, it's just the two of us; you don't need to fix enough for an army. Sheesh, you could feed a small country on the leftovers we have. But, *today*, Mother, you now have your army. The small country will have to do without for today." He chuckled at his own comment. Eli could see age creeping up on his parents. It was subtle, but he could see it.

Rachel and Desiree returned from the beach as talkative as they were when they left. Eli watched as the two interacted, but it amazed him that he, too, had a special bond. She managed to maintain relationships with all three of them, alike but different. She was a child but a woman at the very same time. He turned his head in just enough time to catch his mother watching *him* watch her.

He could see the all-knowing expression on his mother's face; suddenly, he felt guilty, almost perverse. He knew deep down inside he lusted after Desiree from day one, and it wasn't until the afternoon on the couch that there had been an awkward moment where he felt the attraction might be mutual. Even then, the heightened moment may have been crisis-induced. Was it real? Could it be considered as *real*? He managed to complicate everything in his mind.

"Central, 26; Reported Signal 30, Le Chateau. Unknown exact location. Report to front desk."

"Unit 26, 10-4." This was one of the calls he hated the most it was usually some drunk tourist overtaken by a hustler, and like so many, it hadn't ended pretty; however, what he didn't know was this crime scene would set him back a few steps.

The room looked virtually untouched. The bed was still tightly made, and there was no evidence anyone had been there except for the men's clothing in the closet and the ominous dead body slumped on the floor next to the lounge.

"Awww, jeez, Simone," he hung his head, slowly shaking it from side to side. The other officers were making smart-ass comments used to lighten the tension.

"Sarge looks like your girlfriend was playing around on you. What you do, catch him and throw his body in the river?" The uniforms chuckled amongst themselves.

"Right, right, enough, already. Coroner's on the way, and guys don't be touching nothing." He surveyed the room. It was too clean to be Sonny's handiwork, he thought. *Fuckin' Manducci.* "Guys, this smacks of a pro, and fellas, this bird has already flown the coop; you can bet on it."

This new development spooked Mac. He had no way of contacting Desiree. No one knew anything about Simone, where she came from, or if she had a family. The only info they could get would be from the club, but it might be easier to get it from the I.R.S. He was disgusted over the whole mess, and the fact it stemmed from Sonny smacking Desiree around and pissing Manducci off only made him even more nauseous.

Crime scene techs swarmed the room like bees around a honeypot. One called over to Mac, "What ya make of this, Sarge?" When he turned the body over, a slow stream of milky fluid mixed with blood ran from the corner of her mouth.

"Y'all gonna swab her anyway, make sure y'all run everything. Might lead to something, might not, who knows. I'm heading to the Golden Lady club; y'all look like you got this covered. Be respectful."

"*This* is the golden lady of *The* Golden Lady club?" one of them asked.

"One and the same, boys. You've had your hee-haw; *tone it down now.*"

His anger mounted as he drove to the club, partially because he knew it would be a dead-end, not to mention he had developed a fondness for Simone. In her own way, she had touched his heart. Something about her had been naïve and vulnerable, which from all appearances may have seemed a contradiction to her chosen lifestyle.

As he pulled up, a group of punks was hanging outside The Golden Lady. They seemed nonchalant as he passed them and entered the club. He went straight to the office.

"Boss in?" He asked the girl sitting at a table outside the office.

The girl answered he wasn't, but he was expected shortly. He decided to take a load off and wait. Her information had been correct as it was only fifteen minutes until he arrived. Manducci was none too pleased to see Sgt. MacFarland.

Mac followed him into his office and leaned against the arm of a chair. He informed Manducci about the discovery of Simone's body. Manducci put on an air of surprise and concern, but a chilling void twisted Mac's gut. The cold, calculated act of murder was something he would never get accustomed to; it was a totally different animal when it involved the heat of the moment. There was a passion of significance involved in the act. Even the robbery gone bad, he could muster a semblance of understanding, but this, this was the worst. Ordering the hit was as casual to Manducci as ordering dinner; it was nothing special, and the situation's depravity raged in Mac's soul.

As predicted, he obtained very little information about Simone; there was nothing in her personnel file referring to her past. There had to be someone, somewhere, that cared besides Desiree.

He made his way through the Quarter to Simone's apartment. The door was taped; he let himself in any way. Everything in the apartment was neat and tidy; he could smell the fragrance of her perfume. As he looked over the bookcase, photo albums, and desk, a sense of guilt overcame him. On the bedside table was a picture of a young black man and an older black woman dressed in heavy overcoats standing in front of a moderate-looking snow-covered home. The photo had obviously not been taken in New Orleans. The more he studied the picture, the more he realized the strong resemblance of the young man to Simone, less the long braids, make-up, and women's attire. There was a logo of sorts on the parka of the young man. He slid the picture out of the frame and planned to take it to the lab for enhancement; perhaps this might lead to the past.

Desiree awoke to the soothing sounds of waves as they danced along the shoreline. She couldn't imagine a place more peaceful and relaxing. From the kitchen, she could detect the delicious aroma of breakfast. She quickly dressed and made her way to the kitchen.

"You slept well, dear?" his mom seemed to want to know, not just passing morning small talk.

"Yes, ma'am, dis place is like a slice-a heaven. Anyt'ing I can do ta help?"

"What kind of host would I be should I have my guests serving themselves? You go relax and sit with Pops; he's sunning himself on the back deck. I tell him, what, you don't think the sun will make cancer on your skin? He tells me if he hadn't gotten it by now, he won't. What're you going to do? He does as he pleases. And you, you better be careful; our sun is not like your sun. You don't want to look like a prune when you're older, and believe me; there are plenty of prune-looking people around here." She wiped her hands on her apron.

"Mrs. Rosen, I got lotsa olive in ma skin, I don't burn easily, but I will take ya warnin' and lotion up b'fore goin' in it." Her stomach tickled with happiness which made her smile at the thought of a mother caring enough about her.

The old woman walked into the laundry room and came out with a brightly colored straw hat equipped with an extra-wide brim. "Here, you put this on. Not trying to meddle, but a young woman like you needs to think of the future. I see all kinds of kids and women your age and older, my dear, burning their skin. They'll pay for it later in life; I've seen it over and over, but suit yourself, not that it's any of my business." Desiree graciously donned the hat. Mims was satisfied, "It may not be Vogue, but one day you'll thank me."

Pops was sprawled on one of the lounge chairs reading USA Today. He seemed to brighten up when Desiree came out. "Good morning, young lady; I trust you had a good night's sleep?"

"Yes, sir. I was—"

He interrupted, "I see my wife gave you that ridiculous hat to wear.

She's always making people wear her ridiculous hats. You want to wear it; I say go ahead and wear it, you don't want to wear it, say, no thank you, I don't want to wear it. Sheesh, that woman meddles in everyone's affairs."

She wasn't sure what to say, "I don't mind; it's kinda fun."

"It's ridiculous; that's what it is. You a Republican?"

Zing, she thought, where did that come from, but she remembered Alan's warning. "I—" he interrupted.

"I thought so; I can always tell. Lots of you young people go for the Democrats. I say they're kids; what do they know, maybe with age and making money," he winked at her, "then we'll see what they think."

She breathed a sigh of relief when Eli joined them. "Ah, I see you've already gotten the skin cancer lecture." Sporting casual togs, Eli looked younger than when he was in suits.

"Eli, ya dad an' I been talkin' politics." She raised her eyebrows.

"That didn't take long, did it?" he rolled his eyes and mouthed, "Sorry."

Pops patted Desiree's knee, "This one's a smart one, knows whose side to be on, unlike some *other* people I know." The old man looked toward her, "You'd think my son, the big businessman, would want to keep the money he earns, but no, he wants that all of us, after working year upon year, our whole lives, to support—"

"That's enough, Dad. Remember, no politics and no religion makes a good time for all."

Pops waved him off and winked at Desiree, "We'll talk later when mister spoilsport isn't around. What is taking that woman so long with breakfast? It'll be lunchtime soon, and no one will be hungry for lunch." He sighed in exasperation. Desiree enjoyed the unusual banter and flexing of opinions.

"I think we can call this brunch, Dad; that way, none of us need to eat lunch; it saves Mom from cooking an extra meal."

"Sheesh. Come here for a week and want to change everything." He buried his head back in the paper.

"Dad, it's just for today, and it's okay," he knew how to play to his dad's disposition.

The phone rang; Manducci rolled over and picked it up. The general rule was don't mention names or talk too long or detailed; one never knew what line was tapped or who might be listening in. "Yeah, you there?" he listened, "I'm on my way." Short and to the point.

He nudged his latest piece on the side, "Dawlin, time to get your stuff together and get out of here. Don't let no one see you leaving."

She leaned over, gave him a quick peck, and quickly got dressed, "Baby, you got some extra cash, there's a gorgeous dress I saw, and I was thinking—"

"I make sure you got what you need; you got no complaints, right?" he tossed a few hundred her way, "That enough?"

"You're a doll," she slung her purse over her shoulder and headed out the door.

He threw on his clothes and waited in the parlor watching from the window for any signs of his car. Years ago, he had foreseen the need for a hideout, love nest, or whatever situation might arise kind of place, all unbeknownst to his wife or family.

It didn't take long before the car turned onto the street. He made his way down halls, then a back staircase, and appeared as the long black stretch pulled up.

The door opened, and Manducci got in, "You still in town? I woulda thought you'd already be gone." He plopped his hands on his thighs,

"Not to fret, sir. Unlike your boys here, things were left clean as a whistle. Besides, I have a flight booked for this afternoon, and I did need to get some rest and enjoy at least one of the gourmet delights while sleazing around here."

Manducci wasn't sure if the pretty boy was light in the loafers or just weird, but he had come from a most reliable source, and that in itself was worth every penny. He could have done without the obnoxious attitude.

"I want things to settle here a bit, but I got something I'm gonna need your expertise on in a couple of weeks. This one ain't gonna be as easy as the fairy."

"The fairy?" the man scolded, "I'm sure the fairy made you a bloody fortune, and to speak of the dead, especially the gold mine, she was, tch, tch, tch. Tacky, tacky, tacky."

Manducci was getting extremely agitated, "Who you think you fuckin' with, pretty boy? You better just shut your fuckin trap."

The intense young man flipped his long blond mane back, and through an icy glare, his demeanor momentarily leapt to a new dimension, "No, don't fuck with me, Tony." As the car came to a stop, he opened the door and was gone. He virtually seemed to vanish in the crowd.

"What a fuckin' weirdo. Fuck him."

Rachel and Alan coaxed Mims and Pops to take them shopping. Eli and Desiree didn't feel like shopping and couldn't think of anything nicer than relaxing on the beach.

Eli admired how beautifully curved her body was, everything tiny but perfect. After twenty minutes on her back, she rolled over.

"Sha, ya got da lotion? Ya min' puttin' it on ma back?"

He squirted the cold sunscreen on her back and chuckled as she squirmed. "I'm glad you t'ink dis is funny. Jus' ya wait, you should be turnin' ova soon; I'm gonna get revenge. Whad do dey say? Payback is a mutha—"

"Okay, point taken, you win."

Eli massaged the lotion into her back. His hands took up her entire back and then some. He kneaded her small tight muscles, "I shoulda been getting' ya ta rub my back; it feels like heaven. Gawd, yes ya gonna put me straight ta sleep." The massage lasted another few minutes. Mims had been right; the sun was different and forty minutes out in it was enough for one afternoon.

The coolness of the shower felt invigorating as a pulsating spray of water rained against her body. Upon getting out of the shower, Desiree realized Mims had taken the used towels, leaving her in a predicament. She wiped off as much water as possible with her hands then padded her way into the bedroom to cover herself before beginning the search for a clean towel. There was a light tap on the door.

"You decent?" She only had time to grab a top that she held in front of her body.

"Gimme a sec, Eli." Still drenched and barely covered by the shirt, she cracked the door to find him standing with an arm full of towels.

"Thought you might need one," he passed a few through the crack in the door.

"T'anks," she turned away from the door, dropped her shirt, and began to wrap the towel around her naked body. The bedroom door slowly crept open as Eli turned to walk away; he caught a glimpse. In that instance, he couldn't help but notice the beauty of her nakedness. She turned her head, and their eyes met for just a blink of time.

Curiosity took over; she turned around, dropped the towel, and stood before him, her body still glistening with small droplets of water. He watched as one tiny drop of water slid from the end of a curl and slowly trickled down the curve of her body. "Sha, ya like?' her voice wavered with a seductive whisper.

He froze. Where did it go from there? His mind exploded with a thousand thoughts, "Oh, yeah, *sha*, I like."

She slowly walked toward him; his heart pounded so hard and fast for a moment, he thought it would leap from his chest. Standing directly in front of him, she took his hand and placed it on her breast, then reached up, pulled his head towards her, and gently kissed his lips.

He had dreamt of a moment like this, fantasized about the eventuality, but here he was, opportunity literally at hand, and he fumbled, paralyzed by his own thought. He tried to kiss her back but couldn't; he wanted to caress her tenderly but failed miserably. He wanted her desperately; he could hardly breathe.

"It's okay, ma frien', jus' not the right time. Dat's cool." She winked at him with coyness.

She pulled back from him. He couldn't let the moment slip away, but he didn't want to say anything too lame like, *are you sure?* Hell, yes, she was sure. No one made her drop the towel; besides, he knew she'd been around the block a few times, and she knew what she wanted. He pulled her closer, and with all the pent-up passion that raged in his soul, he kissed her. He could feel her body succumb. And like a fragile doll, he cradled her in his arms, gently placing her on the bed.

"Ya got some moves fa an ol' fella."

"Old fella, you say? I'll show you old." Nothing he liked better than flirty banter in the bed. It cut all the tension leaving room for pure pleasure.

UNEXPECTED

The long black car slowly pulled up in front of the club. Manducci sent his driver in for one of his boys. Within seconds, one of them quickly flew out of the door.

"Yes, sir, you wanted to see me?" His voice trembled.

"Just checking on the place; anything I should know about?"

"Whoa, yes, sir! Ya boy, Sonny, come by a coupla days ago. He told me to tell you that he's righting his wrong, and then he's going out of the country until the heat dies down. Then he says, get this; he wants you and him to bury the hatchet. I told him, boss, that he was stone-cold crazy. A dead man walking, ya know?" His fingers drummed against his side.

"Bury the hatchet, interesting choice of words. He say where he was stayin?" The boss showed no expression. He was cold and lacked human qualities.

With a stuttered, nervous sputter, he said, "No, sir, but he was riding with his crip friend; I think his name was Busta or Bubba, one of them names."

"Yeah, I know about the kid. Doesn't seem like someone Sonny'd hang with. I tell ya what," Manducci slipped him a $100 bill, "He comes by again, you bring him in for a drink, then call me. Capiche?"

"You bet, yes sir, Mr. Manducci. You bet. Anything else I can do for you, lemme know."

The boss patted his hand, "That's all for now." The window began to glide up as the car pulled away.

"Shit, I can handle this," he pocketed the hundred and went back into the bar.

Since the untimely demise of the golden lady, the atmosphere in the club was heavy. The club manager had promoted one of the more talented dancers into the main act, but it paled in comparison to Simone. He would need to find another talented trannie to become the new Golden Lady. The wanna-be wiseguy clan was still sitting at the same table talking the same talk when he resumed his seat at the table.

"What the boss want?"

"Just checking on things. I told him about old Sonny-boy coming by. In fact, if y'all see him, let me know. Manducci said for us to play nice with him. He wants us to bring him in for a drink. Instead of waiting for him to show, I say, let's go find his ass. We got anyone that knows where the crip lives; he'll be the best to ask where Sonny's at. Boys, this is an opportunity of a lifetime. We help the boss, and who knows, maybe we might earn ourselves a rise in the rank."

The days of holiday bliss flew by. It was good fortune Rachel and Alan seemed caught up in their beach ratting, which gave Desiree more alone time with Eli. Their relationship had entered a new dimension, and she loved it. Unlike all the other men she had been with, Eli was by far the best lover. It wasn't just getting his jollies; it was making love, a foreign concept for her, even when she and Sonny had first hooked up. This was a different experience. His tender touch and sensitivity to her needs were something she had never experienced before. She felt safe and secure in his arms.

The thought of their return to New Orleans was in the back of both of their minds. As far as they knew, no one was aware of the change their relationship had taken, and they felt a great deal of apprehension in the prospect of revelation. There was not just the home aspect, but then the work situation. Many at the office were already suspicious; it would only make things more awkward. They'd have to lay low about the whole thing until the timing was right. The issue wasn't Alan; he wouldn't care one way or another, but Rachel was a different kettle of fish. The only one who knew was Mims, but it was more conjecture than actual knowledge. Not much got by the old gal. She seemed to catch their subtle glances and quiet chats.

The last night, Mims and Pops made reservations at one of Miami's finest restaurants. Desiree was busy readying herself for the big night when Mims tapped on the door.

"You mind if I come in while you get ready?"

"Heck no, do I min'?" Desiree plopped on the bed and patted the spot next to her, "I figure ya'd want ta talk ta me eventually. Whad can I do fa ya?"

"Not that I'm trying to meddle in my son's affairs, God knows he's a grown man and can do as he pleases, but you, don't you worry, you're too young for him? You're a smart woman, Desiree. You see the stability he offers, but I ask you, will that be enough? You have to think ahead, not that I'm trying to tell you your business, but I see before me a young woman, wide-eyed and full of life. Are you sure you want to strap yourself with a man that'll be old when you're still young? Surely, you'll want children; you want for their father to be an old man? Who'll play ball with them in the backyard, you? Trust me; you'll find a nice man your age, marry and have children. The things we've seen, especially here in Miami with all the gold-diggers, old men going for young women. Plain as the nose on your face, the world sees what's going on." She held Desiree's hand.

"I understan' whad ya sayin' an' I mean no disrespect, but it wasn't until this time here that I looked at Eli a different way. I'm not sayin' this whole t'ing won't poof an' disappear when we get back, ya know, who knows? I hope it works, Mrs. Rosen, 'cause I like ya son a lot. Neither of us knows whad'll happen once we back in N'awlins, but I promise ya I'll t'ink aboud whad ya said. Also, I wanna clear da air. I ain't lookin' fa no meal ticket if dat's whad ya t'ink. I been takin' care of myself since I was a little kid an' sure as hell don't need no man ta take care of me. I do jus' fine. Me an' Eli got a good t'ing as frien's anyt'ing else is lagniappe."

Mims explained how broken Eli's heart had been when the kids' mom left, and she couldn't bear to see it happen again. She not only was looking out for her boy but the kids as well. "But what do I know?"

"Don't sell y'sef short, ya know a lot an' believe me, I'll put a lotta t'ought inta ya suggestion. It's nice ta have some motherly advice; I neva really had any b'fore. Closest t'ing ta a momma fa me eva was Simone. Mrs. Rosen, if t'ings work out well fa ya son an' me, I promise ya I'll take good care of him. T'ank ya fa everyt'ing. Don't be surprised when he denies, denies, denies."

"Tell me something I don't know." His mom smiled warmly.

The phone rang with a high pitch shrill, "That fuckin' phone of yours is enough to give me a heart attack." Sonny whined.

Busta ignored him and answered the call, "Yeah, you got me. I maybe could find him; why?" He listened some more. "Ya don't say; I'll look for him. Gimme a number to call back." He hung up the phone. "Son-*ny*, that was one of the boys from the club. They're looking for you. Word is the big man bit, and maybe it's real, or maybe you get hit, but it sounded real. You'll maybe be able to tell when you call them back. Oh, and he wants to talk to you tonight."

"I'll call, alright. Maybe it's real, maybe not. I won't know 'til I get there, right? Better believe I'm gonna cover my ass; you can take that to the bank, son." Sonny kicked his feet on the dilapidated coffee table.

He managed the call, and from all accounts, it sounded legit. Despite his hard-ass talk, he agreed to the club. Sonny got Busta to drive him to the club for ten that evening. He then gave him Mac's number, "You don't hear from me by noon tomorrow, you call this man and tell him about the meeting between me and my unc." He took a long drag off his cigarette, leaned his head back, and exhaled the smoke straight upward.

"Me call a fuckin' cop, man; you must be smokin' your socks. Like I'm gonna turn on Manducci; what kinda asshole do you take me for? Not gonna write my own death warrant. Sure thing, Sonny." He started to roll into the kitchen, mumbling under his breath.

The sarcasm was thick.

"Ya call him from somewhere's else, asshole. What's wrong with you? It's not like you're giving him your name or anything other than about the meeting and then hang up. Besides, I don't think things'll go down that way anyway. I gotta good feeling about this. All I gotta do is play it smart, and I'm back."

Manducci called a meeting before Sonny was to arrive. He told the boys Sonny was returning as head bouncer, and things would fall back into place like they had been; they were to answer to Sonny. This news wasn't what they wanted to hear, but Manducci was the boss, and there was no arguing the point; after all, blood is thicker than water.

Little did they know the big man had an altogether different agenda. He would be keeping that to himself and one other. He was well aware this group of misfits was big on mouth and little on action. If he wanted to keep everything clean, he'd have to keep them in the dark—their hopes of rising in rank sunk in an instant.

Sonny had mixed feelings about meeting with his uncle. He became more anxious as the time drew near. As agreed, Busta dropped him at the club. Sonny wasn't quite sure how things would go down, but he was determined to keep a close eye for anything funny. Nothing had changed in the club. As he walked in, the usual gang acknowledged him as though nothing had ever happened. One of the boys made his way to him.

"Don't know how ya did it, my man, but you did. I gotta hand it to you; I didn't think it would go down like this. You know as well as me, Manducci don't give no second chances, but you did it," he patted him on the back. "I think he's in the office."

As he began his walk back to the office, the question, in his mind, was the nature of his welcome, bullet or open arms. Would they bury the hatchet? The door was open, and he could smell the stale odor of cigars, but this was a good sign. He rapped on the doorjamb.

Manducci looked up, "Glad to see you, my boy. How the hell have you been?"

"I've been fine, Uncle Tony," he didn't know whether to sit or stand.

"Take a load off; we got some matters we gotta go over." Sonny sat but was jumpy as a trapped animal.

"Yeah, I know. I want you to know I'm gonna take care of the mess I made, and I give you my word it ain't gonna never happen again, I promise, unc."

"Water under the bridge, kid." He rapped on the desk in front of him. "You're young; some lessons are harder to learn than others, but you learned, right?" shrugging one shoulder.

"Yes, sir, I'm gonna keep my fuckin' trap shut from now on." His head bobbed like a hula figurine stuck on a dashboard.

"Good. Onto other business. You want a sandwich or something?" His uncle seemed almost friendly, which in itself was frightening.

"No, sir, I done ate already. What you want me to do for you?"

"I need you back at the front door. You'll have to do some real barkin' because the new act ain't making the same draw."

Sonny was shocked by the statement. "The new act? The fairy quit?"

With a conjured look of surprise, Manducci said, "You didn't hear, I guess. Seems like she hustled the wrong John and got her throat cut. I'm surprised you didn't hear. It was a mess, and the cops don't even have a suspect yet." He narrowed his eyes.

"Uncle, you hear anything from your boys on the street? It shouldn't be that hard to find out who offed her. If you want, I'll look into it for you." Sonny was jittery, trying to prove his value. More akin to kissing ass than anything else, but what choice did he have?

His uncle said if Sonny heard something, make sure to let him know. He knew full well nobody would find out anything; that's why the bucks paid were hefty. You want a pro; you had to pay pro prices. He also advised that if he heard anything, let him know and not get involved.

"Yes, sir, I mean, no, sir, I won't be putting myself in the mix. It's all yours. I guess the club's taking a beating. I know she was your big money maker."

Manducci left it precisely the way he wanted, and Sonny was none the wiser.

She felt sad. Miami was blissful; she didn't want to leave all the luxuries. His parents knew how to put on a good time. Miami life was definitely the way to live. Twinkling lights along the periphery of the restaurant created a magical air to the evening. The orchestra played everything from swing to old show tunes. She marveled at her hosts as they, along with Eli and the kids, knew every song the band played. Pops and Mims took to the dance floor. It was great fun watching them trip the light fantastic. Perfectly choreographed from years as dancing partners, they glided around the dancefloor.

Alan surprised her, "You swing?"

"Whad?" she seemed shocked.

"Swing, ya know, like Mims and Pops right now?" then he took a sip of his water.

"Guess so. Why?"

He stood, put his hand out, and bowed, "May I have the honor of this dance, please."

"You gotta be kiddin'; you dance to this?"

"He's pretty good, Des. He's easy to follow; he'll make you look good, don't worry." Rachel chimed in.

"I guess I can't refuse afta a thumbs up from ya sis."

Eli took Rachel's hand and joined the other two couples on the dancefloor. Rachel had been right; Alan was good and easy to follow. She felt like she'd been swinging all her life and had a blast.

Throughout the evening, they swapped partners, and by the end, everyone had danced with everyone at least two times. Toward the end of the evening, the bandleader announced he had a special request dedicated to a young lady from the bayou country of Louisiana. In saying that, they began to play the lively tune, Fun on de Bayou. Desiree took Eli's hand and led him to the floor. It was the perfect ending for this fantasy night.

The night had been better than any she could remember. It was the kind of night that dreams were made from—great food, fun people, and dancing, dancing, dancing. Like all dreams, this, too, would have to end.

Morning came, and the rush to the airport was on. The goodbyes and farewells lasted what seemed to be an eternity. Mims leaned in to kiss Desiree on the cheek and whispered in her ear, "With or without Elijah, you're welcome to our home, my dear. Do yourself a favor and think about our conversation."

"Yes, ma'am, I sure will, and t'ank you for everyt'in. You don't know how great it was, especially fa a girl like me," they gave a final hug.

As they boarded the plane, Eli asked her what the whispering with his mom was all about. She told him it was a tale to tell alone at some time, but nothing important, just words of wisdom.

"One thing is for sure; Mom always has words of wisdom to impart to anyone and everyone. We can talk about it later," he took his seat and motioned for her to take the seat next to him. He pointed to the two empty seats behind them to Rachel and Alan.

As they taxied out, he looked around and gave her a quick peck on the lips, "I been dying to do that all morning." She wondered when his interrogation would begin. After being with his parents, it was clear where Eli learned the Q and A game.

They were in the air in no time; Rachel and Alan decked out with new earbuds from Mims and Pops.

He checked back at them; both eyes closed, listening to their music. They were great kids; he had been truly blessed. He smiled at Desiree, "Do tell, what were the wise words?"

She squeezed his hand, "You know ya momma's been knowin' aboud, ya know—"

"The change in our relationship?" One side of his mouth turned up.

"Yeah, dat's it. Your mom came in da room as I was gettin' ready las' night before we went ta dinna. She wants ta talk, says it's no business of hers," she smiled and raised her eyebrows, "Ya know how dat goes."

"Yeah, right, but?"

"Simply, she don't t'ink we should be together on accounta our age difference and all—"

He interrupted, "I'm sorry. That takes the cake. What, my mom thinks I'm too old for you? What exactly was she referencing? I know she gets to all the whys and wherefores. What did you say?" He turned in the seat so they were face to face.

"Eli, she's lookin' out fa ya. I t'ink she may have t'ought I might be out fa ya money, but den brought up maybe I would want kids one day an' dose kinda t'ings. I was polite; I said I didn't want ya money; I'd been takin' care of myse'f and didn't need no man fa dat. I didn't answer the kids t'ing. Shit, I don't know if I'd eva want children. I'm not the mothery kind, mebbe cause I ain't had one. Who knows? She heard me loud an' clear. Which brings me ta dis question, we real or jus' holiday hotties?"

"Holiday hotties? Hmmm, let me think," he paused for a second, "Desiree, what do you think?"

"I'm jus' wonderin', dat's all, ma frien'." She took his hand.

"Why, what do you want, Desiree? Real or—"

"Yeah, it's real, but," she motioned toward the seats behind them, "We'll have ta see how it plays out, yeah?"

He stroked her hand with a whispered touch. "Let's get settled back at the house, wait a couple of weeks, and then we can talk to the kids if you want. See where their comfort level is. I don't know, play it by ear. Okay with you?" he kissed the top of her hand.

It seemed like they had just boarded when the captain announced the descent, "Gawd, dat was much fasta comin' back."

"No, you were too busy talking to notice the time passing," he grinned. Desiree gave him a quick elbow to the ribs.

It was a rat race at the police station; one could hardly think straight. The crime lab and the investigative team soon deciphered the photo from Simone's side table was Simon Smith, a city planner from the Windy City. They also were able to uncover the last known address and telephone number. The phone and the address were still in the name of Simon Smith. Mac decided to make the call himself.

The phone rang a couple of times, picked up by an elderly woman. "Hello, ma'am, this is Detective MacFarland of the New Orleans Police Department. May I speak with Mr. Simon Smith."

"Simon? Who you say you are?"

He repeated himself.

"You want Simon? Why?"

"I'd rather talk with Simon directly, ma'am."

"Detective, I'm sorry you're just going to have to talk to me because Simon's not here."

"Is there somewhere I can reach him, perhaps?"

"Everything okay, Detective. Is Simon okay?"

"I'm not sure, ma'am; that's why I need to talk with him."

"Simon doesn't live here no more; he hasn't for a long time now."

"Where's he living?"

"Some big city. He moved after his momma passed. I get a card from him now and then; I think I may even have his number somewhere here. He gave it to me in case something went wrong with his house."

"I'm sorry, you are?"

"His Auntie. I think I may still have his Christmas card. You want me to look for it?"

Mac didn't think a Christmas card would do any good, but hell, he felt he had nothing else. It couldn't hurt. "If you wouldn't mind, I surely would appreciate it. You have his number handy? I'll hold while you look. By the way, he have any other relatives besides you?"

"No, I'm it. There's no other family. I suppose he had a father, but we never knew who he was. Everyone else have all died off now." She put the phone down to look for the number.

After a few minutes, she returned, "I found the number. You ready?" She called out the number beginning with a 504 area code. Sure enough, it was Simone's number. He sighed deeply. "Mista, I hope it helps you out."

"Yes, ma'am, it does." Proper protocol would have been to have a Chicago law enforcement agency contact the woman in person, but he decided to toss protocol to the side. "Ma'am, I am truly sorry to be the one to bear this bad news, and I was afraid my instincts were right. Ma'am Simon was the victim of murder; I'm sorry." His voice quaked about to break down. He swallowed hard. "Is there anyone you can call to come be with you now? If so, you need to call them."

She ignored him and began rattling off questions about what happened; how was she going to get his body, or was he going to be buried there? Mac gave her the numbers of people she needed to contact regarding retrieval of the body and bid his goodbyes and condolences.

The summer months were typically slow for the convention business in New Orleans. The only large groups booking were associations capitalizing on the lower prices and incentives. In June, July, and August, Class Act compiled their new pricing for the next year, updated vendor files, and did their general house cleaning. The attire was a lot more casual, and the schedule more flexible. The pace slowed, which everyone needed after Spring and their most power-packed time. The past Spring had been banner, and everyone was still exhausted and calculating the final figures.

Lee caught up on all the reports and made a pointed effort to pass by Eli's house every afternoon. Things around the house looked fine, and she'd toss his paper over the fence, so they wouldn't pile up, signaling any would-be burglars the owners were away. Year after year, she had done this for him, but since the waning of the relationship, no actual agreement was in place, but they were friends, and come hell or high water, she would be a friend to the end. While she thought Eli was acting like a fool, she still considered him a close friend. She cut him slack, he was the most stand-up guy she'd ever met, and whatever this thing he had going on at present didn't change her opinion.

On many occasions, the thought of a future with Eli had passed through her mind. She loved his kids, and he seemed to get along well with hers. He never once offered to take her to Miami in all the time she had known him. She knew Mims and Pops almost as well as her parents.

They had invited her many times, but he hadn't. It pissed her off that he included Desiree after only knowing her for such a brief time. The whole sordid thing didn't add up; perhaps it was time for her to cool her friendship with him; after all, it wasn't going anywhere.

Lee called it a short day. Eli was due back in the afternoon, and she didn't want to be in the office when he returned. The first thing he always did was phone her to tell her about the Miami trip and to pass on Mims and Pops' best wishes. Mims always sent a little something to her; they had gotten quite close over the years. She was not going to wait around the office any longer. Grabbing her purse and briefcase, she bolted for the parking lot.

As the elevator doors opened on the first level, she could only hear the loud, angry voices of two men. She cautiously got out, managing to remain unseen. From where she was standing, she could see Salty waving his fist in the air and yelling at someone in an old, beaten-up van. Seeing Salty, she came out of hiding just as the van squealed out of the parking lot.

"Heya Salty, everything okay down here?" His face was still very red from the recent encounter.

"Yes, ma'am, damn boy of mine. I tell you, sometimes I think the worstest thing I did was to let him move back home." Lee tried to look sympathetic, but all she wanted was her car and to get the hell out of there.

"He's giving you a hard time, is he?"

"Ya know it's not him as much as the crowd he hangs with. I not only got his sorry self eating my groceries, but now he's got one of his slimeball friends campin' on my couch. I tell ya, this friend ain't no good. That's what all the hollering was about; sorry if you had to hear the commotion. I told him flat out I wanted his friend, Sonny Ramone, out of my house. He's got Busta, that's my kid, running him all over town biddin' his bad business. That Sonny, he's involved with a nasty group of folks. Anytime he comes around, you can start looking for something bad to happen. Last time he and Sonny hung out was when my boy got shot. Ya know he's a cripple. Ya think his so-called friends come round after that night? Sh-oot, I told him, I did. I warned him they were bad news, but ya can't tell a kid; they gotta learn for themselves." He shook his head side to side with a look of total disgust.

She had to end the rambling, "Kids, what ya gonna do with them?" That was the cue; he retrieved her keys and disappeared to get her car.

The drive through the Quarter was spent in a self-debate regarding a final pass by Eli's house. Why she chose to punish herself was anyone's guess. She pulled into his driveway, and just as she tossed the paper over the fence, they pulled up.

The four of them got out of the car, and each had a glorious beach-bronzed look. She could feel the pangs of jealousy twist in her stomach. Rachel ran to her with arms outstretched, "Miss Lee, my Gawd, it is soooo good to see you."

After Rachel's long hug, Lee commented, "Look at y'all with gorgeous sun-kissed skin you can only get from a real beach," she put out her bottom lip in an exaggerated pout, "I'm jealous."

Eli leaned over and gave her a quick peck on the cheek, "What a pal, I forgot about the paper, had remembered the mail, but forgot the damn paper. Thanks so much, Lee. You watch out for me. What would I do without you?"

There were a million things she would have liked to retort with, but none would have been pleasant; she left it with a smile.

Rachel hooked her arm in Lee's, pulling her toward the door, "Mims sent a whole buncha stuff for you. C'mon."

When they went in, Desiree made herself scarce; she felt too awkward to hang around. She figured she knew how Lee felt about Eli, and she also knew another woman would easily detect their newfound intimacy. She really liked and respected Lee and suddenly felt all too guilty.

Eli began his quick inspection of the house; everything seemed in order, "Anything special going on in the office?"

"Nah, same old, same old. Leaving today, there was a bit of excitement. As I got out of the elevator, I heard this yelling. At first, I got a little scared, but then found out it was Salty yelling at his kid."

"Salty give you the whole run-down?" Eli smiled, knowing Salty's propensity for conversation.

"Of course." She forcibly snickered, "Seems his kid, who's grown, mind you, has let some friend flop at their place. Evidently, this houseguest is a real creep. You know his kid's paralyzed or something? Here he's been parking my car for years, and I never knew about his kid. It's got to be hard, don't you think?" She kept cool but couldn't deny her feeling for him.

"Yeah, gotta be. Salty told me the story once. Bunch of kids stealing beer I think. His boy got shot; I don't know, I got the impression he was a good kid gone bad hanging out with a couple of punks." She kept the conversation going; while it was hardly warm and personal, it was better than the weather or no conversation at all.

"Wow, I didn't know. I can see why he got as mad as he did. You should've seen his face; I was waiting for him to keel over; he was so red. The punk taking space on the couch is one of the boys he was with when he got hurt. The name even sounded like a hoodlum, Sonny something, like Tyronne. Conjured a real piece of work in my imagination."

It made Eli ponder the possibility of Salty's Sonny being Desiree's ex. He made a mental note to tell Mac, just in case.

Lee stayed long enough to get the full scoop on Mims and Pops. Without fail, Mims always sent something with seashells; consequently, Lee had potholders, towels, framed pictures, candle holders, and now a jewelry box with shimmering seashells. Whether she liked it or not, she had acquired quite a collection of these glistening beauties. She bade her goodbyes and headed home.

As he shut the door behind her, he noticed the message light was blinking madly. There were seven messages; six were from Mac, and one hang up. Normally he would have waited until morning, but there was urgency in Mac's voice, followed by several numbers to reach him. Eli figured he better call.

The first number was a success; he immediately reached Mac.

"Eli, Desiree with you?" Mac seemed worried.

"Yeah, not standing here, but I can get her—" he offered.

"Nah. What I gotta tell her has to be done in person."

"Something wrong?" suddenly, Eli was concerned.

"*Ooh yeah,* really wrong. Don't say nothing to Des until I get there, okay?"

"No problem. What's up?" Eli could hear Mac's voice wavering.

"Simone's dead. Happened soon after y'all left town."

Eli got a sickening lump in his throat. "Shit. I can't believe it. I'm not gonna say anything but get here soon. She's going to know something is wrong with me just by looking at me."

"See ya in a sec," and he hung up.

"Damn straight; she's gonna be able to tell somet'ins wrong." She startled him to the point he visibly jumped, "Whad ya not gonna tell me, sha? By da look on ya face, it mus' be real bad, ya gone all sick lookin'." She stood with her hand on her hip, tapping her foot.

"Mac's on his way. I rather wait until he gets here." Eli already hurt for her before she even knew.

"If it's somet'ing I gotta hear, I t'ink it'd be betta comin' from you, don't ya t'ink."

"Not this one, mainly because I don't know what's what. I have no facts or information. I'd be only giving you sketchy patches." He ran his hand through his hair and cleared his throat.

"Sha, jus' tell me whad ya know, so I can prepare, ya know, I mean if it's dat bad. I wanna be ready."

Eli stood silent. He didn't want to argue with her but knew how he'd feel if the situation were reversed, yet Mac had explicitly asked him not to say anything. He remained silent, staring at her as though willing the information telepathically.

She turned her head and sat on the couch. He began rustling through the drawers until he found a stashed pack of cigarettes. She could see his hands tremble as he tried to light up. Tears welled in her eyes; she knew it had to be something beyond bad. Life had gotten once-in-a-lifetime good; the thought of something of ultimate horror was almost unbearable. It wasn't fair.

He ran his hand through his hair, again, still clearing his throat, and then turned toward Desiree. He cast his eyes down to her, "Oh God, I 'm sorry," his voice cracked as he tried to force the words out. It was a scratchy whisper, "Simone's gone."

"Is dat whad dis is all aboud, I know she's gone, she tol' me she was leavin'. It's okay, sha. She said she'd call when she could. Eli, you are too sweet. You worry way too much, sha." Her face took on an almost angelic look. He touched her soul. He cared enough to try and save her feelings when she had already known.

"No, Desiree, she's gone," he paused, "dead."

The angelic look turned into confusion, "No, you wrong, she tol' me she was leavin' ta get away dat's all. She ain't dead."

Eli shook his head, "Yes, she is. I'm so terribly sorry. Mac told me and told me not to tell you. He wanted to talk to you."

She sat down and started to think, "Can't be true, no way. Gawd, no," she dropped her head. "How's he know, mebbe he's wrong. Dat has to be it." She stared off into space.

"That's why I didn't want to tell you. I don't know anything." His eyes were pleading.

There was a knock at the door. Desiree lunged to her feet, racing to the door. One look at Mac's face said it all; there was no doubt, now. She backed away from him, trembling, "Nooo, say nooo." Collapsing on the floor her body heaved with sobs, "It's all my fault, oh Gawd, nooo."

Eli crouched next to her and held her in his arms, stroking her hair. The hysteria brought Rachel and Alan to the front. Confused and concerned, they, too, went to her side.

"Dad, what's wrong? What's wrong? Is Desiree okay?" He motioned for them to back away. He gently coaxed her from the floor and assisted her onto the sofa. Rachel was quick to grab a box of Kleenex. Even though she had no idea what was wrong, tears rolled down her cheeks as she bore Desiree's pain. She looked to her dad for reassurance. Mac had taken a seat in a nearby chair. He waited quietly as the members of the household settled themselves. Although controlling the tears, Desiree's tiny body still spasmodically jerked as she tried to gain control of her breathing.

"W-w-when?" she sadly asked. She wanted to understand.

Mac had a calming effect on everyone. Eli took a quick second to introduce Mac to Rachel and Alan. As a side note, he told them they could stay, and he'd fill in the gaps they may have later.

"Thursday night, sometime after the show," Mac kept his answers simple. From many years of practice, he found it best when delivering bad news to remain calm, matter-of-fact, and not cloudy the waters with hypotheses, just stick to the basic, very basic, facts. Follow-up conversations would go into more detail. But the survivors were in shock and could only absorb so much, if any at all. It was best to keep it simple for everyone.

Desiree was confused, "In da dressin—"

"No, Desiree, she had already left the club and gone to a hotel." He stated in a soft but factual tone.

"She was leavin' the nex' day, ya know? Yeah, she was gettin' da hell outta dis shithole, she tol' me, she did. Oh yeah," she nodded, "She was gonna be a gone pecan. She had it all planned out." She pushed the tissue against her eyes.

"We can get to that later." With the most sincere look of compassion, he slowly nodded with his eyes closed. "Right now, I'm making sure my little coon-ass friend is okay." He winked at her.

"Ya know me; I'll be okay, sha. I'll be okay. I can't believe she's gone." The tears trickled down her cheeks, and her nose was stuffy but running." Her voice wavered, and she cleared her throat. "Where's da body? I wanna see her."

"If that's what you want, I'll make it happen." Mac nodded.

"Mac, how'd it, ya know, happen? A g-gun?"

"No, her throat was cut," he stated facts concisely.

"Dat mutha-fuckin Sonny, ya know he tried ta do me dat more n' once. Ya got da son-of—"

"Desiree, it wasn't Sonny; it was a pro. They set her up. Sonny ain't bright enough to do that." Mac was right.

"Den who? Manducci?" Her eyes were full of questions.

"We don't know anything yet, but we will find out. I wanted to tell you in person; I know y'all were close. I'm sorry, she was a nice lady."

"Yeah," her voice stretched again as the outpouring of tears took hold, "she was. She was the momma I neva had."

Mac stayed for another hour. He told her about contacting Simone's aunt, and they had not determined the burial. They left the conversation, saying they would meet the next day. She should contact him in the morning. He'd arrange for her to see the body.

CHANGE IN PLANS

It was as though nothing had ever happened between Sonny and his uncle; if anything, it appeared they had gotten closer and spoke more frequently. Sonny's old posse had turned coat again and was back to being his entourage. It was amazing how quickly things could turn from good to bad and then back again. What it boiled down to was there was no such thing as allegiance in the wiseguy business. Everyone was out for themselves, and nobody could trust anybody. The bartender called Sonny to the phone.

"Yes, sir. Sure thing, sir. I'll be waiting for you, sir."

It was good to be back in the boss' graces. He sat at the bar to wait. He couldn't help but wonder what Manducci had on his mind. Munching on pretzels, he waited. Time seemed to drag to an almost standstill. He felt conspicuous sitting there alone. One of the boys made his way over.

"What ya got going?" he tried to warm up to Sonny.

"Nothin. I'm waiting for the old man, that's all." His answers had a slight chill to them.

"Yeah, what'd he want?" Sonny thought, another question, really?

"Don't know." Cool as a cucumber.

"Son-ny, I been wantin' to talk to ya. I hope you ain't got hard feelings from when ya were on the outs. I wanted to help ya, being paisans, but it would have been my ass if the bossman woulda found out, you know how it goes." While Sonny crunched his ice, the other punk ordered a beer.

"Yeah, I know how it goes." His voice was cold as ice. He made his point. Manducci made his entrance, and without a *screw you* or *see ya*, Sonny turned his back on the no-good chump and joined his uncle in the office.

"You eaten yet, kid? I'm gonna send for a muffuletta."

"Sure, thanks. That would be great, Uncle Tony." The bossman had the bartender make a call to Central Grocery.

"I need ya help, Sonny, with a small matter. Last we spoke, we left off you sending a message to our esteemed governor." He pointed a finger at Sonny, jabbing the air with each word for emphasis. "Listen, this thing I need you to do is important; ya gotta know up front, no mistakes, and ya gotta keep it under ya hat. We, my partners, and me got a lot invested." Manducci told Sonny to close the door. "What we want to do is turn the building next door into a casino. It'll be a small place but top drawer for high rollers only—first floor for gambling and the rest for one of them boutique hotels.

"We got the go-ahead on the hotel, but the governor's tying us up putting the casino to some kind of vote. You see our little problem here?"

"Yes, sir, I sure do." He was so far up Manducci's ass anything he said was perfect by Sonny.

"What we gotta do, is get a message to him, one letting him know he needs to play ball. I got it on good information; he's got a piece on the side." He tossed a brown envelope; inside were pictures of the governor in most compromising situations.

"As you can see, the governor's wife or, let's say, the media might love to get their hands on that. Perhaps after seeing the photos, he may be more inclined to see things our way." Manducci was right; this bit of blackmail could be most damaging in the wrong hands. Things looked pretty chummy between the gov and his masked boyfriend.

Sonny rocked his head back and forth in disbelief. "Whoa! I never had any idea he swung that way. He sure don't seem like," and he grasped the back of his neck, "that way. Who's the blond cat? The boy's hanging some sausage, that's for sure. Where'd ya get this?"

"Don't know; it just showed up on my desk. I guess a friend must have dropped them off." Manducci turned up his hands and shrugged his shoulders.

"I got this, no problem, Uncle Tony."

It was hard for her to comprehend Simone's death. Desiree questioned herself about seeing the body; she didn't want the last memory to be sad and stuck in her mind for the rest of time. There were way too many good times they'd had, and she wanted to preserve those memories with all her heart. If she didn't see the body, would there ever be closure? She had to see it.

Eli lightly tapped on the door, "You decent?"

"Yeah," as she slipped into a top.

He slowly opened the door. "I meant what I said; if you want me to go with you, I don't mind."

"Nah. Mac'll be wit' me. I'll be okay, sha. I promise." Desiree tilted her head slightly and closed her eyes.

"I can at least drop you off, right?" He solemnly nodded.

"Dat ya can do. I'll be ready; just hang on a sec."

Within minutes she was ready, and off they went. There was no point in trying to make small talk on the way to the morgue. The trials and tribulations of the past six weeks had seemed enough for a lifetime. As Eli thought about it all, it was hard to fathom Desiree had only been a part of his life for a little over a month. The bond they shared and the closeness of their relationship felt more like something from years of knowing someone, and while he still didn't know her entire history, he knew enough to know what kind of person she was, and he had fallen in love with her.

Mac was waiting out in front of the morgue. He leaned into the open window of the car, "Ya sure ya wanna go through with this? Ya don't have to."

"Yeah, I wanna." She leaned over and gave Eli a quick kiss. "T'anks fa da ride, ma frien'. I'll see ya at da office when I'm done, okay?"

"Call me if you need me?" Eli looked concerned.

The heat bounced off the pavement, creating a suffocating feeling. Desiree patted the car, sending Eli on his way. "Dis heat is a mutha." She looked to her side at Mac.

"Yeah, you right, and the sun ain't even all the way yet." Biting his bottom lip, he nodded, just barely. "I'm warning you; it ain't pleasant. You sure you up to it?" Desiree dropped her head to her chest and muttered yes.

They made their way down the hall. Mac had been right; the morgue had a distinct antiseptic or chemical smell. He held the door open for her. Upon seeing Mac, the attendant opened one of the cold metal drawers. A lump formed in the back of her throat; she glanced at Mac. He put his hand on her shoulder, giving her reassurance. She couldn't turn her eyes toward the metal drawer. She whispered to Mac, "Whad am I gonna see? Does she look bad?"

Since Simone was in the drawer feet first, the slash on her neck looked like a crease in her skin. It had been razor-sharp and executed with complete precision. "She don't look good, but you don't see nothing gory."

With every ounce of intestinal fortitude, she slowly looked toward the drawer. "Gawd, Mac, she looks so grey. I know dis soun's sick, but I'm waitin' fa her to sit up an' say 'gotcha.' Like dis is some big joke on me. I know she ain't. She stroked Simone's cold gray cheek. "Girl, I don't know how dis happened, but I will fin' out, yes indeed, I will." She touched her friend's long slender hands, "Good Gawd Simone, ya broke one of ya nails. I'll make sure dat's fixed up fa ya goin' out."

The attendant told Mac that Simone's aunt had arranged to transport the body to Chicago. Desiree blurted out, "You can't do dat, she got no one dere' cept her auntie, an' she's not all dere if ya know whad I mean."

"Desiree, she is next of kin, at least legally." Mac reminded.

"She sure as hell can't go like dat, not wit' dem braids and long nails. Can't I call the aunt an' see if I can keep her?"

"Keep her?" both Mac and the attendant said in unison.

"Bury her here. I'll pay fa her burial. Da aunt don't want to see her, all she was ta Simone was a pain in da ass. She lived rent-free in her house. Simone paid all the electricity an' gas, too."

"I can see, but don't count on it."

Mac had a hard time pulling Desiree from the body. He suspected she would have stayed there all day if given a chance. She completely broke down as they left the morgue. Her tiny body heaved with heavy sobs; his heart broke for her.

Between gasps, she cried, "She's all I had, ya know?"

"Yeah, dawlin' I know." He put his big husky arm around her and pulled her in close.

"Whad dey gonna do wi' her stuff, ya know, at her apartment?"

"I'm not sure; I guess it's up to the landlord. They usually hire a mover. I do know the aunt doesn't want the expense." He knew there would be some kind of comment coming back.

"Whad I tell ya? I want some of her t'ings dey come wit' stories, sha. Her aunt can kiss ma ass." She looked at Mac for an answer. "Also, I can pack up her t'ings, tell dem I'm her sister from anotha mutha. I'm more kin."

"I'll see what I can do. One way or another, I will get something worked out for you."

He held the phone to his ear, waiting for someone to answer. Finally, Busta picked up.

"Almost hung up, padna."

"Where ya at, Sonny?"

"The worm has turned, my friend and I'm back in. Look, I'm gonna pass by later to get my car. Things cool now on the home front. Boy, you were a lifesaver, ma man, a real lifesaver, and don't think I won't remember. You know I'd done the same thing for you, huh, paisan?"

"Sure thing, Sonny," and he hung up the phone. He looked to the ceiling, "Thank you, Gawd." It saved him from having to throw Sonny out; his pops had had his fill and had given the order. If Busta wouldn't tell him, then the old man would. In any case, it wouldn't have been pretty.

Busta gathered up Sonny's few belongings, "It'll be good to have his punk ass out of here." He dug the phone from his pocket, "Well, I done it, Pops; I told him he had to leave. Things'll be back to normal; I wanted to let you know."

While it was a good thing Sonny was leaving, Busta felt torn. Having Sonny in the house made him feel alive again, instead of sitting around doing nothing but collecting his government check. It was no kind of life. Even though tagging along with Sonny was living on the edge, at least it was living.

He called Sonny at the club, "What time you comin' for your car?"

"Dunno, maybe four. Why you got plans?" he could hear the sarcastic smirk in Sonny's voice.

"Nah, just wanted to be here when ya came, that's all." Seemed he was back to being a bother now that Sonny didn't need him.

"I guess four," Sonny was such a dick.

"Cool. I been meaning to ask ya about the club. Ya think there might be an opening? I could stamp hands at the door. I gotta get out of here, or I'll go fuckin' nuts." He was almost pleading with him.

"I dunno, I gotta talk to the boss. Being you're a crip, not that I care, I don't know what the boss will think. I'll get back to you on it." It felt like Sonny was blowing him off.

"It's hard for me to say, but I think my old man wants me out of here; I thought maybe I could move in with you just till I get some money. Ya know, flop on your couch."

"Man, I wish I could, but there's not enough room in my shithole for my stuff. You know I would if I could. The boss is looking for me; I'll get back to you on the job thing."

That was the end of that. Busta looked around the dingy room, talking to himself, "What a cocksucker. I shoulda never put him up here. Fuck him."

Desiree was silent during the drive back to Eli's office, disturbing Mac. It wasn't her personality to be quiet. Although to herself, he could see the wheels of thought churning away. "What you got goin' on in that head of yours? You're too quiet, must be up to no good."

"Mac, I'm not t'inkin' nothing; I guess I'm in shock or somet'in'. I got to *process*, as Eli would say." It didn't sit well with him.

"It's the processing that has me concerned." He looked over at her for a second. "You not planning anything stupid, like looking for Simone's killer. Desiree, that's my job, and I promise you I will give it all I have."

"Even if I wanted ta, whad could I do ta Manducci? Nuttin'. Dat, is da whole pissa of dis whole t'ing." She became restless in her seat. "He'll neva have ta pay fa whad he done, neva an' Simone'll become one of da many unsolved murders of N'awlins. I aks ya, whad could I do?" There was silence. "Ma point exactly, Mac, so why da fuck even t'ink aboud it, right?"

New Orleans was a strange place, almost like a drug. Just at a glance, locals knew home-grown and visitors. The natives were constantly dogging the city, profusely complaining about everything from the government to the streets to the crime and the filth, but they wouldn't do anything about it but moan. In the same breath, let an outsider speak ill of their beloved city, and the fight was on.

They waited at a red light where a myriad of folks crossed the street. Both Desiree and Mac silently sat as they watched the parade of pedestrians stream across. Maybe it was the section of the city or perhaps even the attitudes, but it appeared as each face had the same forlorn look of hopelessness and despair. They gazed ahead with an empty stare.

"Whad wit' dese people? Dey walkin' round like dey walkin' ta dere death. Ya know, people jus' don't know how good dey got it. Since I been at Eli's, I've learned much. Dey watch a TV channel dat shows all dese far away places like Africa. Dose people, dey goddit bad. Half da people dyin' an' here ya look at dese fools all dey lookin' fa is a handout. It makes me sick."

"Yeah? When you get so political?" He put one of his big meaty hands on her shoulder. "You know what I think, I think it's done you good to be with the Rosens, it's made you smarter, or should I say, more aware? I've always known you were smart."

She couldn't help but acknowledge he was right. Life had taken on a whole new outlook, not the daily drama of the club, she was meeting real people with real lives that had direction and motivation, and she found herself adapting to the change well. Never in her wildest dreams would she have seen herself in a political discussion with one of her co-workers. The girls at the club were more interested in getting high or finding a sugar daddy. No, Desiree wanted more now. Even if things were different with Manducci, she could never go back to the lifestyle of the club; she'd grown too much.

Eli's mind was going in a thousand directions, but when he pulled into the parking garage and saw Salty, he seized the opportunity.

"How you doing, Mista Eli?" Salty said, walking towards the car.

"Real good, Salty, no complaints." He shook the old guy's hand.

"Ya had y'self a good vacation?"

"Real nice, thanks. Salty, you mind if I ask you something?"

"You go right ahead, sir. If it's about me and my boy—"

Eli put his hand up, "Family stuff, we all got it, right? It's about your son's friend." As though looking back in his memory, "What's his name? Oh, right, Sonny." Eli put his hands in his pockets.

"Yeah, Ramone, Sonny Ramone. He's a real piece of work. Sombitch was holding out at my place, but I told my boy to t'row his nasty a—" Eli saw the redness climbing up Salty's neck.

"Good, I hear he can be trouble; I'm glad he isn't staying by you anymore."

Salty had a ruddy complexion and deep grooves in his skin from years on the sea while in the Navy. They looked more like smile or laugh lines than scowl. He was a good, hard-working guy. "Don't get me wrong, Busta, my son, ain't no golden child, he got a buncha crap with him, but he don't got that mean streak like Ramone. Sonny gives me the creeps and being around the docks, I've seen some creeps; Sonny'd fit right in ova by them."

"Glad to know he's gone. You take care, now."

"You too. Have a good day, Mista Eli."

The files and messages were piled high on his desk. It never ceased to amaze him how one week away could produce such a wake of paper. He began going through the first stack when there was a light rap on the door.

"Got a minute?" he was relieved when he saw it was Lee.

"Sure, By the way, thanks for the newspaper favor, but I wish you would've done something about these," he grinned, pointing to the stacks. He clasped his hands behind his head and leaned back in his chair. It felt comfortable and familiar.

"No problem; what are pals for? Which is why I want to talk to you. Before y'all left, I felt bad about the way things had gotten; I mean, we go back, and to tell you the truth, I missed having my friend. Whatever happened, can we put it behind and get back where we were before?" Her eyes filled with tears. He could see she was fighting them back.

He got up and came from around the desk, "I've missed you too, pal-y. I think this calls for a hug." He hugged her; it felt good; he had missed his friend. Things had been weird, but the onset of the weirdness was with him.

The hug was interrupted by the phone. Lee turned to leave. "W-wait." He answered the phone. It was Mac letting him know he had just let Desiree out of the car, and she'd be on her way up. Eli motioned for Lee to shut his door.

"What? What's so secret we need to shut the door?"

"I got a lot to unload; you willing to be my ear?"

Sonny was careful not to make a mistake. He had taken the photos Manducci had given him to a self-copy place. Donning latex gloves, he made four copies of each picture. The first set he'd deliver directly to the governor, the second sealed in an envelope addressed to the wife, the third to the media, the original back to Manducci, and the last copy he'd hide for safe-keeping in his apartment.

If the gov wouldn't play ball, he'd post the one to the wife, and if that didn't work, he'd send it to the media. Eventually, one way or another, Sonny would make sure his uncle got what he wanted. He knew he couldn't do it himself, the connection to Manducci was too easy, but the question remained, who could he use? The answer came to him quickly; he picked up the phone.

"Hey paisan, I've thought about your situation, and hell, you helped me out of a tight spot, sure you can crash at my place, but I'm warning you, it's small. You won't believe how small."

Busta was in utter shock; Sonny had come through for him. He had always thought it to be a one-way friendship; maybe Sonny had looked at himself and decided to change.

"Thanks, you still comin' around four? I guess we can work out the details, huh?"

"Yeah, nothing to work out; just have your stuff when I come by, and we'll bolt. Later."

It all came too fast; Busta wasn't sure how it would work. He was his Pops ride to and from work. The thought of him having to take the bus downtown didn't seem right. He felt all too guilty. He had a few hours to think it over before making any big decisions.

When Desiree got upstairs, she went to Eli's office; the door was closed. She figured he must be with someone of importance; she continued to her desk. She'd buzz him a little later. Inside his office, Eli had Lee's undivided attention. The more he unraveled the story, the wider her eyes became. When he got to the part about the attack on the street, she put her hand to her mouth with a gasp. Within a half-hour, he had her up to speed, leaving out the intimate moments with Desiree. The story ended with a brief description of the happenings after she had left his house the night before.

"I don't mean to rush through all this, but I wanted to give you a head's up. The detective took her to see the body this morning; I'm sure she'll be a wreck." He looked sad.

"Poor kid. She's got a look that says she's been around and seen a lot, but she's had it rougher than I thought." She hesitated a moment, "What you've done for her is a good thing, but you really need to watch out for yourself and those kids of yours. Face it; she's not your responsibility. I'm not wagging my finger or nothin', but you gotta think it through, Eli. You got a lot at stake." Lee nodded at him.

"I know you're right, but I don't think it's the right time to send her on her way. Not after—"

Lee interrupted, "Give it a week or two and then help her find a place of her own. Shit, she's making enough. You gotta start putting some space between y'all. You may have to help her with deposits and that kinda stuff, but at least it would be better than having all this shit in your house. Hell, there may even be an efficiency in one of those big houses near you. I'll keep my ear to the ground." She got up to walk out and then turned, "Am I supposed to know any of this or what?"

"Keep it quiet for now; I'll let you know," his phone buzzed as Lee left his office.

It was Desiree. "I'm back."

"Want to talk?"

"Yeah, ya don't mind?"

She was better off than he anticipated. She went through the morning's experience step by step.

"I tol' Mac that he's gotta make damn sure Simone don't go home like she is. Shit, no one dere knows her as Simone. I wish they'd bury her here; I could visit. He's gonna let me get some of ha stuff, don't know whad will happen ta da res'."

He attentively listened as he rolled a pen in his palm. "We have a small shed in the backyard. You could store some stuff there until you get your own place. Hell, that'd save you from buying furniture, and I'm sure Simone would want you to have it. You'd have a bit of her around you always." His eyes sparkled with warmth.

"Mebbe. I t'ought aboud tryin' ta take ova ha lease, but even if I could afford it, which I can't, I couldn't live dere, no. Too many memories, plus dat would be da firs' place people start lookin' fa me, ya know?" Her eyes looked sad. His phone buzzed again; it was the receptionist looking for Desiree.

"I'm here; pass it ta me, please."

She had a call on line two from Mac, "Dis is Des—"

"I'll be quick; I wanted to let you know I talked to old auntie in Chicago, and she says she'd appreciate you handling the burial and anything you want from the apartment to go for it; it's all yours. She's having the papers sent. You better figure out what you're gonna do and get on it fast. I have a feeling the landlord is gonna want to rent it asap."

"Mac, t'ank you. Dis means a lot ta me. I'm gonna get rightd on it."

He had been right; he only kept her on the phone thirty seconds tops.

Desiree wasn't quite sure where to start, but she'd get it done—it required the utmost discretion. It was good there wasn't much going on in the office; it allowed her to start making the calls to get Simone laid to rest.

The conversation between Eli and Lee rolled through his mind like an endless loop. He knew she was right about Desiree, but he also knew he didn't want to be away from her. If anything, he wanted her to move from the couch to his bed. He wanted to exclaim to the whole world she was his lady—not the right time for such an announcement.

Four o'clock came; Busta wasn't sure what he wanted to do. Part of him longed to get from under his old man's thumb and move in with Sonny for a taste of real life, but the other part felt the bond of allegiance to his aging father. With dread, he waited for Sonny. He watched from the window as a cab pulled up to the house. Sonny had regained his air of superiority and had a distinct cockiness to his gait.

Sonny called in through the screen, "Where ya at, Busta? You ready to bolt?"

Busta rolled to the door, "Gotta go pick up da old man, better you go on without me; we'll catch up later."

"Don't tell me you're backing out on me. Man, we got places to go and women to do. C'mon, I'll take you to go get your old man." Busta knew bringing Sonny to pick up his dad was an unwise plan.

"Better if I meet you after. You'll be at the club?"

"Okay, see you there."

The rumbling sound of Sonny's car echoed through the tiny house. Busta watched from the front porch as the beaten-up Trans Am peeled rubber onto Banks. Perhaps he'd hang with Sonny and crash at his place on the weekends. That way, he wouldn't be letting his old man down and still be able to have some kind of life.

As he navigated through the city, he felt good about his decision.

Salty was waiting for him as he pulled up to the garage. Busta watched him as he climbed into the van. It was like he was looking at him from a different perspective. He had never realized just how old his father was getting. Salty had an empty, worn look in his eyes, a look that spelled years of hard work with little or nothing to show for it. It wasn't fair; the old guy had paid his dues. It was now his time to sit back and coast, but there he was day in and day out catering to the white collars. Between both of their government checks, they barely paid the bills. His dad had no choice; he had to be the one to put food on the table. Perhaps hanging with Sonny might present some employment opportunities, and then his dad *could* take it easy.

"Boy, it's been a hot one today. No breeze, no nuttin', just steam bouncing off the pavement. It's damn smothering; that's what it is, smothering." Busta nodded in agreement.

Most of the way home was silent. The two of them listened to the traffic report, making small talk about the potholes.

"I take it all went okay getting Sonny out the house?" Salty had his eyes closed, and his head was resting back.

"Yeah, a little strained, but okay."

"Who's he gonna mooch off now?"

"He ain't; he's going back to his place; he got back in his unc's good graces."

Salty shook his head. "He's even more stupid than I thought. Mr. Anthony Manducci don't forgive no one nothing, ya hear? My bet is he's setting the boy up. Like they say, what goes around comes around."

"Pops, it doesn't look like no setup."

"Of course, it don't; if it did, it wouldn't be no setup," the old man shook his head again in disbelief.

"Whatever, Pops. Sonny might be able to get me some work under the table."

With that, Salty opened his eyes and sternly looked at Busta. "You leave that boy alone, I'm warning you, stay clear of him, he ain't nuttin' but trouble, ya hear me?"

Silence fell upon the van for the rest of the ride. When they pulled up to the house, Salty reminded Busta, "I hope you heard me, boy. You stay clear of Sonny; for once, do something smart and take your old man's advice."

"I will," there was no point in getting into it with him; he'd never be able to make the old man understand his lack of a life. Something was better than nothing.

No sooner had they gotten home, Busta headed out the door, "Be back later."

Sonny and the boys were tossing down some brew when the boss showed up. A few regulars sat at the bar, and a few watched the bored strippers, but other than that, the place was dead.

The bossman strolled out of his office. "We gotta drum up some business boys instead of throwing back profit." He pulled Sonny to the side, "You come up with any ideas?"

Sonny began spewing off about ads on the radio and something about a name act. Manducci interrupted, making it clear he was less than impressed with Sonny's ability to comprehend the question. "Stop; I was referring to the thing we discussed earlier." Sonny could see his uncle's temples pulsing.

"Oh that," with smug confidence, he added, "I got that in the bag. No problem."

"I sincerely hope so because if anything goes wrong, you'll take the fall. Believe me; they'll nail your ass; there'll be no getting off. I walk away like I don't know you, capiche?" He went through the motions of dusting his hands and had a threatening look.

"Yes, sir, definitely capiche. I won't be anywhere near the governor's office. I got someone else to do the delivery. Got it covered; this time tomorrow, it's gonna be a done deal."

"You better make sure you got the right patsy, and I sure hope it ain't one of them stooges out there," he jerked his thumb in the direction of the bar and the posse, then stiffly patted Sonny on the cheek and left.

Just as Manducci was leaving the club, Busta rolled in.

Sonny met him halfway, "You and me, we gotta talk." He grabbed a beer for the two of them and then led the way to a table on the far side of the club, "You still thinking you might want some work around here?"

"Yeah." Busta nodded excitedly.

"I gotta little something you can handle." Without leaking important information, he told Busta he needed him to run him to Baton Rouge; they had a delivery to make, and then they'd turn around and come right back. "You'll be back in time to pick up your pops, and you'll have yourself an extra three hundred bucks to put in your pocket. That's if you want it. If not, I'll get someone else; I just thought I'd make the offer to you first."

"Hell yeah, I want it, a trip to Baton Rouge for three hundred, no problem." He raised his bottle to Sonny, "Here's to the first bit of business and more to come."

Sonny figured if they traced the prints on the envelope, it would give them nothing. Busta had never been in trouble; he was a juvey when the accident happened. At the time of the accident, the bar owner was so torn up he dropped charges. But if they somehow linked it to Busta, he'd never give him up. Looking at the worst-case scenario and Busta mentioned Sonny's name, there would be no prints on the envelope or pictures to incriminate him. It would be Busta's word against his, and neither held any political weight; it would end up a wash.

They arranged to meet the following day after Busta dropped off his dad.

Simone's burial arrangements came together much easier than Desiree had anticipated. The city provided a public burial area for those who couldn't pay. She would be laid to rest the following day, which gave Desiree time to pick out the perfect burial ensemble for Simone. She felt sure it would have been Simone's wishes. Eli insisted he go with her in the event she had unexpected company. She would have preferred to go by herself but decided this would not be one of the battles she would fight.

Being back at Simone's sent shivers down her spine. It was eerie; she was expecting Simone to come around the corner in her pink robe and fluffy slippers at any moment. Despite the weirdness of the experience, Desiree felt a sense of calm, and upon opening the closet, a rush of Simone's scent filled the air. Quickly she stripped one of the garments from a hanger and nuzzled her face into the silky cascade of fabric. Her eyes began filling with tears; she felt alone.

Eli was only steps away in the front room, but the loneliness had nothing to do with space or time; it was a hollow insatiable void pained with a gnawing ache that stole her very breath. In an instant, a slight cool feeling traced across the back of her neck. Desiree knew the feeling she had it once before years ago after the death of her godfather, whom she loved dearly, but she had only been a small child; no one took her seriously. She had heard of people with the gift but had never considered herself one of those.

Quietly she whispered, "I feel ya, sha. I'm not scared, no," again the coldness crept up the back of her neck, followed by a resonant hollow sound. While there were no formed words, a vision materialized in her mind. She could see Simone leaving the club with a most handsome blond-haired man. Simone turned her head and looked right into Desiree's eyes. While she said nothing, Desiree knew the man in the vision had been her killer. His face imprinted in her memory, and she would hunt him down.

"I got da message. We'll get da bastard; ya can bet ya bottom dollar," she paused, her body falling backward as she gasped for air, and in a snap, the vision, the coldness, and the presence were gone.

"Desiree, who are you talking to? You okay?" Eli poked his head into the room.

"I'm fine, it's nuttin, no, I'm crazy talkin' ta m'sef, that's all."

She managed to pull together an outfit perfect for the occasion. Simone would have agreed. As hard as it was going to be, and she knew it would, life *would* go on.

It was a humid morning with no sign of even the slightest breeze. Busta pulled up to the club after dropping off the old man at work. He was excited; it felt good to have a purpose. There was no doubt in his mind this mission of sorts was dubious at best. It had to be; it was Sonny's kind of business. Nonetheless, it translated into excitement. Sonny slinked out of the club and climbed aboard the van.

"Son-ny, you look pretty rough, bud. Must have been a good time." Busta remarked.

"Good enough," he instructed Busta to head to the government building in Baton Rouge, 900 North 3rd.

Sliding down in the seat, he put his shades on and settled himself for an hour's nap. Within minutes Busta could hear the rhythmic snores of his paisan. As they approached the state building, he gave Sonny a nudge.

"We here, bud. What's next?"

Sonny directed him to go straight in and head toward the governor's office. Security would probably stop him along the way; he was to say that he was merely a delivery boy and was given strict instructions not to deliver the package to anyone but the governor's assistant. Sonny explained he'd have to go through security and even undergo an inspection of his chair to stay calm and collected, and it should all go down as planned.

Sure enough, Sonny had been right. He passed through the metal detector and x-ray booth; they inspected his wheelchair, but other than that, no one had much to say to him. Busta thought, *so much for security*. When he reached the appropriate office, he found several people gathered in a huddle of disagreement. Something had obviously gone amiss, and it was up to them to put out the fire. When Busta asked for the governor's PA, a young gentleman raised his hand, quickly took the envelope from him, assured him it would get in the right hands, and resumed his position in the huddle, no questions asked. It went like clockwork; maybe he didn't look like a threat; mission accomplished.

He made it back to the van, and within minutes they were back on their way to the city. What Busta hadn't realized was security cameras captured the face of everyone entering and exiting the building. If, and that was a big if, the gov's assistant were to remember him in any way, the security camera would provide a clear picture and certain identification. On the other hand, Sonny knew all about the security cameras; however, he felt it was of little concern; it would be Busta they would come after.

TOO
CLOSE

Everything came together without a hitch, and as far as she knew, no one was any the wiser. Simone had been laid to rest in a quiet, small ceremony, her apartment had been cleared out and stored in Eli's back shed, and life was, for the most part, back to normal. It had been the better part of a week since she'd heard from Mac. Desiree was most curious about any developments regarding Sonny, so she arranged a lunch date with Mac. They met at a small sandwich shop just doors down from her work; in fact, the last time she had been there was with Simone.

"Where ya been at, ma frien'? I ain't seen ya since da funeral, no." She stared at him, waiting.

"Nothing personal, Des; I been beyond busy, that's all. In truth, I was glad when you called. It's good to see you." Regardless of what shirt and tie he had on, it was always stained or wrinkled.

She raised an eyebrow. "Ya run into Sonny? It's been a while dat he's been on da loose. I done everyt'in' y'all tol' me ta do, and y'all ain't got him yet? Like ya tol' me, ev'ry day he's on da street, I'm in danger." She ordered her lunch.

"We'll get him. We will." He tried to reassure her, but she wasn't biting.

"I hope so, sha. Now," she looked around. "I got somet'in' ta tell ya. Da otha night I was by Simone's place, I got eerie chills. I know ya gonna t'ink I'm completely out da box. Simone was dere, I felt her. She got in ma head. I could see her walkin' from da club wit' dis tall light-haired man, good lookin', yeah. No one I eva seen b'fore. All of a sudden, she stopped while she was walkin' and looked inta my eyes like I was dere, but not. Dat guy was da one who killed her. An' dat quick," she snapped her fingers. "Da feelin' an' da picture in ma head were gone. I tell ya, I see dat guy on da street; I'll know him. I have his face stuck in ma brain."

Mac sat there looking at her.

The server brought their sandwiches. "Ya t'ink I'm crazy, yeah? I tell ya, I saw whad I saw, it was real, ma frien'. I don't care if ya believe me or not."

"Wait a second; I never said I didn't believe you. Calm down, Desiree. You tell me that's what happened; then I say okay, that's what happened. There's nothing I can do about it." He took a few bites of his lunch.

"I know you can't do nuttin; I'm not expectin' ya to; I'm jus' tellin' ya I know whad the killa looks like. I got a feelin' I'll see the guy again, and when I do, I'll call ya an' say, he's here an' ya come. Deal?" She punctuated her thought with a bite and a few swallows of Coke.

"Deal. Desiree, but don't do nothing stupid."

"Ya gonna let me know when ya have Sonny?" She said with a mouth full of food.

"You betcha." They chewed the fat for the next half hour, drank their soft drinks, and finished their sandwiches. It was a leisurely lunch, and they reminisced about Simone.

Manducci paced back and forth along the side of his desk with a most irritated look on his face. A ring of the phone broke the silence.

"Yeah," he listened, "You were already supposed to be in the city. What you mean tomorrow?" He listened again, "So be it." He slammed the phone down.

The assassin had come highly recommended; even if he was the best, Manducci had his fill of the cocky foreigner. After his blond friend finished his assignment, he'd have to teach the boy some manners. The more he thought about it, the angrier he got. Obviously, this guy didn't know how the game was played and who the players were. Didn't he know you didn't square off with the Mob? He was working for them, not the other way around. Yeah, he thought someone would have to teach this punk a thing or two.

The phone buzzed, "You got a call from the governor's office; sorry to bother you. Do you want to take it, or should I tell them you stepped out?"

"Put it through."

It was the governor himself, "Tony? Sterling here." The conversation continued with the common civilities of two friends, which led to the crux of the matter: "We need to get together, Tony. I know you are aware that if it were just up to me, the casino would be no problem, but I have people to answer to."

"As do I, and my people are getting extremely impatient. Time is money, am I right?"

"Look, I'll do what I can, but first, I'll need your assurance your correspondence of late will go no further."

"Correspondence, what correspondence?"

Silence hung from the other side of the phone like a damp rag. "Don't play with me, Tony; we go back way too far. The pictures, that's what," there was a weariness in his tone.

"Pictures?" he hesitated. "You got someone giving you problems? You need my help; say the word."

He could hear the confusion on the other side of the phone. Either way, the guy was over a barrel. If Tony hadn't sent the pictures, which he believed he had, then to have him rid of the problem would leave him obligated. If he did send them, then to assure they wouldn't get into the wrong hands, he would once again be obliged to maneuver a permit without putting it to a vote and perhaps jeopardize his re-election. Whatever he did, he was fucked.

"What's it gonna take? I make the permit happen; then you assure me this whole picture incident goes away?"

"I asked if you needed my help as a friend, and you insult me like this? You are under no obligation to do anything for me, but I would be most grateful if you think you can get the permit. Permit or not, you want my help, say the word." He really had the governor confused by this point, exactly where he wanted him.

The Governor cleared his throat, "You'll have it by next week." If his tone indicated how he felt, Manducci surmised his dear friend would be searching a toilet to purge his gut. He had a nauseated sound in his voice.

"What a friend; I knew I could count on you." He wondered how the gov would deal with the media frenzy once the news got out about Manducci's gambling permit, but that kept the spin doctors with a job.

He loved toying with the politicians, it gave him a sense of power; it was reminiscent of the good old days when it was the norm to have politicians in his pocket. Things had gotten messy with all the new protocols and everyone being afraid of exposure. The media was out of control and on the wrong people's payrolls. Too many people had forgotten the meaning of respect; this new attitude was bad for business.

The summer months at Class Act were not only a time for gathering information for the coming year but also the time the sales force took to the road cementing client relationships and nailing down contracts for the coming year. Eli, like the others, was scheduled for a few out-of-town meetings. In light of all that had gone on, he was less than comfortable with the idea of leaving the family—a vast array of what-ifs ran through his head.

There was some comfort in knowing Mac would keep a watchful eye on his little tribe in his absence. Following her lunch with Mac, Desiree had planned the afternoon with Eli honing in on all that would need to be accomplished while he was gone and making sure he had everything he needed for his trip out west.

Desiree knocked on the doorframe of Eli's office. He looked up, "Your lunch with Mac went well; I take it?"

"Yeah, sha, he tol' me ta relay ta ya dat he'll stay on toppa t'ings while ya gone an' not ta worry none." She sat down and watched as he continued to flip through the stack of papers she had given him earlier.

With a longing smile, he said, "I'm gonna miss you; promise me you are gonna behave while I'm gone." He said with a half-smile.

Desiree cocked her head to the side. "Whad ya don't trus' me? Ya only gonna be gone fa a coupla days ya make it soun' like it's a month."

"I know, things are weird, to say the least; I worry." Eli knew how careless she could be and how hard-headed she was about the whole Sonny thing.

"Ya soun' like ya momma, sha," she teased him.

He put the final papers in his briefcase and buzzed Lee's office to confirm he was ready anytime she was.

"Mebbe I should be da one worried, no?" she felt a slight twinge of jealousy about him and Lee traveling together.

"Please!" he shut the door, pressed against her, and delivered an intense kiss, "I'm gonna miss you, and you have nothing to worry about, okay? This trip is business only, understand?" He opened the door, "You have my itinerary and my number; call if you want."

She watched as the two of them walked out of the office. With little left to do, Desiree called it a day and headed home in Eli's Volvo. Still without a license and a bit unsure at the wheel, she carefully drove through the streets. As she pulled into the driveway, Rachel came out onto the porch. The distraction of Rachel and her natural ill-ease behind the wheel made it easy for the vehicle behind her to go unnoticed.

Alan had plans to spend the evening with friends, making it girl's night. They planned an evening of the usual chick flicks. Rachel had them all, from Steel Magnolias to Beaches, Bridesmaids, and Fried Green Tomatoes. Donned in their favorite nighttime tees, they made a tasty dinner salad and settled in with a bottle of Merlot, French bread, and a box of Kleenex. The two of them leaned their backs against the sofa with the shared box of Kleenex between them; Steel Magnolias won the honor of the first video. They indulgently watched amidst laughter, held breath, and tears. Still glued to the screen, they readied themselves for the heart-wrenching scene where Sally Fields goes into complete meltdown following the funeral.

Desiree whispered, "Rach, shh, mute da box." They sat in silence, "Ya hear somet'in?"

"What am I supposed to hear?" A slight creak, an almost scratching sound from the back, got their attention. Desiree took the remote and put the volume back up. She quietly stole into the kitchen and grabbed one of the big knives from the carving block. She motioned for Rachel to dial 911.

A loud thud came from the direction of the back door as though the screen had banged close. The operator picked up, Rachel whispered that they had an intruder. The operator told her to stay on the line, and a unit would be immediately dispatched.

Desiree stood to the side of the hallway door, ready to lunge. They could hear footsteps slowly moving toward the front, taking a few steps then stopping. This went on for what seemed forever.

A loud banging on the front door caused both women to jump nearly out of their skin. And with the knock came a scuffle from the back of the house. Rachel managed to open the door and caught sight of Desiree as she took off down the hall, knife in hand. Next came a series of bangs and booms as doors opened and slammed. She could hear someone making tracks along the side of the house. The noise of an apparent scuffle drew Rachel onto the porch, just in time to see a policeman fall and the perpetrator bolt down the street. Beyond any control, she screamed from the pit of her being.

Within the next two minutes, several police cars pulled in front of the house and an ambulance for the injured officer. The officer inside the house surmised someone had broken in, and his presence had spooked the intruder, who ran through the sideyard and into the other officer. The downed officer sustained a stab wound to the gut, enough to bring him down, but no risk of anything life-threatening.

Desiree held Rachel, "You okay, sha?" Rachel trembled in her arms. "Rach, we okay. It's all ova now. You okay, girl," she stroked her hair, softly cooing to her.

The first officer approached the two women with a series of questions. "Look, Mista officer, I know ya jus' doin' ya job, but ya need ta back off a bit right now, 'til we get ourselves more betta. Ma frien' here's all shook up; give us a bit of space, please."

He was more than understanding but told her time was of the essence; his partner was on the way to the hospital, and all he wanted was info so he could apprehend the S.O.B.

She asked for Mac by name.

That had been too close. Sonny drove back to the club and made a point of letting everyone know he was there and had been all night. To think Desiree had been so close, right under his nose all the time, infuriated him. He felt like it meant she had won and *that* he would never tolerate. She had made him look the fool, and no one did that and stayed healthy. Next time he'd be waiting for her, somewhere with no escape.

He figured it wouldn't be long before some of New Orleans' finest would be snooping around looking for him. He knew they had already gotten a warrant for his arrest, but he'd been able to evade them up until this point, so there would be no hanging around just in case. He left out the back, undetected by anyone. As he suspected, it was only an hour or so before Mac entered, flashing his badge.

"Tell ya padna; Mac's hear to see him."

"You don't say?" the barkeep responded with a smirk, "and just who would ma padna be, officer?" The bartender continued working.

"Cute, real cute." Mac continued toward the offices. "Ya can tell him I'm coming back for his wop ass."

The bartender called to the back, "Sonny here?"

Someone from the back came out and said he had just seen him. "I don't know where he's at, but he's been here all night watching the fuckin' door."

"Whatever, let him know I'm looking for him. Of course, he already knows that. You boys better watch yourselves." Mac nodded with a grin of warning, turned, and left.

Mac began his nightly vigil of combing the streets of the Quarter. He was bound and determined to get the creep. He had told Desiree he would, and he was going to by God. He spotted the Trans Am a block up. Slowly pulling alongside, he got out and put his hand on the hood. It was debatable as to whether it had just parked, or it could have easily been parked there for a few hours and was warm from the hot summer's night.

There was a parking spot caddy corner to Sonny's apartment; Mac pulled in to wait. The place looked void of life. Sonny could be anywhere; the Quarter was an easy place to get lost; there were bars on almost every corner and an unwillingness to cooperate with five-o. Mac's, or any other officer's pending arrival, was always long announced before they were present. The local grapevine kept the bad guys one step ahead. Mac watched as passers-by paraded one by one down the street. They all looked the same with glazed-over eyes and a boozed-up swagger. It was the sober ones that stood out from the rest.

The steadfast stride of a light-haired man caught his attention. He walked briskly, neither glancing from side to side nor particularly bothered by anything. His face was void of any emotion. He slowed down as he approached Sonny's apartment. Looking at his reflection in the closest window, he adjusted his collar, then turned and carried on about his business. There was nothing untoward; however, something lurked in the back of Mac's mind. He instinctively checked his rearview mirror for another glance at the fellow, but he was gone. Mac turned completely around there was no way the guy could have gone that far in seconds, but he didn't see him. That raised even more suspicion; he started his engine and turned the corner. He patrolled the block, circling round and round, to no avail. The mystery man had vanished.

It was one thing to navigate his Trans Am through the narrow streets, but Busta's van was a whole different deal. The more he stewed over the fact that Desiree had been so close, the angrier he got and the less mindful he was becoming behind the wheel. Turning onto Conti, he just missed hitting a tourist.

"Hey stupid, watch where ya going. Fuckin' tourist."

The stranger stood in the street as though staring the van down. Cold, no expression.

Sonny was impatient, "Get the fuck out the way."

The blond-haired man took a few steps backward but kept his eye trained on Sonny, who swerved the big van to the side, slowly passing the tourist, "Fuckin' tourist."

An ominous, almost knowing smile formed on the gentleman's face, which sent an icy chill up Sonny's spine, "Asshole." He checked his rearview mirror; the man was gone, which put Sonny on edge.

Eventually, he pulled around to his place, honked once, then drove around the corner. Within the next five minutes, Busta rolled up to the van. Sonny hopped out, and Busta got in, "Hey, let me know if you need a lift til ya wheels are back in biz, no problem. Where ever you need to go, I'm your man."

"Seen anything funny going on? Has five-o come by?" Sonny was manic.

"Nope. All's been quiet, Sonny."

"Good." Sonny checked both directions, raised his collar, and slinked down the street to his pad. As usual, Busta waved an unreciprocated goodbye.

Desiree tried to keep a calm appearance, but she felt sick inside. She couldn't believe Sonny had found her, she had felt so secure at Eli's, and now she was bringing the trouble to his place. There was only one thing left to do, but it would have to wait until she knew Eli was on his way home, which would be one more day.

She decided to hunt the bastard down and get rid of the problem once and for all. Thinking to herself, she should have done it a long time ago; perhaps Simone would still be alive. No one cared whether Sonny Ramone lived or not. After working for Manducci, who didn't give a rat's ass about him for all practical purposes, he had estranged himself from family years ago. Sonny was merely his nephew, the son of the holy roller sister of his first wife.

His ex and her sister hadn't talked in years. Sonny's mom was a Catholic lady with a houseful of kids. She had been widowed months after she delivered her last child and had done her best to raise them on her own. Four of the five kids had made their way respectably in life, and then there was Sonny, the bad apple. He had gone from bad to worse in the years Desiree had known him. It was sad in one way; all Sonny wanted was the love and respect of a father figure. The stupid son-of-a bitch chose the wrong hero.

For now, she needed to put her best foot forward and tend to Eli's family. She, at the very least, owed him that. She waited until she knew he'd be available, so she called first thing in the morning. He was still sound asleep; she had forgotten the time difference.

"Shit, Eli, sorry. Call me when ya wake up, sha."

He groggily answered, "No, go ahead. I miss y'all."

"Yeah? Me too?" She asked.

"What do you think, ma dawlin'?"

She hated to tell him, but there was no other choice. "Ya may not feel da same afta I tell ya."

Silence.

"Someone was by da house las' night when Rach an' me was watchin' movies. At firs' we t'ought it was somet'in' rubbin' on da screen, but we took no chances and called da police. Dey got here real fas' an' almos' caught da guy comin' down by da side yard, but he got away."

Wide awake now, "Crap, Rach okay? You okay? Y'all call Mac?"

"Yes, yes, and yes. At firs' we called 911, but den I got a holda Mac. Ya know him; he's on it like a pit bull."

"Anybody got a good look at him? Why don't y'all go stay in a hotel until I get home?" He sounded panicked.

"Don't be ridiculous; we fine. I swear. Alan'll be home tonight. I don't t'ink someone would be stupid enough ta come back again. It's ya call; ya tell me whad ya want me ta do. I t'ink t'ings are okay, Eli."

"Stay there then; if y'all get scared, go straight to the Marriott, they all know me there, so you shouldn't have a problem. Let me know if you do, so I don't worry." His voice still sounded shaken.

"Got it, chief."

"I'll be home by six tomorrow evening. Why don't you see if Mac wants to come by for dinner? Maybe by then, they'll have more information. Call him."

"Okay, say aboud seven?" She tried to sound more upbeat.

Desiree had little to no problem catching up with Mac; he seemed delighted with the invitation. She couldn't help but wonder when he spent time with his wife. He worked all the time, day, night, weekends, always.

She couldn't have staged a better scenario to camouflage the execution of her plan. She'd make a gumbo that would cook all day, have a salad prepared and ready in the fridge, and then after Eli called to say he was on the way home, she would tell Rachel that she had to bolt for the bread and the pot needed watching. Once she made it out the door, she'd vanish into the Quarter and hunt down Sonny.

There would be no stopping her. Why she hadn't thought of this earlier was the question that would loom in her mind forever. She would pack a small bag with some essentials, slip one of the kitchen knives wrapped in a towel, and stash it in the bushes for retrieval later. If everything went as planned, she would return to Eli, explain she had to clear her mind, and settle with him for the rest of the time. She hoped he would be willing to take her back.

She called into work and left a message she wouldn't be in; even though she was sure they wouldn't have another visit, she didn't want to leave Rachel alone in the house. Both of them needed to catch up on some sleep. Following her phone call with Eli, the two climbed into Rachel's bed.

"Des, something going on between you and my dad?" Rachel asked.

"Girl, why ya say dat?"

"I heard you on the phone sounded kinda like honey-talk. So? Y'all have been funny since Miami," she listed observations with no good or bad emotion. It was hard to judge.

"I care a lot for ya dad. He's a great guy. I neva gave it too much t'ought," maybe that would suffice, but hell no, she was Eli's kid.

"You kissed him yet?" She pushed.

"I kiss him all da time."

"No, I mean, have you *kissed* him?"

"Anyone eva tell ya dat ya aks too many damn questions?"

"Ah-ha! So, you *have!*" There was a brief pause, "it's okay. I've been able to tell he was attracted to you from the first time he told me about you, after the parking lot thing."

"Shhh. Sha, let's get some sleep."

Sonny turned down one of the brick alleyways, quickly checking to ensure no one followed him. He scaled the brick wall halfway down the path and was over in no time, then dropped to his feet, landing in the corridor that led to his grungy flat. A quick flick of his lighter was enough to find a clear path to his bathroom.

Once the bathroom door closed, he could turn on a light. This cat and mouse game with the NOPD was getting old. He felt confident that once he got Desiree out of the picture, his uncle would assist him in an escape from the city and line him up in one of his other places outside New Orleans.

The bathroom was tiny and most disgusting. It didn't help that he hung his clothing on the shower rod. Sonny didn't dare move things back into the bedroom. It seemed five-o was forever parked outside waiting for some sign he was home; consequently, all lights had to stay off. Sonny stripped down, turned off the bedroom light, and felt his way to the bedroom. He crawled into bed just as the sun broke in all its beauty, announcing another hot and humid summer's day.

The noon hour was approaching, and with it came the sounds of traffic, the incessant noise of loud music, and a brilliant palette of color as the sun shed its rays on the stately old buildings of the Quarter. Yet, Sonny's dark and dismal existence hid him from the rest of the world as he slept long into the afternoon.

So deep was his sleep that he didn't feel the presence of a person looming over him as he slept the day away. Long around five, he began to stir, repeating the same stumble through the darkness into the bathroom, shutting the door and flipping on the light. He tried to rub the fog from his eyes as he slowly cast his sight on his reflection in the mirror over the sink. His heart leaped upon seeing the face looking back at him. Large smears of blood streaked from his eyes, and his entire neck was red. Everywhere he looked, he saw splatters and evidence of his blood. He fitfully threw water on his face and neck; he watched as the red river of water paled to a faint pink. It was hard to believe so much blood could have come from such a tiny scratch on his neck. It looked like a fine incision, but the only explanation he could derive was that he scratched himself or something cut him in his bed. It wasn't fathomable to think someone could have come into his apartment, let alone slit his throat and leave undetected. Surely, he would have woken up. He reasoned himself to comfort, but deep in his mind, he couldn't help but feel as though there *had been* an intruder. The face of the crazy tourist from the evening past came to the forefront of his mind. He immediately shook it off as paranoia and went about his business.

He wasted no time in getting the hell out. From the alley, he called Busta.

"Can you come by? Same place."

It only took him twenty minutes to make it through the traffic.

Desiree woke around one and began preparing the night's dinner. Her plan rolled over in her mind as she thoughtlessly threw the gumbo together. Gumbo was one of those things that didn't require much thought. Once she made the roux, she threw the rest of it in the pot and let it do itself. She took the opportunity while Rachel slept to pack her bag and hide it in the side shrubs. She expected Alan soon and, quite frankly, was looking forward to having a male in the house, even if he was only a teenager.

With each passing hour, the knot in her stomach seemed to tighten. By the time four o'clock rolled around, Rachel had awakened, Alan had come home, and Eli had phoned saying he'd be home near five. As per the plan, Desiree slipped into the choreographed script. With the ruse of needing French bread, she scooted out of the door with the promise of a speedy return.

Throwing her backpack over her shoulder, she made her way into the Quarter. She desperately wanted to turn around but knew it would never end unless she took the situation into her own hands. Over the years,

Sonny had pissed off many locals with his crude behavior and wannabe wiseguy attitude; she knew she could find safe harbor for a few hours, long enough for the veil of night to shroud her path to his apartment. Once behind the brick wall leading to the corridor of his place, she was good as in; it had been a routine she knew all too well. The weathering of the old brick wall made it easy to climb. She'd have no problem.

As dusk approached, the Quarter began its nightly transformation, the streets packed with bumper-to-bumper suits on their mad exodus to suburbia held ransom by the hoards of tourists meandering between vehicles, oblivious to their role in the massive traffic jams. Ever-so-slowly, drivers would inch their way with the hopes of eventually reaching the outskirts and Esplanade Avenue, the promised land.

The Golden Lady was recovering from the death of the star, and after hiring a few new dancers, it was on the upswing, making it easier for Sonny to bark the crowds inside. After luring a few takers into the club, he'd position one of his flunkies on the street, and he would fall back inside the door. There were eyes all over, scoping the scene for five-o. Undercover or not, their presence was always detected long before they reached the club, giving Sonny plenty of time to slip out the back. If they were ever to get him, it would be by fluke alone; there were too many places to duck out of sight.

Sonny ambled into the club with a peacock strut. "Where y'at, y'all. Looks like we already got some business. Good work, boys."

He pulled out a cigarette, and as though on cue, one of his wannabes flicked their lighter. "Geez, Sonny, what the fuck happened to your neck? Whoa, must have been one hell of a bitch you had riding your pony. Go ahead, ma man!" He raised his hand for a high five.

He took a drag, "Some kind of ride, what can I say?"

"The old man's here; you might want to go see him; he was just looking for your ass."

Sonny cruised to Manducci's office; the door was open, so he tapped on the frame. "They said, you looking for me, sir?"

His uncle leaned back in his chair and puffed on one of his big Cuban cigars. "Yeah, I was looking for you." A plume of smoke hung over his head.

He tossed a heavy white envelope to Sonny, "You done good in Baton Rouge. Here's a little thank you from me to you. Now don't go spending it all on some skirt."

He wanted to look in the envelope, but instead, he tucked it deep into the front of his pants. He could never let on and wouldn't show just how puffed up he got from his uncle's praise. Manducci reached into the bottom drawer of his desk and pulled out a thirty-eight, sliding it across the desktop toward Sonny. Bewildered, he stood there.

"Looks like I got another something that needs taking care of," and he winked at him. "Ya think you're up to it? Don't feel obligated; this ain't no command or nothing. I thought you might want to make a little more scratch." His uncle raised his chin and eyebrows at the same time.

"Uncle Tony, you know, I do anything for you. Just say the word."

"Shut the door and take a load off."

He slid a manila envelope like the one he had with the kinky photos of the governor. Sonny opened it. There were two pictures, both of the same blond-haired man.

"Damn, you ain't gonna believe this shit, unc. I seen this man; I almost ran over him last night. Shit, if I woulda known then, man, I woulda gunned it. Who is he? I've never seen him before last night."

"He's just someone that pissed off the wrong people; that's all you need to know."

"You know where he's stayin at or where I can find him?" Sonny was itching to make his mark again.

"No. All I know is that you will see him again, and then, badda-bing, badda-boom, capiche?"

"Yes, sir."

DECEPTION IN THE FIRST DEGREE

Totally consumed by a John Wick movie, Alan and Rachel hadn't noticed Desiree's return was long overdue. It wasn't until Eli came in that thought was given to the amount of time Desiree had been gone. He was most anxious to be with them and had been nervous since the intruder scare. Speaking with his family on the phone was one thing, but holding them and seeing they were alright was a whole different thing.

"Where's Des?" Eli started to head into the back.

"She left out of here for some bread, but it's been a while. Rach, what time did she leave? It's been a while, don't ya think?" Alan started to seem concerned, and Eli turned back toward the front room.

"I dunno, but it's been too long," there was a slight quake in her voice, "I shoulda gone with her."

"Guys, y'all are overreacting; she probably got caught up talking with someone at the store; y'all know how she is. I'm gonna change; she'll probably be back by then. Mac'll be here soon for supper." He went back into his room and called the store; the girl said she hadn't seen Desiree all day. He stripped off the dress button-down for a knit golf shirt and made his way to the front tucking in with each stride. He had heard the knock on the door and the sound of Mac's voice.

"I hope I ain't too early," looking toward the kitchen, his eyes sparkled. It was more than evident that Mac enjoyed a good meal and had. He rubbed his thick hands together with excited anticipation, "Somethin' smells great, y'all. Where's our little coon-ass cook?"

"Good question. The kids said she left a while ago to get some bread, but no sign of her."

The switch flipped, and he was back in detective mode. "What time she leave outta here?"

Both kids shrugged, "Don't know," came from both of them.

"What y'all doin' when she left?"

"Watchin' a movie," Alan answered.

"And what time was that?" Mac looked back and forth from one of the kids to the other.

"It's still on; I guess it's a five to seven movie. It wasn't long after it started, so guessing it was around five-fifteen or so." Alan felt the angst in the situation but was still a bit confused.

"Y'all mind to the stove, make sure the gumbo don't scorch, and I'll spin around the block, see if she's girl-talking." Mac walked to his car.

Desiree was infamous for dawdling in conversation. What would take another person ten minutes to do, Des would be a least half an hour, that is, if there were someone to talk to; otherwise, she'd have it done in five minutes rather than ten. His gut told him differently; it told him something was amiss. He circled the block and went down a few more.

Eli couldn't handle waiting. His insides were writhing with worry. "Y'all stay by the phone; I got my cell. You hear something, call me." He took off. He knew right where he was going. He'd go to the club; he felt sure Sonny had something to do with her disappearance. Maybe he grabbed her when she was walking to the store.

His tires squealed as he pulled up to the side service entrance of the club—the screen door banging behind him as he walked in. A few people were hanging in the back. They all seemed to startle as the screen slammed shut. One of the guys went for something in the back of his pants.

Eli looked him square, "Don't even think about it. Where's Sonny?" The guy motioned to the front; Eli passed the office and through the club. Sonny was near the door. Eli walked right up to him and planted his foot in the small of his back. Sonny went flying out the door. Before getting up off the ground, Eli kicked him in the ribs, tossing him over like a dead fish. "Where is she, Sonny? What the fuck you do with her?" He tried scrambling to his feet, and Eli kicked him again each time, knocking him off balance. The moment seemed to drag as though in slow motion. Eli had no idea where the gun came from, but all he could hear was the pop and the smell of smoke. Sonny had missed.

Through the madness came a familiar voice, "Drop it, Sonny, drop it now." Mac was standing behind Sonny with his gun trained on him. In a blink, Sonny swept Eli from his feet, and as the big man began to fall, Mac put a hand out to slow the fall, losing Sonny amid the chaos. Eli lay on the ground, looking up at Mac. "Just what you think you doing, Eli?" He gave him a hand up, "You got any idea how much trouble you could be in? I could arrest your ass for obstruction or assault; there's a lot of stuff I could get you on. You do this stupid thing again, and I *will* arrest your ass, no doubt about it. You coulda gotten yourself killed. You got two kids to think about, Eli, do you hear me?"

"Yeah, I just wanted—"

"Yeah, I get it, but what you need to do is get home to your kids and let me do my job already."

By the time he got home, his kids were in hysteria, "Oh my God, Dad," Rachel threw her arms around him, "It's my fault I shoulda gone with her, and none of this would have happened."

He held her tight, "No, I'm glad you didn't because then I'd really be crazy trying to find you. Mac's hot on it; if anyone can find her, it's Mac. Y'all eaten yet?"

Rachel shot him a look, "As if."

Once inside Sonny's apartment, the smell of funk and mildew raced old memories to the forefront of her mind. Why she had stayed with him as long as she did was something no one could answer. Simone had told her time and time again to leave him and to stay by her place. If only she'd listened, Simone might still be alive, and none of the current shit would be an issue. She guessed everything happened for a reason because she wouldn't have met Eli or gotten a new start in life. Unfortunately, her old world was poking its way into his world of normalcy.

She planned to hide in his apartment and wait for him to come home. He more than likely would be tired and drunk. She'd get him a good one in the back, and when he fell, she'd finish the job; otherwise, there would be no peace. There was no point in only wounding him in hopes of sending a message; he wasn't bright enough to pick up on it. Besides with his overstated machismo, he'd never let things go. She crouched down in the back of the pit he called a closet. She knew it would be a long wait and got comfortable.

Sleep must have overcome her. She awoke with the creaking sound of dilapidated old wood floors as they gave way under the weight of someone moving around the apartment. She remained completely still. She had rehearsed the attack in her mind over and over. She'd have to be motionless until it was time to act, and then she'd have to move with darting speed, agility, and precision; there would be no second chance. The timing had to be perfect; she waited as the sound came closer.

Through a crack in the door, she could catch a glimpse of a silhouette. It was too tall to be Sonny, but she didn't recognize the individual. She studied the figure as he positioned himself between the set of bookcases. He appeared to be waiting for something or someone. Quietly she sat and waited.

It couldn't have been more than half an hour before the door creaked open. Desiree recognized the pattern of Sonny's steps as he made his way to the bedroom. He had to pass both the closet and the bookshelves to make it to the bathroom. She found it strange he hadn't turned on any lights. Had he put them on, he would have had at least half a chance against the stranger, but he hadn't.

She remained still, waiting to see how the whole thing with the intruder would play out. Sonny passed the closet; he was close enough she could smell him. He had the funky smell of cigarettes, too much booze, and too many hours of hanging in the club. Sonny stopped at his makeshift dresser, took something from his pants, and continued on his way to the bathroom. He had no sooner passed the bookshelves when the stranger grabbed him from behind. Although not a very big man, Sonny was wiry, enabling him to pull away from the intruder.

"I guess you ain't had enough, have ya boy?" Sonny reached for his gun. The big man knocked it aside with ease. As the tussle ensued, Sonny grabbed the taller man's head, loosening the mane of long blond hair.

In one fell swoop, the blond stranger had him off the floor by his neck with one hand, plunging a dagger deep into his gut with the other, then dropped him to the floor. It took everything she had to keep it together. Surely the intruder was unaware of her presence; had he known, he would have already killed her. Sonny lay on the floor, his body twitching as the life quickly escaped his body.

The stranger gracefully exited, taking whatever Sonny had left on the dresser. She got a good look at his face as he passed by the closet on his way out. She could hardly believe it; it was the same man she had seen in her vision of Simone. Pure hate raged through her. All she could think about was avenging Simone's murder; she'd have to set him up and go for the kill, just as he had Simone. Before anything she had to get out of the apartment unseen. Now Sonny was out of the picture and no longer a threat; she could return to Eli's with a clear conscience.

Mac had been all over the Golden Lady, interviewing anyone and everyone who could have possibly known Desiree's whereabouts. With each line of questioning, he was left empty-handed. He needed a full twenty-four hours to make an official report, but he knew each passing minute painted a more discouraging picture. He was waiting for the call stating her body had been found floating in the river or in the bottom of some dumpster or slumped in the doorway of a French Quarter building along with the homeless and street urchins. He arranged for a few uniforms to patrol the streets. His radio went off. Part of him didn't want to hear what the officer had to say, but he listened.

"Hold her. 10-4."

They had found her alive. Mac couldn't believe it; immediately, he called Eli and said he would be bringing her there. Despite the lack of sleep and the ordeal she had witnessed, she was no worse for wear. Now that he knew she was okay, he got pissed.

"What the hell were you thinking? Jesus Christ, Desiree, don't you got more sense than that? You got everyone up in arms. Where you been at?"

"Walkin'. Whad ya up ma shit fa? I didn't do nuttin'."

"Oh, well, excuse the fuck outta me. I forgot its normal for someone to go out for bread and then disappear, poof, no word, no nothing. You lied." He looked over at her. She'd never seen him so angry.

"I ain't sayin' dat, don't be stupid. All I could t'ink aboud was how close Sonny came ta hurtin' me n' Rachel. Afta all Eli's done fa me, I could neva look him in da face if somet'in' were ta happen ta her, bein' ma fault. I t'ought 'I'll get outta dere lives. Mebbe dey'd be hurt at firs', but dey'd be betta off. See?" She turned her hands up.

"I don't know if I'm buying or not. Something don't smell right, Desiree."

"Sha, dere ain't nuttin else ta tell, ya t'ink whad ya wanna, ya gonna anyway. I may be a lotta t'ings, but I ain't no liar, no," she turned her head with a pout.

They pulled in front of the house; the door flew open as Rachel, Alan, and Eli came racing out. She noticed tears filling Eli's eyes. He put his arms around her and picked her up off the ground, squeezing her tightly only to break the clutch for a quick kiss on the lips."

Rachel broke the moment, "I guess that answers *that* question!" Desiree pulled away and hugged Rachel. The group moved into the house.

Mac grabbed her arm, "Hey, Des, don't be doing this again, understand?"

No one spoke of Desiree's disappearing act. They all wanted to put it behind them and only look forward; now, the scare was over.

Sitting behind his desk with his feet propped up on an open drawer, he quietly spoke on the phone. He didn't hear the intruder enter; he didn't hear anything to suggest someone was coming into the office.

"You're looking rather dapper, Mr. Manducci. I'm glad I caught you in the office. I wasn't too sure you'd be here."

Manducci watched as the blond took a seat. "I sure as hell didn't think I'd see your mug in here." He said with a sharp edge to his voice.

"I wanted to let you know personally; our business is complete. Now for your end?" He questioned softly.

"I don't got it all here, now. I'll meet you later with the rest. Where you stayin' at?"

The handsome stranger raised an eyebrow, "You *really* expect me to answer that? Nice try, but that's not how the game is played, now is it?" He held a cold smile.

Manducci could feel his face as it began to flush. He had his fill of this foreign punk. Just the mere sound of his voice made him want to draw his Baretta and pop him a few in the chest, do the rest of the world a service. As far as Manducci was concerned, this was the most arrogant bastard he'd ever encountered.

"Kid, I'm gonna give you the benefit of the doubt, being as you're not from this country. You better watch how you talk to people around here. You don't watch your mouth; who knows where it'll get you. Catch my drift? You're starting to piss me off. Ask around; soon, you'll see I'm not a man you wanna piss off." Things tensed.

"Nor am I, sir. If I have insulted you in any way, please accept my sincerest apologies. As you said, I'm not a native of these parts, and how should I put this? I find it rather tedious, not to mention a complete bore, to associate myself with such crude and ignorant people; perhaps it has rendered me a bit cross and impatient. I suppose it's the downside of the profession. I will expect an envelope addressed to Adrian Smythe left at the concierge desk of the Bourbon Orleans no later than 5 p.m. It was a pleasure."

He stood, his back to Manducci, smoothed his hair, picked up his valise, and walked out of the door. He had provided the perfect target and opportunity, but Manducci froze. He turned at the door staring the older man square in the eyes, "I didn't think so." Enraged, Manducci lurched out of his chair, but the blond-haired man had disappeared by the time he had gotten from behind his desk.

The reunion back at the Rosen house was going well, but on the back-burner, Desiree thought of nothing but avenging Simone's death. By four, her nerves were raw. Knowing her new family would be confused by any nighttime outings on her behalf, she would have to devise something entirely plausible.

She wore her perplexity like a mask, "You got something on your mind, little lady?" Eli sat on the back of the sofa and still was six inches taller than Desiree.

"Not really, I was jus' t'inkin aboud someone I ran inta las' night, ya know a frien' or should I say an acquaintance from da pas'. Dey saw me at ma wors', mebbe dey might be worried since I was such a wreck." She draped her arms over Eli's shoulders.

"Not like I'm trying to tell you what you should do, but I think the right thing to do is to call them and let them know you're alright. Like I told you before, you're more than welcome to have friends over here." He gazed into her eyes.

"Ya prob'ly right, the problem is, I don't know how ta get in touch, mebbe

I should go fin' dem. Whad ya t'ink?" cocking her head as if to question.

"It's up to you; I don't like the idea of you going out alone, at least not while Sonny's still on the loose. I'll be glad to give you a ride if you want." He kissed her softly.

"I can't aks ya ta do dat, sha. Mebbe I fin' dem, mebbe I don't. I wouldn't want ya sittin' in da car all night, no." She shook her head.

"You asked my opinion; now it's up to you. Promise me one thing, call me if you're not coming home tonight; otherwise, I'll be up all night worrying." He patted her butt.

"Eli, ya worry too much, sha. I tell whad I'm gonna do. I'll go out fa mebbe coupla hours; if I can't fin' dem, I'll come straight back. If I do fin' dem, I'll call ya, an' we'll go from dere, yeah?"

"Yeah." He nodded.

It only took her an hour to bathe and ready herself. She dolled herself up, going for a hot sexy look. An easy pull-off for her; she'd lived a sexy-looking kind of life for a long time. When Eli saw her coming down the hallway, he gave her a double-take.

"Ya know, I never did ask if these friends were men or women." He waited for an answer.

"Sha, don tell me ya getting' jealous, no? Ya too funny, ma frien'."

"Well?" he asked.

"Dey's both boys and girls, "she laughed. He grabbed her by the wrist and pulled her in close.

"You just look too hot, way too hot. I wish you were staying and not going out."

"Yeah? Are ya tryin' ta make me a bedda offa?" She put her hand on his crotch and winked. "Hol' dat t'ought. I'll be back soon." She threw her purse on her shoulder and was out the door.

Desiree carefully navigated the streets in his car. She was still quite

189

uncomfortable behind the wheel. It was nearing six, and the traffic was still fairly heavy. She wasn't sure where she was going, but she felt Simone would lead her. Listening to the small inner voice was going to be crucial. In a whisper, she called out to Simone. "C'mon, girl, tell me where I gotta be. Gimme a sign, sweet Simone." She felt the need to pull over and stop. She sat silently in the car waiting, waiting for what; she wasn't quite sure. Was it nerves from driving, or was it some message from Simone? There was a tap on her window; a woman asked her for directions to the Bourbon Orleans. "Hon, it's just dere," and she pointed up the street. The woman thanked her and went on her merry way. "C'mon, Simone, gimme some kinda sign." She watched as the woman entered her hotel. To her surprise, just as she entered, the blond man emerged. "Gotcha muthafucka."

She got out of the car and started across the street. She faked an ankle twist followed by a high-pitched squeal. The plan worked; she had gotten his attention. She continued across the street. The closer she got to the guy, the easier she understood why Simone had fallen for him. He was perhaps one of the most handsome men she'd ever seen, and he had a way about him; his mannerisms, the way he walked, he oozed sex appeal. She tossed him another flirty smile.

"Mademoiselle, I trust you are alright? I couldn't help but notice you turned your ankle. One has to exert extreme caution when walking in this city. You never know what will be in your path." He looked down at her with mesmerizing eyes.

She threw the Cajun on heavy, which she could tell intrigued him. He replied, "Oh, I see you are from these parts."

She giggled in a flirty girlish manner, "Oh no, sah, nod rilly, ya know—Ma home ees down de bayou. Ah come fa a weeken' of shoppin'. Da shoppin' by ma houz it's nod vary good, infac' it's pitiful. Now Houma has some good shoppin', mais oui, but, I ratha come ta da city. An' you, I can tell, sha, awe nod from dese parts, no? Ah say mebbe London?"

"Not London, a small village in the English countryside, *cherie.*"

She batted her eyes and slightly wrinkled her nose, "Ya makin' da fun of me?"

"No," he took her hand and kissed it, "I find it most enchanting."

"Yah fladda me. It wuz a pleasure meetin' ya an' enjoy ya stay in N'awlins. Oh, an' wen ya cross da streets here ya mightd wanna watch ya step." She pulled together the sweetest, sexiest smile she could, holding the look for a punctuated moment.

"*Cherie*, don't break my heart." He still held her hand. "Perhaps you would like a companion to escort you? Certainly, you wouldn't be shopping at this time; all the good sales would have been picked over by now, correct? Please do not think me too forward, but if you have not already made plans, would you consider dining with me tonight?"

"Ya too kind, sah, bud Ah do have plans—"

"Cancel them, then." The way he commanded suggested he was a control freak.

"Cancel dem?" she giggled, "Whad makes dinna wid ya, sah, worth cancelin' ma plans?"

He kissed her hand again, "Because I will take you places you've never dreamt of going."

"Now how do I know, ya not some kinda ax murderer, plannin' ta do me in, or mebbe some perverted sex fien'?"

"Guilty as charged," he flashed a smile creating a tingle from her head to her toes. The blond stranger was one smooth operator. "I'm going to call my car now. If you are interested, I'll know because you will be in the car with me; if not, *parting is such sweet sorrow*." He beckoned with a graceful wave, and a long black car materialized from around the corner.

She didn't want to lose her chance. "W-wait a minute; I gotta make a phone call. Where we goin' so ad leas' someone knows ma whereabouds?"

"Fair enough. Dinner at Windsor Court, then jazz at Snug Harbor. Okay, by you?" He raised a seductive eyebrow.

"Lemme make a call." He produced a phone from his pocket. Desiree quickly called Eli and told him she had run into her friends and would see him before midnight. She turned her back to the stranger and whispered into the phone, "Dere's somet'in I been wantin' ta say ta ya an' haven't ya don't need ta say anyt'in' jus' listen—I love you." She disconnected, smiled, and turned with a look of eagerness.

"Your chariot awaits, m'lady," he slid in next to her and instructed the driver.

"Nice caw, bud, b'fore we go any furtha, we gotta have names here. Whatcha name, sah?"

"What do you want it to be?" He coyly asked.

She pouted, "Whad no name? You, sah, mus' be hidin' from da law if ya got no name. Dat makes ya more interestin' if ya know whad I mean." She leaned away from him and studied his face, "Whad shall I call ya? Somet'in' posh an' international soundin'."

He smiled, "Bond, James Bond."

She nodded in approval.

"And you are Miss Moneypenny. Now that we've established our identities, tell me, Penny, what would make this date better than any other date you've ever had?" He had a way of looking into her eyes that, under different circumstances, would've made it intriguing.

She started to speak, but he shushed her with a kiss before she could get a word out. It was perhaps the most passionate kiss she'd ever received. He ran his fingers through her hair and pulled her head back, dusting her neck with soft feathery kisses. He whispered, "Don't answer just yet; let me fantasize throughout dinner. It'll be enlightening to see how close I come. Yes, Miss Moneypenny, I believe we are one in spirit, two of a kind. Would you say the perfect match?"

The evening was taking a spin she didn't anticipate. She had to keep reminding herself she had just witnessed this charming gentleman savagely gut another human being without the slightest hesitation. He was the monster that had brutally murdered her best and dearest friend. Desiree had to keep her guard up, but the more she tried, the easier he maneuvered through the wall. He gave her a strange, scary feeling like he knew her every thought; he had unveiled her intentions. She was supposed to be laying the trap, not him.

The dinner was exquisite, and her escort was undoubtedly well-versed in almost any subject. The beautiful man had been educated at the finest schools in Europe and had insinuated that his family's wealth was near royal proportions. She was cautious not to give any factual information about herself throughout the conversation, which made her question the validity of the portrait he painted. He had never come right out and said anything definitive but implied enough; he knew she could read between the lines. What he didn't realize was his blue-blood upbringing wasn't important, nor was it impressive to her.

He took both her hands in his, and with a soft sensual whisper, he looked directly into her eyes, "All evening, I have let my thoughts toy with me. You, my dear Penny, are a most difficult lady to read. *However*, if I were a betting man, I'd place my wager on you having *no* interest in listening to jazz, and any dancing tonight would only take place in the privacy of my suite. How close am I, my dear sweet Penny?"

"Too close, too close, sha. Unfortunately, I mus' take a raincheck; you'll be in town tomorra?"

He looked somewhat surprised, "Actually, I had planned—"

She interrupted with a twinkle in her eyes, "Change dem."

She could tell he found it all amusing. "Then changed they are. What can I anticipate for the morrow, may I ask?" The gorgeous stranger, ever-so-lightly, stroked her hands while holding them and gazing intently into her eyes, invading her soul. Her body involuntarily shivered.

"Wanna start wit' coffee n' beignets at Café du Monde, say nine o'clock? We'll play it by ear from dere. But, I promise ya, sha, it'll be da kinda day *ta die fa*. Not dere by half pas' nine, ya miss out on da Cajun cookin'," she laughed light-heartedly.

"I'll be there, not to worry. It sounds all too promising," he kissed her hand and led her to the lobby, "My car will take you wherever you need to go, and until tomorrow, Miss Penny, adieu."

The limousine took her straight to Eli's car. She hoped it would still be there, boot-free. Luck had been on her side, no boot, no ticket; she tootled her way back to the house. What a strange evening it had been; she looked forward to the next day when the adventure was bound to get even more interesting. Desiree roughly sketched the plan in her mind; she'd fine-tune it as the day played on.

All was silent as she entered the house. The lights were off, and the only sound came from the ticking of the hall clock. She tip-toed past Eli's room to the bath. His door slowly creaked open, and a hand emerged with a daunting finger beckoning her inside. She obeyed to find Eli comfortably clad in cotton sleeping pants, standing at the door.

"Since your phone call, all I have been able to do is think about you. Desiree, I can't begin to tell you how much I love you." He took her into his arms, "You have no idea."

From the depths of her heart, she embraced him, "I love you, too."

Desiree quickly fell asleep as she snuggled into the form of his body. A sweet, subtle duet of slumbering breaths filled the air in no time. There was an indescribable peace as she drifted into the world of dreams.

It was as though she was watching herself; she was in Jackson Square with Eli; they strolled along the sidewalk admiring the multitude of sketches, paintings, and pastels until they came to a row of portraits handsomely displayed along the wrought iron fence of the square.

Her eyes glanced at a portrait with a resemblance to Simone. Mesmerized, she studied the fine lines of the painting and observed in awe as a single tear rolled down Simone's cheek, causing smears and streaks in the paint as it passed over each stroke of the brush. She tried to get Eli's attention, but he seemed not to see what she saw or understand what she was desperately trying to tell him. As dreams often can, the background, along with Eli, blurred out of vision, leaving Desiree alone with the living portrait. A haunting cold feeling came over her as the picture began to speak. "It's over."

Desiree was in a panic, "What's over?"

Again, the voice from the painting replied, "Over."

"Simone?" she wanted to talk to her in the worst way. Not once did it seem ridiculous that Simone would be talking to her from a painting, but then again, the impossible often goes unnoticed in the land of dreams and is taken as truth. Nothing seemed unusual or odd about the whole interaction. She begged and pleaded with Simone to come from the painting, to tell her what she meant. What was over? The deal with Sonny, yeah, she knew the nightmare was over. What Eli? What was over? "Sha, I found the man, da one who killed you. It's his turn now, ma frien'. I got dis."

The voice echoed, "Live," then drifted away as the background of the square and Eli once again took on resolution.

"No, don't leave, no! Whad's ova, tell me, please, please, please." She woke with a start as her lips continued to form the word, please. She shook the dream from her thoughts, snuggling even closer to Eli, and drifted back to sleep.

The morning came, and his rush to work was in full throttle. Eli went through his customary morning ritual as he had every morning for the past twenty-five years. He moved with precision, and it all came together picture-perfect. Desiree, on the other hand, was moving in slow motion.

"Girl, you better get a move on, you 're gonna make me late, and you know I don't like being late."

"I don't feel so good, sha. I jus' can't get m'sef goin' dis mornin'. I don't know whad's wrong."

He felt her forehead, but no sign of fever. "Think you're sick or just tired? There's something to the old adage, burning the candle at both ends, you ever stop to think maybe you been burning both ends?" He kissed the top of her head.

"Yeah, yeah, I feel yuck, plain old yuck." She was already feeling guilty about lying to him; any further expansion of her alleged sickness would make her even more guilty.

He pulled back the comforter on his bed and flipped on the TV, "Then, Miss Priss, get yourself back in the bed; we'll make out fine in the office. You feel better." She climbed into his bed, snuggling down into the nest of pillows and fluffy comforter. "Now you take care; that's an order!" He leaned over and kissed her goodbye. "Seeing you in bed makes it very hard to leave, love." He kissed her again.

She waited almost an hour before setting off on the day's adventure. It was a spectacular day, it wasn't overly hot, and the breeze off the Mississippi River was just enough to cool any perspiration away. It seemed every face she passed had a smile and a bright, cheerful good morning greeting. Indeed, this must be a good omen; God was on her side and gave His seal of approval with such a glorious day. Had it been dark and dismal with the usual suffocating humidity, she may have needed to reconsider her plans, as that too would have been a sign, a sign of displeasure. No, she was right with God.

The French Quarter was coming to life. Bleary-eyed tourists filed into the famous Café du Monde. While they seemed to enjoy themselves, the genuine appreciation was from the locals. Good coffee was easy to come by in the city, but nothing could compare with the rich, full flavor of café au lait at the French Market.

She sat at a corner table under the awning and watched as a mime began his set-up for a day of performing. The street entertainers always amused her; they seemed to be in character from the time they stepped onto the street to when they returned home. Although she had seen them for years and knew they knew her, their silence remained golden.

He was right on time. Desiree watched as he approached; he had a smooth, stealthy gait like a lion in the wild stalking his prey. The world was his oyster, and he was going to have it. Almost every head turned in admiration as the mysterious stranger walked by. Men may have preferred to be called handsome, but this man was beyond; he was exquisite. Perfect features, body, great hair, and dressed to die for, and yet for all the pluses, he might as well have been the devil incarnate, the way he ruthlessly killed. She could only imagine how betrayed Simone must have felt; it made her heart ache.

"Bonjour, mademoiselle," he gently kissed her hand. "Comment c'est va?"

"Tres bien, merci, et tu?"

"Tres bien, *now* that I'm sitting with the loveliest of lovelies in all this fair city. I trust you slept well." His eyes glittered most seductively.

"Oh, but, yes, to be sure."

"I'm here," he made a bowing gesture, "Completely and totally at your disposal, do with me as you will." He had a titillating naughtiness rather than the bleak shadow of a ruthless killer.

"I t'ought we could see some sites, no? Like da 'quarium, mebbe go fa a boat ride, ya know act like da otha tourists. I've neva done dat, you? Den I t'ought we have a private lunch, mebbe, in ya hotel room and we could see whad went from dere. Soun's good?" She tried to keep a flirty girlish smile.

"Marvelous, Moneypenny."

"Okay, double-o-seven, it's off ta see da big fish."

Walking along the river would have made for a most romantic interlude had the situation been different. If the man had any suspicions about her, they appeared at rest. Although still quite cosmopolitan, he seemed more at ease and not quite as formal. Desiree lured him in closer and closer as she poured on the spunky charm. She could tell he was falling for her. With cooling sno-balls in hand, they retired to a bench overlooking the river.

"Penny, oh my dear Penny, I haven't had this much enjoyment since, well, quite frankly, I don't know when."

"Sha, not da way ta a long life. Ya know dere is somet'in' ta da eat, drink and be merry? But, I guess ya too caught up in work, yeah? Whad ya do? I bet you're a lawyer, no?"

He shook his head, "Please tell me I don't look like a lawyer."

"Nah, mebbe an accountant," she giggled.

"Are you purposely trying to insult me?" he put his arm around her shoulder.

"Nah, I t'ink a supa in-ta-national model. Gawd knows ya pretty enough." She gave an elongated bat of the eyes.

"Sorry to disappoint you, but it's not quite so glamorous. I actually demonstrate the use of knives for a German company." He put his arm around her, pulling her close. His scent was delicious.

"Dey gotta lotta restaurants and fancy chefs here, ya mus' make a killin'." That was about all she could say to that. In her mind, all she could think was she had seen his demonstration, and it was time to put his showman days to an end.

"Wife?" she asked suspiciously, purposely acting the part as though she cared, keeping the ruse going.

"It's been great so far, don't spoil the moment, Penny, with such mundane questions. Neither of us, if I'm reading this situation correctly, really cares if the other is attached. I get the impression you're the type of adventurous young lady that wouldn't think twice about joining me on a whirlwind jaunt to Jamaica or perhaps Paris; you would pick up and go. The only thing we need to know about each other is what is good for the moment, which, my dear Penny, is where the intrigue lies. Take for instance," and he pointed to a couple overlooking the river, "I imagine those two at one time saw each other for the first time, and something stirred deep inside—*the intrigue*. Then after a few times together, they began to muck it up with questions of the past, plans for the future and totally forgot about the day. Why? Why would someone want to ruin that? The allure is the mystery, the unanswered question, is it not?" His eyes and the tenor of his voice were hypnotic.

"I don't know aboud dat, sha. Da mystery mightd be da attraction, ad firs', but den da more ya get ta know someone da more ya like 'em or don't. If ya like 'em den mebbe ya wanna spen' more time together, ya neva give up *all* ya secrets, keepin' some *mystery*; ma thoughts on da madda." She took a deep breath as though basking in the idea of romance.

"Tell me you don't *love* the intrigue. Look me square in the eyes and tell me you don't find it completely titillating, enthralling?" He looked back at the couple leaning against the railing. Watching their body language and the lack of affection, it became patently obvious there was no excitement, and they were merely going through the motions; a sadness filled her heart. "Miss Moneypenny, tell me, is *that,*" referring to the couple, "what you want? There's something to be said for living for the day, do you not agree?" He took her hand and stood, "I'm feeling a bit peckish; perhaps we should go back to the suite for a bite of lunch. She felt a passion burn in her stomach, part of her wanted to get up and run, run as fast as she could away from this monster, but she had a mission, and with all the fire burning inside, she knew it would be the catalyst she needed to accomplish her task.

THE SHARP EDGE

Sonny had promised him there'd be other jobs, but it had been a while since he had heard from his paisan, so he decided to wake this fair-weathered friend. He knew Sonny was out for himself, but he was the closest thing he had to a friend other than his pops. Busta motored over. The place was dark, but then he knew Sonny was keeping it with the look of being unoccupied on purpose. Busta pulled out the key to the apartment; Sonny had entrusted him and proceeded inside.

"Jesus Christ! What in the hell stinks? Man, oh man, this is the pits. Shit! Sonny, where y'at, ma man? Your fuckin' place stinks worse than anything I ever smelt. Yo Sonny, where y'at?" He knew the rule, no lights, so he slowly rolled through the apartment. "Get ya lazy ass up, man; this is gross. Yo, Son-ny." His chair came to an abrupt stop. He tried to wheel it forward, but there was no moving anywhere. "Sonny, ya gonna have to put at least one light on; I can't see shit. I'm stuck on something." There was no response; Busta leaned over to try and move the object out of the way. "Jesus, Mary, and Joseph."

He quickly backed his chair to the light switch on the wall. The contrast from the blanket of darkness to such bright light was nearly blinding, but he could see clearly enough there was a body on the floor and judging from the amount of blood, he surmised a dead body at that. "Oh man, Sonny, what the fuck happened here? Jeez." He pulled out his phone, "Yeah, I got a fuckin' dead body over here. I don't know what to do. Look, lady, I really got the creeps, it's my friend, and no, I don't want to hang around." He listened for another second. "Okay, I'll be waiting outside; tell them not to take their sweet ass time, neither."

He rolled out onto the street. "I knew I shouldn't have gotten messed up with this shit. Man—" He was more than freaking out, and passers-by kept their eyes straight ahead as they passed the crazy man in the wheelchair. It took the police only minutes to get there. They instructed Busta he'd have to wait until the detective arrived, and maybe then he could go, *maybe.*

Mac knocked on the door, then rang the bell; no one came to the door. Hitting redial, he called Eli again. He listened as the phone rang. "Dammit, Desiree." As he waited for Eli to answer, he peered through the lace sheers, but there was nothing to indicate anyone was home. Eli finally picked up.

"Eli, you did say Desiree was home, right?"

"Yeah, she's not feelin' too good."

"I don't know how to tell ya this, brotha, but she ain't here."

Eli commented perhaps she was in the bath; they had an understanding. The only other explanation was she started feeling better and went to get something to eat. He wasn't worried. Mac's radio went off just as the conversation concluded—possible murder in the Quarter. The murder rate seemed to go hand-in-hand with the thermometer. The hotter it got, the more violent it became. Duty called; he made a mental note to check on Desiree later. He scribbled the address on his notepad. It hadn't sunk in until he read his chicken scratch, and then it struck a chord, and well it should, as it was the address they had under surveillance for over two weeks.

Like many of the old buildings in the Quarter, Sonny's apartment had an old mildewy smell compounded by the stack of dirty dishes and the pungent heaviness of death stench. So stomach-churning was the smell of death and bodily decay, especially in the New Orleans heat, that all it took was one exposure, and the scent would forever be etched in one's memory. Dirty clothes, weeks'-old food, and assorted garbage littered the hellhole of an apartment. It was hard to fathom that a person resided in the filth.

All indications suggested some sort of struggle that left Sonny on the losing end of the stick. The perpetrator had almost gutted him like a pig and left him to bleed out. Blood was everywhere, and still gripped in Sonny's hand were a few long strands of blond hair. Shivers ran up Mac's spine, and there was no doubt in his mind that this was the same stranger Desiree had told him about in her vision of Simone. Certainly, it was more than a coincidence that he had seen a well-groomed blond-haired man only nights before outside Sonny's apartment.

Mac remembered having a cagey feeling about the stranger. In his mind, he also knew that the specimen swabbed from Simone would more than likely prove to have the same DNA as the hairs in Sonny's hand. Questions ran through Mac's mind; who was this guy, and was he doing Manducci's heavy work? If that was the case, and he was pretty sure it was, the only piece of the puzzle missing was Desiree. He had to find and warn her.

Clearly, the friend in the wheelchair was just that, nothing more, nothing less. He took Busta's number and excused him. He couldn't help but feel bad for the guy; he looked like he had lost his only friend.

Class Act was beginning to speed up as summer was coming to a close with only a few more weeks remaining. The tariffs and pricing books were on the final edit. The staff from the war room had assembled the marketing packets and readied them for a mass mail out. The word came out only that morning, although unofficial, that due to the success of Lee and Eli's meetings Class Act had been awarded the contracts from a few massive incentive houses.

Buried deep in a review of the pricing schedule, Eli tuned out to the rest of the world. Her first knock didn't get his attention, so she rapped harder.

"Hey, pal-y, ya gotta come up for air sometime. Heard the news?" Lee had returned to her playful self.

"News?" He asked with raised eyebrows.

"Yeah, word is we got Sampson *and* Wexon, and get this, *World Air!* This coup, my friend, calls for a celebration. You know what it'll do for sales; oh, my Gawd, Eli, you'll make company history."

"Not definite yet." He warmly advised with a grin.

"Close enough that I'm gonna spring for lunch, and I'm not taking no; now get your lanky ass up and let's beat the crowd." It took a few minutes, but they got there quick enough to get a good table at the Palace Café.

After ordering a glass of wine, Lee asked, "So, how're things goin' on the homefront with your guest? Things okay when you got back?" Her tone sounded sincere.

She would have to ask *that* question, he thought. That one question sparked what would've turned into a long, involved conversation that could've gone on for hours had his phone not rung.

Before he could say hello, Mac started. "Eli, you'll neva guess where I'm at. Ya friend, Sonny, got whacked. Thought you'd like to know."

"No shit." His eyes popped wide. "Well, at least Desiree won't have to worry about him anymore." He nodded to Lee, who had questioning eyes.

"Where you at, I gotta talk to ya. Talk to Desiree yet?"

"No, I'm at the Palace, you're welcome to come here, but I gotta warn you that I have someone with me."

Mac sounded puzzled, "Like a date?"

"Nothing like that. Lee, from work; she knows everything. Maybe it won't hurt to get a woman's read on it?"

"Whateva, see ya in a few."

Mac was good for his word, as it was minutes later that he walked into the restaurant. He had met Lee before, but Eli went through the polite introductions. It didn't take long for Mac to figure out that while Lee may have known most everything in the Desiree saga, there was one fact Eli had kept to himself. She had no idea that Desiree had become his lover. What was even more curious to Mac was Lee's obvious feelings for Eli, workmates or not. Whether Eli would admit it or not, Mac could definitely see a reciprocated affection. He wondered why the game.

Eli commented with great interest. "So, Sonny got his comeuppance. I can't say it surprises me, nor does it break my heart." Eli turned to Lee, "He was a real S.O.B."

Mac broke in, "S.O.B. or not, I still got some concerns, y'all. Think about it, Manducci gives Sonny an order; the stupid schmuck blabs in fronta Desiree, then Des, afta getting the shit beat out of her, tells Simone. So now, other than Manducci, who knows?" He put his hand up and sequentially raised three pudgy fingers. "Simone dead, Sonny dead, and then there's Desiree. See my point?"

Eli took a long draw on his water. "If he wanted her, don't you think he woulda gotten to her by now?"

Mac shook his head, "Eli, whatcha talkin' about, she done disappeared right inta the protected, incognita life of Eli's World."

Lee laughed, "Eli's World? People come and go outta our office; you could have a tribe of bandits rape and pillage; trust me, no one would notice, and I mean no one. He coulda gotten her easy-peasy."

Lee and Eli's lunch arrived. Mac took a fry off of Eli's plate. "I'm starving, hope ya don't mind. But, back to what you was sayin, y'all, he wouldn't have known ta be lookin' for her there." Mac cleared his throat. "Here's this street kid; all she knows is the street. I bet ya; he had every one of his wannabe's lookin' for her. Every time she has walked the streets, he's known. Now I'm not sayin' she's his top priority. He's fryin' his own fish; it's been all over the news. He's putting in his casina, so whoever may have heard or known of his comment about threatening the governor is in a hot seat; he ain't gonna leave it too long." He looked back and forth between Eli and Lee and stole another fry. Eli slid the plate of fries in front of him and winked at him, putting his hand out to say, *they're yours*. "Anyway, the story gets weird. I walk in; Sonny's dead in a pool of blood. The killer did a real knife job on him, but some long blond hairs got stuck between Sonny's dead fingers. He musta gotten a handful of the killer's hair." Mac looked at Eli, "Des tell ya about what happened at Simone's?"

"When?"

"When she went ta get her clothes for the funeral."

"I was there; nothing happened."

Mac nodded his head. "Ya mean, she didn't tell ya what happened. The vision?"

"Um, that would be a no."

"Simone came to her mind, and she saw, plain as day, Simone walking next to a tall man with long blond hair. Like she was sayin', this here is the guy that killed me. Y'all, I'm not one ta go for da spirit kinda thing 'specially when it's foul play, but Desiree described this guy to a tee, and then, I remember seeing him outside of Sonny's while I was doing surveillance. The guy made my skin crawl, and that don't happen; I've seen all kinds of creeps."

Eli and Lee glanced at each other.

"I don't give a rat's ass if you don't believe me; I'm just telling you what she told me, and that's what I saw the night I saw him. When I turned back to get a good look, the guy poof disappeared. So, I circle the block, figuring I'd catch a glimpse of the guy, but nope. Like a ghost, I tell ya. The thing is, I know what his sorry ass looks like now, and believe me, I'm gunnin' for him."

This newfound friend of hers became more charming as the day went by. His was, without a doubt, the most palatial hotel suite she'd ever seen.

Everything from fresh floral arrangements to the hand towels was first class, all the way.

"Oh ma Gawd, Bond. I bet this beauty is settin' ya back a few bucks. Ya must make good money demonstratin' dose knives of yours." She busied herself exploring the suite, then plopped on the bed. "Heaven, dat's whad dis is. Yes, indeed." He lounged beside her on the bed, gently twirling her hair through his fingers.

"I only wish I had more time, Miss Moneypenny. I find you refreshing and natural." He slowly began to undress her. Instinctively her hands went up to shield her body. "Shy? How perfectly quaint; I thought we might be in for more of an adventure. Are we getting cold feet?" He had a sly, almost prowling look on his face.

"But no, sha, I just like to be in chawge. Ya know, *dominatrix*." She arched her back, brought her body to a sitting position, and then gave him her most sultry look. "Unless dat's a problem, 007?"

He grinned. "Forgive me, Miss Moneypenny; I humbly beseech you to forgive your servant. Tell me, my mistress, what delights may I bestow upon you?"

She sat in one of the Queen Anne chairs next to the side table near the bed. Dramatically, she crossed her legs and pointed with an authoritative tone in her voice. "Slave, take off your clothes."

Mystery man eagerly responded. There was no denying his physical perfection. Every muscle was precisely defined—most stunning. She got up and circled her prey, studying the lines of his body. "Tie back your hair." He followed her command, unleashing a leather bracelet that provided a tie to hold back his hair. "To your knees." She glanced down at him with a wickedly sensual smile, then walked back to the window. She removed the tasseled silken ropes holding back the lavish draperies and ordered him to lie on the bed. Taking the cords, she tightly wrapped his wrists and tied them to the bed. She straddled him and leaned forward with a taunting whisper. "Do I make ya nervous, sha?" He didn't answer; he remained without emotion. She slapped him across the face, "Answer me, damn you, does da mistress scare ya?" He continued with the silence; she struck him again. The more she slapped him, the more aroused he became. She couldn't help but think this was one sick bastard.

Standing over him, she slowly removed the rest of her clothing while whispering promising obscenities. She watched as he admired her body, "Dis whad you wan'?" She delicately ran her hands along the curves of her body. His eyes sparkled with delight as he nodded. "Not yet, slave." She teasingly moved her body across his, tempting him, skillfully dismounting him. She stood at the foot of the bed. It would be easy to get the gun from her purse, which she'd taken from Sonny's after the monster gutted him. She'd aim and pull the trigger, but that wasn't enough, she wanted him to be afraid, to have those moments to regret, and then, yes, perhaps she would shoot, merely wounding him, watching him writhe in pain. Would he beg for mercy, would he feel remorse? She would tell him that this was payback for the cold-blooded murder of her most precious Simone—an outstanding talent with a passion for life, she didn't need to die, but he, on the other hand, deserved the terror and suffering. Yes, this piece of shit more than deserved to die.

"You've been such a good boy; Mistress has a reward fa ya obedience." She slithered between his legs, coming mere centimeters from his already hot erection, but then she stopped, went to her purse, and slipped the gun out. Concealing the pistol behind her, Desiree sashayed to the bed, moving slowly between his legs. With light flutters of her tongue, she made her way along the insides of his thighs. Then crouched on her knees and pressed the barrel between his eyes. He made not a sound, not a whimper, nothing. "Aren't ya gonna beg ya mistress, fa ya life?" Silence. She traced his face with the barrel. "Oh, sha, what a waste. You're so beautiful; it's a shame I've got to kill ya." He blankly stared at her. "Shocked? Don't be; ya made a fadal mistake when ya kilt ma Simone. An' now, ya gonna pay." She felt her finger gently squeezing the trigger.

It happened in a blink; one second, she was squeezing the trigger, and the next, she was pinned on her back, his muscular legs commanding the breath from her body. The gun had gone off and fallen to the floor. All that came from the firing was a small hole in the wall.

"Things were going so well, my sweet Desiree; why'd you have to go and ruin it? We could have had a most delightful afternoon. So, where do we go from here? I'm afraid it's become most awkward, wouldn't you say?"

"Fuck you." She growled.

"That's not attractive, Desiree; you should try to refrain. Frankly, it makes you sound cheap. Don't tell me you're going to get all pissy now. You're the one that changed the mood of this encounter, not me, but now you're going to be angry with me. Not good form." He tutted with a shake of his head, then managed to free his hands, turned his body, and pinned her to the bed. "What do you say? Why don't we put all the ugliness behind us and enjoy what appears to be the ending of a most interesting encounter? I promise it'll be one fuck you'll never forget."

She struggled beneath his weight and began to scream. He clasped his hand over her mouth until the sound was a mere muffle. "Let me go," she tried to say.

"Open your mouth once more, and playtime is over, understand?" She nodded; she understood all too well. "You're a funny little thing. Now that the table is turned, you don't want to play. Sorry, that's not how it works, I'm afraid."

He grabbed her hands and tied them to the bed. Then he went to the closet, retrieving two neckties. "You see, my sweet, you failed to secure me. Too bad you'll never have a chance for another go at it. He took one ankle and began tying it to the bedpost. "Yes, you have to tie *both* the arms and the legs for that real bondage experience." He cupped the other foot in his hand and brought it to his lips—"Such dainty small feet. I must commend you, dear; you got the dominatrix part down pat. You do bitch so well, but turn around is fair play."

After securing the other foot, he straddled her hips, supporting his weight. He leaned into her gently, kissing her cheeks and eyes with wispy touches, then moved to her lips. It would've been the kind of kiss that would render heartthrobs to the observer's eye or perhaps be the perfect ending to a lovely fairytale, but Desiree seized the moment and, with the striking speed of a viper, bit a chunk out of his lip. Bright red droplets of blood rolled down his chin. He slapped her across the face, then stroked her hair. She desperately tried to pull from him. "Don't be a sore loser; nobody likes a poor sport, Desiree. Now, let's try it again. Remember how much you liked my kiss in the car? We both know how this story ends, so let's do our best to make it spectacular; why don't we?" He leaned in to kiss her again. She lay there statue still, void of any emotion. "Well, you could've made it more enjoyable, but I will have my way one way or the other. Face it; you're not in a position to object," She helplessly tugged at the cords binding her wrists.

He pressed his body against her breasts, leaning forward slightly to place himself for penetration. With everything she had, she threw her head forward and latched onto his neck, sinking her teeth deep. He tried to pull away, but it only served to tear the flesh even more. He put one hand to her throat and squeezed; she could feel her windpipe begin to crush under the force of his grip. The more he tried to pry her loose, the harder her jaw clenched. She could feel the force of his blood as it seemed to spray in pulsating waves. The sheet beneath her was saturated, and the blood was beginning to pool. With one last-ditch attempt, he tried to pull from her and, this time, had success. Clutching his neck, he stumbled to the bathroom. She could hear as he turned the faucet on, violently cursing her. She knew if she was going to act, it needed to be quick. The once-tight cords had stretched during the struggle. Slipping her hands, she managed to untie one foot before he re-entered the room. He came toward her with a menacing approach. She thrashed her arms and kicked with her one free foot.

He held a bloody towel to his neck. "Fucking bitch." He turned from her and went to one of the black leather cases in the closet. "Let's just get this over."

Desiree took that brief second to loosen the tie, almost enough to slide her foot out. She tugged again, and the foot came with an audible crack.

"Shit. Oh, my Gawd." The pain was immense. She stood on the good foot and lunged for the gun on the floor. Although her back was to him, she felt him coming up behind her. She knew what would be next. He grabbed her shoulder, pulling her to him; being so tiny and agile, she could turn her body so she was facing him. Desiree shoved the muzzle of the gun against his stomach and pulled the trigger.

In one sweeping motion, he swept the knife across her throat. She couldn't believe there had been no pain, so he must've missed, but how could he? She watched as he stumbled, his chest streaked red from the draining wound to his neck. He reached for his stomach, dropping the blood-stained knife on the floor. He had a look of complete and utter bewilderment. Seeing the blood on the edge of the blade, she put her hand to her throat—he hadn't missed. Desiree's eyes filled with tears as fear raced through her. Trying to take a step, she moved on the broken foot, falling hard to the floor. He watched her as the tears rolled down her cheeks.

The room began to grow dim. The only sound was their labored breaths, intermittent and slowing, creating an almost calming silence. Unable to move, she lay absorbed in the passion of her death. His hand touched hers ever so gently, barely moving her head; Desiree looked into his eyes. She could see the suffering and fear in his eyes, yet she felt no rest from his pain. Maybe there had been remorse after all. Her body began to drift upward. Looking down at the room as though in a dream, she observed the two motionless bodies, fingertips barely touching. There was no more sadness, only peace. She felt loving arms embrace her. It was a familiar presence, one that had soothed many a tear and made quiet the fearful, racing heart of a young girl. "I've missed you, Desiree." The Lord had sent Simone to welcome her to the afterlife.

The check finally came, and as the three of them began to leave the restaurant, Mac's radio went off again. There was a reported disturbance at the Windsor Court Hotel. In all his years on the force, he had only one other call to the Windsor; it was such a first-class operation that rarely was anything out of order. The elite clientele was too civilized for anything violent; those disputes were settled in the boardrooms. Mac bid farewell, planted the beacon on the roof of his unit, and off he went, siren screaming.

It only took a minute or two to get there. The General Manager and head of security greeted him. They quickly ushered him to one of the service elevators and proceeded upward. On the way, they explained that a concerned guest heard what they thought was a gunshot. Security was on top of it. The hotel did not want to alarm their guests, so they merely called it a disturbance. The head of security assured him that nothing had been touched as the Manager unlocked the door. Mac slowly entered; he couldn't help admiring the loveliness of the suite; this was the first time he'd seen firsthand the private comforts of the rich and famous. It wasn't until he pushed the half-opened bedroom door aside that the tragedy hit home.

He felt paralyzed. He had let her down. All that ran through his mind was that while he was eating and discussing the case, which was unethical, to say the least, his precious Desiree was battling the demon alone. There was no need to rush in and feel for a pulse; there was no question; she was gone. The two of them, covered only by streams of blood, lay with fingers touching, creating an unfathomable scene. How had this gone down? Mac surmised that Desiree must have lured him with her irresistible charm or had he seduced her; no, *she* did the luring as a means to avenge Simone's death.

There were too many unanswered questions. Mac's mind flashed to Eli and the kids; there was no way he could prepare them for this; hell, even with his years of seeing death, he didn't know how to handle it. There was something extraordinary about Desiree, something you couldn't put your finger on. He supposed it was just the whole package.

He called the station and assured the hotel they would do everything possible to keep their investigation discreet. The hotel was one step ahead and in the midst of transferring guests to a different floor, offering a host of comps for their inconvenience. The only thing Mac had to request was the name of the person who had reported the gunshot. Although reluctant, due to the reputation for privacy and anonymity, they complied in consideration of the extenuating circumstances. Then he asked to be left alone.

He surveyed the bodies from different angles in the room. What he thought he'd accomplish was irrelevant; he just had to do something to move, or at least go through the motions of being busy. His upright morality told him to at least cover their nakedness, but as an officer of the law, he couldn't compromise the integrity of the scene. Two leather bags were in the closet; one had fallen to the ground, spilling the contents in plain sight.

Without moving anything, Mac could see several passports, a few stacks of cash, a couple of brown envelopes, and what he surmised to be the handles of knives. The case still hid the actual blades. It wouldn't be long before the place would be swarming with more officers and the entourage from the Crime Lab. He could only imagine the host of comments regarding the nude bodies. He'd make a stand, there would be no disrespectful slurs, and he'd ensure they were covered as quickly as possible.

Emotion filled his heart. He leaned back against the wall and allowed his tears to flow freely. His big body heaved with mournful sobs. "Dammit, Desiree, I told you I was gonna handle it; you promised me, now look at cha. Jesus, Desiree, I le'cha down, didn't I? I woulda gotten him, I woulda." He hung his head, "Dammit."

"Yo, Sarge, where y'at?" The first of the official entourage had arrived. He wiped the tears from his eyes and cleared his throat.

"In here."

The young officer entered the room and couldn't help but respond upon seeing the sight. "Whad da—Jesus, Mary, and Joseph."

"Don't go there, ya hear me, and ya betta warn ya cohorts they betta watch their mouths. This one here is personal. Goddit?" Mac punctuated his comment with squinted eyes and a rigid posture.

"No problem, sir," he cleared his throat. "I'm sorry for your loss."

Mac acknowledged the condolence with a nod. Retirement was just around the corner; the way he felt right then, it couldn't come fast enough. The Medical Examiner arrived, checked out the scene then took a closer look at the bodies.

Crouching next to the body of the blond-haired man, he called to one of the techs. "Take a look at this." The young man leaned over to get a better look. The M.E. pointed to the mangled and torn neck of the man.

"What the hell?" and stood up, shaking his head.

The M.E. looked up at the tech. "Looks like our sleeping princess bit right through his carotid before shooting him."

Standing close enough to hear the comment, Mac felt a strange sense of pride. She hadn't gone without a fight, that was for sure. "She was one feisty little coon-ass, she was." He nodded as he caught a single tear beginning to roll down his cheek.

The M.E. turned to him, "You knew her? One of the regular whores?"

The temptation to kick the shit out of the examiner ran rampant through Mac's heart, but he refrained. "No, nuttin' like that. She was a friend, kinda like the daughter I never had."

"Sorry, I didn't know. No offense meant."

Mac cleared his throat, "None taken." Inside he felt outraged and wanted to say a lot more, but there would be no point, so he let it go and figured the best thing for him to do was leave, in case someone else felt the need to comment, and maybe he wouldn't be able to contain himself any longer. He went looking for the woman who reported the shot. He also knew he needed to break the news to Eli but didn't feel stable enough at that moment. It would be heartbreaking, no matter when he broke the news.

The interview went pretty much the way he thought it would. While the woman heard what she thought sounded like a gunshot, she offered nothing else. The only two people that knew what had gone down were the two that lay dead in the room, case closed.

If he thought he could link Manducci, he would, but that would be most unlikely. The identity of the mystery man had still not been ascertained, and he doubted seriously if any of the passports bore the correct name. With the speed of technology, it wouldn't be long until they knew the name of the blond male. Mac was pretty sure Interpol would have some information on the guy if they didn't. No matter who he was or how he came to murder Simone, Desiree, and Sonny, would be forever unanswered. A haze had come over him, and all he could feel was numbness and disbelief. It was like the whole damn thing was a nightmare. The elevator doors silently parted just in time to see them rolling the body bags out.

One of the officers put his hand on Mac's shoulder. "C'mon, let's get out of here. Buy you a cup of coffee?"

"Nah, thanks. I got something I gotta do." He walked over to the M.E. wagon; Mac pointed to the bags. "She's?" The man unzipped one of the bags. Mac leaned in and kissed her forehead. "I'm sorry, ma girl." Head down, he turned and walked to his car. He had to gain some composure before getting to Eli's. Aimlessly he drove the streets, raking over in his mind how he could've changed things. The longer he drove, the more he tortured himself. Mac crashed his fists with a thunderous blow against the steering wheel. "Dammit."

"Thanks for going to lunch pal-y" She nudged him in the ribs, "I had full intentions of picking up the check, ya know? But no, you gotta be Sir Gonad and do the manly thing, pick up the bill. Eli, ya gotta get more up with the times." She looked up at him with a raspy laugh.

"Yeah, yeah. Now ya sound like the girls in ma house. Can't a man pick up the check if he wants? Look at it like this; I just saved you a few bucks. All ya gotta do is say thanks. Don't be waving your burning bra in my face; I like being a gentleman; besides, Mims gets drift of me not buying lunch, trust me, not a pretty sight. Off the subject, I'm calling it a day; see you in the AM?"

She kissed him on the cheek, "See ya."

Eli tootled along; it had been such a good day. It felt good to be back with Lee; he had missed her company. As he pulled into the driveway, Eli noticed Mac's car pulled up to the curb. He figured he must be visiting Desiree. After sorting his things to bring into the house, he turned to get out of the car. Mac was standing there. "Shit! Mac, don't do that. You scared the shit outta me." It wasn't until his heart stopped racing that he could tell something was drastically wrong with him. It appeared as if he had been crying. "You okay?" He lumbered out of the car.

"Not really, we gotta talk."

"Sure. Sure. C'mon in." He led the way to the side door calling behind to Mac. "Don't mean to be insulting, but man, you look bad. What's up?" Mac remained silent. Eli pushed the side door open and called to anyone in the house that he was home and not alone. He dropped his things on the table while Mac grabbed one of the chairs.

"Ya betta sit."

Perplexed, Eli sat. "What's—" his voice trailed off, and then with a burst of panic, he tore off to the bedroom, calling as he ran down the hall, "Desiree, Desiree." He threw open the door only to discover an empty bed. Confused, he turned back to Mac, "Where is she? Where? Is she okay?"

Mac swallowed hard, "No, she's not okay, Eli." Mac's bottom lip began to quiver. "She's not," he cleared his throat, "Okay."

"Where is she? The Medical—?"

Mac put up his hand. "Gimme a sec."

Eli sat completely bewildered. His face took on a look of dread as tears filled his eyes. "She's not? Tell me she's not—"

Mac shook his head, "Gawd, I'm so sorry." He wiped his eyes and tried to continue but couldn't.

"What happened? I thought you said Sonny was dead. Who, how, oh, God, no." He put his face down and held his head in his hands. "Are you su—"

Mac nodded.

The two men sat in silence. The gory details seemed of little importance; the message had been received loud and clear. A stillness fell upon the room; both men paralyzed in silence. There was nothing to say. Over the next few hours, very little verbal exchange was made; the kids poured into the house full of life and vigor but instantly comprehended the horrifying reality of the day. They all sat in silence, treasuring their memories and feelings of sorrow. The impact of her life on theirs had been tremendous. It had been one hell of a summer, one never to be forgotten. Life and all it had to offer took on a whole new perspective.

AND LIFE GOES ON

A month and some had already passed; Labor Day weekend and all its usual madness had left the city no worse for wear, but life, was a different matter. Their lives had taken on a new outlook. No longer would they view life through rose-colored glasses afforded them by their middle-class world. No longer would they assume everyone was in the same boat; they weren't. There was a much clearer and more realistic understanding, and they were grateful. Until that summer, the Rosen family had remained protected in their cocoon, blind to certain aspects of their city. Naïve as it may have been, that was all they knew until Desiree.

While the absence of her cheerful presence saddened the office personnel, nothing had really changed, and the convention world marched on. Eli was grateful that the busy season was nearing; there would be no time to think about his loss with as much business at hand. The kids were back in school, and while their lives had been enlightened and the blinders removed, things at school went on just the same. The world had not come to a screeching halt. When it all boiled down, the Desiree saga was just a brief story on the evening news, only to be forgotten by the rest of the world the next day. For the most part, other than a select few, no one really cared.

He hadn't heard the alarm clock, but he woke with a startle and looked at the clock, "Shit!" Calling out to the kids, the morning race had begun. After a quick scramble to get ready, he headed straight for the hotel without his morning coffee.

By all accounts, Percy should have had at least one of the trucks offloaded. Of all mornings to oversleep, this was the wrong one. Pulling into the parking garage of the Magnolia, he found an all too familiar scenario. Someone in hotel sales had screwed up, and the dock had been double booked. His trucks waited behind some plant company as a single man slowly offloaded. Hurriedly he turned, his tires screeching as he threw it into park.

He called to Percy, "Dammit, what's the deal here? Don't botha; I know what the deal is. Dammit."

Eli went straight to the house phone and, as expected, was greeted with the same obnoxious whine from the front desk, "It's a beautiful day—"

Eli interrupted, "Wrong! Sorry, hon, I know it's not your fault, but would you kindly connect me with Dick Dixon's office? Thanks." The debacle of the double booking compounded Eli's already aggravated mood from oversleeping.

Dick picked up, "I'm already on it."

"Excuse me? Dick, it's Eli."

"I know; that's why I told you I was already on it. I'll be down in a minute."

Eli motioned to Percy. With a quick word, Percy and the rest of the crew joined the guy offloading the plant truck. It was just about when Dick showed up with eight-plus members of the catering staff, and they, too, jumped into action. In minutes the truck was empty, and Eli's guys started offloading his client's event.

Dick walked over to Eli and handed him a cup of coffee. "Thanks, Dick; I needed coffee this morning."

The two men rested against a stack of crates, observing the organized pandemonium. After a brief spell of industry gossip, Dick brought up the last event they had done together. "That was one crazy night, huh? I wonder what eva happened to the girl, remember?"

"Remember? That's something I'll never forget. But, to answer your question, she died about six weeks ago. Her name was Desiree."

Dick seemed confused. "I thought you didn't know her."

"I didn't."

"So, like, how'd you know—"

"It's a long story, but she was a really fun girl, and I miss her a lot."

"Oh, wow, I'm sorry, I had no idea."

Seemingly aloof, Eli looked off to a distance, "It was *one of dem t'ings,* ya know?"

It was time to find the client, so off they went into the hotel. The crew set the room in less than six hours, and, per usual, the client was thrilled. If he had to say what he liked most about the business, it would have to be the expression on the faces of the guests as they entered—that more than made up for the hassles, the loading dock nightmares, demanding clients, and long hours. It was more than a job; it was part of him. After a couple of hours into the party, Eli excused himself, making his way to the loading dock.

He sat on one of the crates and lighted a cigarette. His mind began rolling; this was where it had all begun. What if he hadn't been on the dock that night? What if he had stayed at the party an hour longer or left an hour earlier? Fate was such a strange thing, he had never given much thought or credence for that matter, but his perception had changed, no grown. Even though she was gone, he felt more alive for just having known her. His mind recalled some of the special times they had spent together. In total, he hadn't known her for more than ten weeks, but the impact felt more like a lifetime. It was odd how things worked like that. Perhaps, Desiree was the tool used to open his heart. Before she had shattered his peaceful little world, he was content, content to go on day after day, year after year, just he and his two kids. The reality, and he could see it so clearly now, was that they were growing and getting ready to set out on their own, and he would be left alone. The thought had never occurred to him. Being with Desiree had opened his eyes to the world; he had regained his masculine identity. He had shunned avenues before that perhaps he would be more open to now. His black and white world had taken on some color, perhaps not as structured as it had been, but that was good.

As his mind continued to drift, something caught his attention. He had detected some kind of movement at the entrance to the parking garage. He wasn't sure if his mind was playing tricks on him, but it seemed like he could see a woman's silhouette walking toward him. He rubbed his eyes, trying to shake away this apparition, but it refused to leave. Eli watched as it moved closer. It wasn't until she came closer to the overhead light that he could clearly see. He slowly let out his breath.

"Stopped by to say hi. Wanna buy a lady a drink, pal-y?" She cocked her head to the side.

"You betcha." He hopped down from the dock and offered her his arm.

MANY THANKS...

To the love of my life, my husband, Doug, for all his help and support, in every way, shape, and form. Thanks for your guidance in the rules of law and enforcement protocol.

To our children and grandchildren who make me feel like the real deal and for spreading the word about my books and the myriad of signings and events.

To my dad, who shared his office with me when I wrote the first edition of Price To Pay in 2003. The memories of our time together make me smile and bring joy to my heart.

To the editors that keep me on the straight and narrow. G. Lee, Paige Brannon Gunter, and K.N. Faulk.

To Cyrus Wraith Walker, the designer of my covers and interior formatting. You're the best!

To the many readers of my books, thanks for sharing in this crazy journey. Thank you, thank you, thank you. Please keep spreading the word— your thoughtful reviews have made all the difference.

As always, I wish you love.

Reviews are appreciated, and please visit my website corinnearrowood.com

MORE BOOKS BY CORINNE ARROWOOD

Censored Time Trilogy

A Quarter Past Love (Book I)

Half Past Hate (Book II)

A Strike Past Time (Book III)

Friends Always

A Seat At the Table

COMING SOON

Untouchable Love

BE ON THE LOOKOUT IN 2023

Leave No Doubt

Fit The Crime Series

ABOUT THE AUTHOR

Born and raised in the enchanting city of New Orleans, the author lends a flavor of authenticity to her story and the characters that come to life in the drama, love, lust, betrayal, and murder. Her vivid style of storytelling transports the reader to the very streets of New Orleans with its unique sights, smells, and intoxicating culture. Once a masterful event planner, now retired, she has unleashed her creative wiles in this suspense-filled story...*Price to Pay*.

www.ingramcontent.com/pod-product-compliance
Lightning Source LLC
Chambersburg PA
CBHW031522310726
48971CB00008B/2328